"W   Dead man's ranch : a   , and
the   Ralph Compton novel   ning
tow   eath
him   as Junior looked down at him. No thought at all came to Junior as he drove downward with the pistol's clublike
handle at the boy's temple. MacMawe was stilled with
the single blow—it felt to Junior like a death blow—and
he turned back to who he hoped was the lesser of the
two adversaries.

"Say, what's the matter here?"

As Junior spun, he swung the pistol low and hard and
connected with nothing but chill night air. The force of
his swing spun him backward and over Brandon's unmoving legs. The big stranger was nearly on his feet now,
and Junior managed to rise to his knees. He grabbed the
pistol with his left hand and spun it in his palm, the
deadly end pointing at the dark hulking mass in front of
him.

Ralph Compton

Dead Man's Ranch

A Ralph Compton Novel

by Matthew P. Mayo

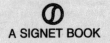

A SIGNET BOOK

SIGNET
Published by New American Library, a division of
Penguin Group (USA) Inc., 375 Hudson Street,
New York, New York 10014, USA
Penguin Group (Canada), 90 Eglinton Avenue East, Suite 700, Toronto,
Ontario M4P 2Y3, Canada (a division of Pearson Penguin Canada Inc.)
Penguin Books Ltd., 80 Strand, London WC2R 0RL, England
Penguin Ireland, 25 St. Stephen's Green, Dublin 2,
Ireland (a division of Penguin Books Ltd.)
Penguin Group (Australia), 250 Camberwell Road, Camberwell, Victoria 3124,
Australia (a division of Pearson Australia Group Pty. Ltd.)
Penguin Books India Pvt. Ltd., 11 Community Centre, Panchsheel Park,
New Delhi - 110 017, India
Penguin Group (NZ), 67 Apollo Drive, Rosedale, Auckland 0632,
New Zealand (a division of Pearson New Zealand Ltd.)
Penguin Books (South Africa) (Pty.) Ltd., 24 Sturdee Avenue,
Rosebank, Johannesburg 2196, South Africa

Penguin Books Ltd., Registered Offices:
80 Strand, London WC2R 0RL, England

First published by Signet, an imprint of New American Library,
a division of Penguin Group (USA) Inc.

First Printing, March 2012
10 9 8 7 6 5 4 3 2 1

THE IMMORTAL COWBOY

This is respectfully dedicated to the "American Cowboy." His was the saga sparked by the turmoil that followed the Civil War, and the passing of more than a century has by no means diminished the flame.

True, the old days and the old ways are but treasured memories, and the old trails have grown dim with the ravages of time, but the spirit of the cowboy lives on.

In my travels—to Texas, Oklahoma, Kansas, Nebraska, Colorado, Wyoming, New Mexico, and Arizona—I always find something that reminds me of the Old West. While I am walking these plains and mountains for the first time, there is this feeling that a part of me is eternal, that I have known these old trails before. I believe it is the undying spirit of the frontier calling me, through the mind's eye, to step back into time. What is the appeal of the Old West of the American frontier?

It has been epitomized by some as the dark and bloody period in American history. Its heroes—Crockett, Bowie, Hickok, Earp—have been reviled and criticized. Yet the Old West lives on, larger than life.

It has become a symbol of freedom, when there was always another mountain to climb and another river to cross; when a dispute between two men was settled not with expensive lawyers, but with fists, knives, or guns. Barbaric? Maybe. But some things never change. When the cowboy rode into the pages of American history, he left behind a legacy that lives within the hearts of us all.

—Ralph Compton

Chapter 1

Mortimer Darturo shook his head and waved away the cards offered him. He rapped his chest and worked up a low belch, then beckoned the fat barmaid. *A good girl for remembering*, he thought, as she set before him a whiskey in milk. She turned to go, but he grabbed her thick wrist and waved a finger at the other three men also seated at the baize table. She nodded and left. She was afraid of him, he knew, for her eyes, the color of a high summer sky, looked liquid, on the verge of tears, her lips set to scream. Good.

He raised the squat glass to his mouth and looked over the rim at the other three. To a man, they looked at him, unbidden disgust sneering their mouths. He smiled as he sipped. *Keep them guessing*, he thought, and almost laughed.

The girl brought the drinks to his game-mates. They each raised their glass to him and sipped. *Fine, fine, fine*, he thought. *Drink and talk. Get to it*. He would sit out this hand. The belch was the least of his worries. He wanted to hear more from the loudmouth lawyer sitting across from him. Mort sensed there was something boiling up in the little fat man, itching to be told. The night was still green and Mort was still sober and this man had something to reveal. Many times in the past he'd heard useful information at the games tables just because he listened.

A tall man in a gray hat and striped gray suit immediately to Darturo's left arranged his bad cards two, three times. *They won't get any better no matter how often you rearrange them*, thought Mort. *This much I know. I've tried.* Then the man cleared his throat, sent an expert stream of brown chew juice dead into a half-full spittoon by his chair legs, and said, "You were saying, about New Mexico Territory, I mean. . . ." He nodded toward the little fat lawyer in the green suit. The lawyer nodded back, barely looking up from his cards.

Go ahead and talk, thought Mort. *Talk before the booze makes you quiet and sad. For surely yours is a sad little life.* He almost smiled then, but instead he concentrated on making the man talk.

As if to prove that such a thing could be forced, the green-suited lawyer downed the last of his drink and said, "New Old May-hee-co, yes. Why do you ask?"

"Oh well," said the man who spoke first. He continued shuffling his five cards. "I have to sell my wares elsewhere soon and I wonder what the situation with the savages is like these days. Might try my hand south of here."

The third man, a scruffy character in a greasy buckskin shirt that looked to Darturo as if it had been dipped in a gut pile and then dried, said, "You'd do as well to stick with Denver. This town's got it all."

"And what makes you so expert?"

"Never said I was expert at nothin', but I been down to New Mex before and it ain't no treat. Can't trap a critter to save my ass down there. Ain't a cent to be had thataways, leastwise not from pelts, no, sir."

The green-suited lawyer spoke up. "I cannot speak of pelts, naturally." He winked at the men. "But regarding land, I beg to differ, sir." He pulled the chewed cigar nub from his mouth and set it on the table edge.

It looks like something a sick dog would have left in the alley, thought Mort. *Now continue talking*, he urged as he stared at the man.

"I have a client down there. He's a landowner of righteous proportions, and besides being dead . . ." This last comment seemed to him a funny thing, for he snorted through his nose, then apologized. "He was my client. Now he's just a dead landowner . . . or something like that. Big mess with his family, though. God, remind me never to have children. Always grubbing for money. . . ." He set his cards down, facedown, and thumped the table as if he were in court.

You are drunk and a fool, thought Darturo. *But keep on talking, little man*, he urged him with his mind, with his eyes. *Keep talking*.

"Kids ain't worth the time, if my client's life is anything of an indication. . . . Prime land all over the good Lord's creation and what does he get? He's dead and his beneficiaries can't find their asses with both hands. . . ." This was funnier to him than his last funny statement, and the little fat lawyer laid his head right on the poker table and laughed, pounding the surface with a plump fist.

"You ain't gonna play, then call out. Otherwise, I take it as an open offer to let me see your cards. So here." The smelly trapper slapped down his cards. "I call." He grinned.

Darturo grinned too. *I want to hear more before the night is through*, he thought. *Now that I know there is more worth hearing. For maybe I need a new plan, a new way of doing things. A new way around the old tree, as the man once said. Hell*, he thought. *Why go all the way around it? Why not just cut down the tree?*

Maybe it is time I find a place to call home, a ranch perhaps. He had taken things that were plenty bigger than the deed to a ranch, so why should this be any different? *After all, I am a powerful man, am I not? And all powerful men need a place where they operate from. And if the ranch happened to be one of the best in the region, and one of the biggest too, naturally, then who am I, Mortimer Darturo, to argue? Perhaps I will become a judge, for that is what land barons do.* He almost laughed, even as a plan flowered in his mind, opening as if in full, hot sun after a soaking rain.

Two hours later, in an alley a few buildings down the street from the saloon, Mortimer Darturo slipped a thin, three-inch blade in and out of the drunk attorney's gut five times before the man thought to scream. Red bubbles rose from the fat mouth that opened and closed like the lips of a fish. *Every time it's the same,* thought Mort. *Like jabbing a sack of meal.* Would no one ever lash back? Had they all grown so soft as to take such a thing as their own killing as something not to be bothered with? He sighed. For as long as he lived, Mort knew that he was destined to be disappointed by people. He would never understand them. Never.

"It is hard to speak when your throat is so full, huh?" Light spiking down from a whore's upstairs window that overlooked the narrow alley let Darturo stare into the man's wide eyes. *I made this happen,* thought Mort. *It is only right that I am the last thing he sees.* When the lids relaxed, Mort let the fat little lawyer ease to the dirt, wiped the blade on the dead man's sleeve, and as he straightened his own jacket he looked up at the window. Nothing shaded the world from such a private act that, from the looks of things, was nearing its end.

He half smiled and thumped his chest, working up a fresh belch. "Animals," he said as the gas bubble emerged.

As he strolled from the alley, wiping the blade clean on the inner hem of his frock coat, Mort snorted a laugh. He walked to the livery, pockets filled with fresh cash and his mind filled with a sudden urge to see New Mexico Territory.

Chapter 2

The steel wheels of the Santa Fe and Rio Grande Western screeched low and long as they churned to a stop. Steam valves released, pluming at the ground and swirling the dust.

The last passenger to step down from the train's club car stood on the gravel, an oversized white kerchief pressed to his face, his wide chest convulsing in coughs.

"Who's the dandy?"

The station agent squinted through the dust, looked down at a note in his hand, then up again at the stranger.

"I said ... who's the dandy?" The chunky little man speaking looked up at the station agent from his seat on the nail keg.

"Huh?" said the agent, still squinting at the stranger, who hadn't moved but was now staring at the brocade bag just dropped at his feet. "You say something, Squirly?"

The man on the keg crossed his feet and leaned back. "Nah, nah. You know me, Mr. Teasdale. I don't speak unless spoken to."

The agent looked down at his companion with raised

eyebrows. "Why don't you make yourself useful and retrieve the man's bag? If it's who I expect, then we ought to welcome him, make him feel at home."

The pudgy man looked as if he'd just been forced to drink from a spittoon. "Just who were we expectin'?"

But the station agent had already gone back inside his office for his official coat and hat. Squirly looked again at the stranger, who seemed well and truly lost. He stood like a lost steer, thirty yards down the track, and finally looked back at Squirly.

"This better be worth my time." Squirly grunted to his feet and clumped down the platform, the few remaining fringes on his old buckskin coat wagging with each step.

"Well, this wire told me to expect . . ." Teasdale looked down at the nail keg to which he was speaking and shook his head.

Squirly grabbed the leather loop handles of the man's bag and made for the platform. "Teas—uh, the station agent tells me you're expected." He didn't turn as he spoke.

"See here." The stranger caught up with Squirly, grabbing his arm with a gloved hand. "Just where do you think you're going with my luggage?"

The pudgy man looked down at the hand on his arm and said, "Was headed for the platform but now looks like I'm headed for the calaboose."

"If that's a hotel, then—"

"It ain't. It's the jail."

"The jail? Why?"

"'Cause I'm 'bout to drop you like a sack of cornmeal, mister. Less'n you back off."

Then he felt the bag being pulled from his grasp from behind. "What the . . . ?"

"I'll take it from here, Squirly Ross. Thanks for your help."

The squat older man rasped a pudgy hand across his

chin. "Dry work, Teasdale. Luggin' them fancies." He gestured at the woven bag.

"What's going on here?" said the stranger.

He was a tall man, the agent noted. Broad in the shoulders, and judging from his light whiskering, he had the red hair to boot. Hard to tell under that derby hat, so tight was it pulled down. He'd give him that much; it was a windy day.

"Welcome to Turnbull, sir."

The man ignored Teasdale's outstretched hand and leaned out past the edge of the little depot building to look up the main street. A fresh gust whipped the mouse-colored derby from his head and carried it like a runty, determined tumbleweed straight up the dirt track.

Teasdale smiled and looked at Squirly, then nodded at the young man's hair.

Squirly squinted, looked hard at the young man. "It ain't . . ."

Teasdale smiled, nodded slightly, and rocked back on his heels, a hand in his pocket.

The young stranger turned back to them with a mix of surprise and scowl on his broad face, green eyes ablaze, and the wind tousling a mass of red hair.

"It is!" Squirly took a step back, hand over his mouth.

"My hat . . . the wind . . ." The young man waved a broad hand up the street in the direction the hat had traveled.

Station Agent Teasdale stepped forward and smiling, said, "Welcome to Turnbull, Mr. . . . um . . ." He looked down at the note in his hand. "Mr. Middleton, that's it. Welcome home."

Chapter 3

"I assume you received my wire," said the tall young man.

"Yes, indeed." Teasdale shook the note as if drying it. "And I took the liberty of reserving a room at the hotel for you."

The young man turned his back on them once again and held his hand up, visoring his eyes and staring up the street. A chestnut horse stood at a hitch rail, bowed against the gale. Dim light shone through the darkened panes of the windows in front of them. On the opposite side of the street, two mules drooped before their flat wagon, each with a rear leg canted. Beyond them two women progressed up the boardwalk, skirts snapping like laundry on a line, with hands clamped on their respective headgear. The thinner, taller of the two had on a broad-brim hat, like a man's. The other, thicker and squatter, wore a bonnet. Low, dark clouds hugged the horizon and rode the little town proper as if tethered there.

"That was a waste of time, sir. I won't require a hotel room." The tall, redheaded stranger smirked at the station agent. "I am heading out to the ranch today. Now, where can I hire a hansom or some such conveyance to bring me there?"

"This just keeps getting better." Squirly snorted and, patting Teasdale on the sleeve, stepped off the platform. "Dry work, Teas, but I figure I been paid." He hunched up, his open coat flapping, wisps of silver hair trailing behind his bald head like ragged yarn. As he trudged up the street, shaking his head, the wind carried his voice back to them. "Hire a hansom. . . . Ha! Wait'll I tell the boys."

The station agent cleared his throat. "Fact is, Mr. Mac—Mr. Middleton, you need the better part of a day just to make it to your father's property. You're in luck—the Maligno's passable lately. With a good horse and an early start tomorrow, you can make it to the ranch itself not too long after dark. Stays light late now, so that'll help you."

"I don't plan on being here that long. I made this god-awful journey despite the insistence of my grandfather to the contrary and at the urging of a pathetic Denver attorney who claimed to represent the dead man's interests. I will deal with estate matters, liquidate what I can, and address the remaining headaches from the comfort and safety of my home in Providence, where I fully expect to return within two weeks' time."

He drew himself up to his considerable full height and tilted his head to one side, regarding Teasdale as one might a troubled child who doesn't understand the explanation given him. "Now, before I embark on my trip to the property, perhaps you will be so good as to tell me at what time tomorrow the next train arrives."

Teasdale could only think of the fact that Squirly was right. "First time for everything," he said in a low voice as he hefted the bag and headed down the street.

"See here," said the young man, laying a big hand on Teasdale's arm. "Where are you going with my luggage?"

Teasdale smiled up at the young man and said, "The next train? Why, that's scheduled to pull up, oh boy, let's see. . . . Yes, that would be a week from today. So, next Tuesday, Mr. *Middleton*."

"What do you mean? I have appointments to keep. I have important work to do!" As he spoke he followed the older man. "See here," he said again, but the words whipped from his mouth in a gust of bitter wind as soon as they were uttered.

Minutes later, Teasdale led him to a set of wide wooden steps. The older man bent down and plucked something from the shadows beside the staircase, slapped at it a few times, then presented it to the young man. "Your hat, sir."

For a brief moment Teasdale saw unadorned delight in the young man's eyes. Then their gazes met and Middleton snatched the dented, dusty thing and mumbled, "Thank you."

Teasdale smiled and led the way up the steps and into the foyer of a narrow, two-story building with the simple word HOTEL painted on the facade. He plopped the tall man's bag in front of the sign-in counter. "Heya, Harv," he said.

The man behind the counter, nearly bald and with a fleshy red face, stood crouched over a large ledger he scratched in with a pencil. He didn't look up. Teasdale winked at the stranger and shook his head and rang a little brass bell. The melodic chiming sound echoed in the large room and the man behind the counter looked up. "Teasdale, good to see you today."

The station agent just nodded. "Harv, this fella here"— he nodded toward the stranger—"needs that room I spoke to you about. Just for the night. I'm guessing you can help him out."

The hotelier's smile dropped from his face and his bottom lip thrust forward. He grunted and licked a finger before turning pages in the big green ledger. As far as the other two men could tell, there was no sequence to the page flipping. He finally turned it back to the page he began with and said, "Well . . ."

Teasdale stood off to the side, hands in pockets, and smiled.

"What's wrong? In fact, what's wrong with everyone in this town?" Middleton shook his head and snatched up his satchel.

"Why, I was about to tell you that you're in luck, sir. I have—"

"Never mind. I'll find accommodation elsewhere tonight."

"I doubt it."

"What?" said Middleton, turning on Teasdale. The stranger's shoulders sagged. "Why?"

"Because this is the only place in town with rooms to let, Mr. Middleton." No one said anything for another few seconds; then Teasdale moved to the door. "I'll leave you to it, then, Harv." He nodded at the hotelier, then looked at the stranger and touched a finger to his hat brim. "Mr. Middleton." He closed the door behind him.

Before either man could address the other, Teasdale poked his head back in. "Almost forgot. You'll want to talk with Silver Haskell at the livery. He'll fix you up with a horse in the morning. Good day." The door rattled closed again, but not before a gust fluttered the lace curtains on the windows beside the door.

"I'd like your best room."

The hotelier stared at the tall stranger. "God, but you look familiar."

"A room, please."

"Oh, right. Sorry. Best, you say? They're all the same. Some better in some ways, others in others."

"Just give me a quiet one."

"Well, now," said Harv, spinning the guest register toward the stranger. "Depends on the time of day. Street's busier along toward midday and afternoon, whereas the back's busier in early morning and, of course, nighttime, when the boys are in town. Too much whoopin' and we put 'em out back on the bench in the alley for a spell. We call it an alley, but it ain't really. More like a—"

"Any room will do." The young stranger stared down at the bald hotelier.

"Four could work."

"Four sounds fine."

"Four, then?"

The tall man narrowed his eyes and drew in a breath through his nose.

"Good. Sign here." Harv tapped a pudgy, ink-smudged finger at a blank line. The stranger noticed the date of the previous guest's sign-in was nearly a month old.

"I almost hate to ask. . . . Do you recommend a dining establishment? Preferably not too far. I've had a long day and I am tired."

"Big, young fella like you? My word. I was your age I could go all day in the saddle on Pap's ranch, scrub off the dust, and ride into town most evenings for a game and a snort."

"How fortunate for both of us that you are not me."

Harv grunted and said, "Well, your best bet, not to mention your only one in Turnbull, is Mae's Dinner House, two doors down. My sister-in-law runs it. She's a German but she can cook up a storm. Married to my brother. Course, he took up with my wife, though. Been gone, oh, let's see now—"

Middleton hefted his satchel and walked away while the pudgy bald man spoke.

As he mounted the stairs, he heard the hotelier say, "Well, I never. . . ."

Chapter 4

As was his habit when riding long distances, Mortimer
Darturo passed the time by musing about his life, his
hardscrabble past, and how far he'd come. He knew that
others regarded prideful thinking as shameful, but he
didn't care in the least. He reached down and patted the
neck of his horse, Picolo. The buckskin responded with a
head shake, as if to dispel an irksome bee. Darturo
laughed and lit a short brown cigarillo and settled back
in the saddle to the steady motion of the horse over this
dry but forgiving land that stretched sandy and rarely
green for miles around him.

He wore a black, flat-crowned hat and a tailored
black suit sporting accents of brocade, with thin gray
stripes running the length of the trousers. He had been
mistaken many times for a Mexican gambler. Mortimer
Darturo was not of Spanish descent, however, but Italian to the bone. He had been born thirty-four years before of fisherfolk in Ancona and shipped to the Land of
Promise as a crying youth, with little more than hollow
assurances from his father and mother that they would

soon follow. If they did, he never knew. From the hour of his tearful departure aboard the stinking ship filled with his ragged countrymen, he had been made to work, scrubbing tin cookware, hauling slopping buckets of waste topped with flies so thick at times they settled on his face like a moving mask.

Young Darturo had been born to working people, and though the work was distasteful to him, he assumed this was the deal his parents had struck for his passage, the best their sacrifice could render for him, in order to get him, their beloved son, to the Land of Promise. At least that is what he thought at the beginning of the trip.

The two months at sea seemed to take years. Mortimer had suspected for half of that time that the captain, a slack-bellied tyrant covered in black, curling hair that trapped droplets of sweat, had plans to keep Mortimer aboard, secured in the hold with chains, until they were back at sea. The captain liked how hard Darturo worked.

By the time they docked in Boston Harbor, Darturo had formed a plan. Once the ship had been emptied of cargo and passengers, the captain led him under pretense to the far reaches of the hold, as Darturo knew he would. The big man delivered his usual clouts, his meaty hand smacking Darturo on the cheeks, the ears, the forehead. Darturo smiled and retreated in the dark, waited for the fat man to lunge, thinking he was driving the boy one step closer to the manacles behind him, bolted to the hull, clanking with the gentle motion of the busy harbor.

"You stand there, boy. You know what must be done." There was a wide grin hidden in the dense mat of poking black hair of the man's beard. He slipped off the leather braces from his shoulders, popped free the buckle from its straining belt, and then the sweating bulk of the captain's body stepped in front of Darturo.

As the captain's trousers dropped, he reached for the boy. Darturo pushed upward with all the pent strength of a short life gained working hard for others—first at the docks hauling nets, dragging boats, lugging the catch, then at sea hauling, dragging, and lugging for the ship's vile crew. But now he would be free. As Darturo pulled the captain's own dining knife through the great swinging sack of belly, and as the mass of slick guts slopped to the floor, the boy felt as if something had climbed down off his back. He felt taller and older for the first time since leaving home.

The big, sweaty face moved toward his own, as if to make out a bit of missed conversation, the captain's eyes the only brightness in the dim hold. Darturo bent forward and whispered into the sweat-soaked beard, "Yes, now I know what must be done."

Time stilled long enough for a young man to step aside and draw a breath, his first of freedom, even as the older man groaned and pushed out a final foul breath. The captain pitched forward, his head smacking the manacles, setting them swinging. He dropped to the grimed floor of the hold, his great hairy head matting in the pile of his own sopping guts.

Despite this first triumph, as he came to think of it, Darturo found life in the harbor city a hard thing. He endured other such attacks of filth and disgust, and he spent the next few years working to forget it all, but found that he could not. It occurred to him one night as he clawed his way through the trash pile behind a dining hall, kicking at rats who were nothing more than competition, that since he knew he would never forget the hard life he had now been presented with, perhaps there was a way he could make it work for him. He vowed to spend the rest of his life doing to others what had been done to him. The only bit that amazed him was that it had taken him so long to figure out.

The hat he'd had for six years now. It had belonged to

a man who had explained the promise and allure of the West to Mortimer in such glowing, vivid strokes of conversation one night over a shared bottle and a warm fire in a rail camp that after Darturo had sliced open his gut in much the same manner as he had that of the captain, first clamping one hard hand over the sleeping man's mouth, he'd vowed to take to the road to see if the man had lied to him. He must have, so rich did the West sound to him that night. . . .

From New York he'd traveled, on the man's horse and in the man's clothes, to St. Louis. From there he'd gone, well, everywhere. And he was having the time of his life. The man had been true to his word, and Darturo thanked him every morning when he settled his hat on his head for the day and climbed on his horse.

Along the way he'd learned a few things. Namely that he did not like the South. It was hot and too many things living there tried to sting and bite him—animals, snakes, the people too. And the southernmost of it bordered the ocean. He needed no reminders of life on the shore. The Southwest was little better, but it was drier. Though it too offered vicious, unending heat and vile creatures intent on harming him. Of necessity through the years, he had become capable of all manner of ranch work. However, he dusted off those rudimentary and distasteful skills only when other, less strenuous work was scarce.

His preference was not to work at all, at least for him, and instead consisted of pitting one frenzied person against another in hopes of an outcome that shot sparks high into the sky and money deep into his pockets. He found that desperate, angry people paid money for certain services that with a little thought, they could themselves accomplish. But no matter, he was there to help. And that is what he told the woman in Boulder just two months before he arrived in Denver.

She had been a wealthy chicken, cuckolded for years, who despised her philandering husband. But she didn't know quite what to do about it, only knew that she wanted something to happen to him. Something bad. Something permanent. That task had required Darturo to be more aggressive than he had expected, but so skillfully had he pitted the two against each other that the results would be talked about in Boulder for years. Once their bodies were found, of course, liberated of all their cash and jewels, naturally. *I am not a greedy man*, he thought. Plenty of heavy, ugly furniture was left for their heirs to sell off.

Mort smiled at the memory, and reined up at a small white wooden sign. One end angled upward but still pointed toward the trail ahead.

"Turnbull. Fifty miles." He grunted and wiped grit from his face, taking care not to drag it across his eyes, for then they would sting. "That sounds like the place the fat little Denver lawyer spoke of, eh, Picolo?" He slapped the buckskin's neck and urged him forward with gentle spur taps to the belly. As they trotted toward the far-off place, he smiled, curious to see what would happen next in his life. He had plenty of money left from Denver, but it was his takings from the Boulder episode, as he chose to call it, that allowed him time enough to wait for his next project to present itself.

He'd never had trouble in the past in finding an opportunity. If he had any plan, it was to perhaps visit Mexico. His saddlebags were full of more money than he could spend down there in two lifetimes. And he figured that since he'd already used up this one, there would be plenty for him to enjoy somewhere south of the border. For however long it lasted.

"First, we will see what Turnbull brings, Picolo. If there is nothing to the fat lawyer's chatter and it turns out there are no arguing people, and so, no land for us to take and then sell—or keep for our own and become fat, land-owning judges ourselves—we will move on to Mexico. After we've had a drink or two, and a game or three. Ranch country like this, there's bound to be many clever cowhands looking to strike it rich off a dumb foreigner." Darturo urged the buckskin into a trot. His low, dry chuckle spiraled up and away, breaking apart in a light breeze like old paper over the long, flat plain around him.

Chapter 5

Two hours after he'd checked in, Brian Middleton reversed his journey downstairs and through the hotel's now-empty lobby. He stepped down into the street and looked southward. The wind had abated and darkness crept in. He discovered that the warm, welcoming glow lighting the boardwalk leaked out from the dining establishment that the hotelier had recommended. He pushed open a squeaky screen door and stepped inside.

"Sit anyvere. I bring you coffee."

Middleton realized the fat, red-faced woman in the apron was talking to him, so he nodded and chose a table off to the side of the room. There was no one else in the establishment, but the smells in the close, warm room made him lick his lips. He set his derby hat on the seat of one of the other three chairs at his table and sat down. The table covering was oilcloth, but clean. He had hardly expected wine and candles, but this really was rustic. He looked around, wincing at the crashes and shouts from the kitchen.

"Out. Out of here until I call for you. Useless man. . . ."

From a doorway in the back hurried the little bald hotelier. He saw Middleton and smiled, and as he squeaked open the woodstove's door he said, "So you made it. Good."

Middleton managed a half smile and a curt nod to the hotelier. He wished he had brought a newspaper. There wasn't even a menu to read. The woman came with a cup of steaming coffee and looked at him. "Harvey is right. You look like—"

"Hush, Mae. That ain't our business."

"Oh, bosh."

Harv replied by clunking another hunk of wood into the firebox and slamming the door.

He mumbled something Middleton could not discern, but the woman evidently had heard him, for she scowled at Harv and said, "Enough of dat noise from you. Or no pie."

She turned back to Middleton and with the back of her hand pushed flyaway strands of gray-brown hair from her red face. "You like the beef, yah? And potato, carrots, biscuits—big and fluffy—and more coffee."

"Do I have a choice? No menu from which to choose?" As he said this the door opened and two women entered.

Mae looked up from scowling at the stranger, and a smile transformed her face. "Miss Callie. Miss Gleason. Come in, come in. Harvey vill help you with your things."

"Course I will. I do everything else around here."

"Oh, hush, silly man."

But he strode forward and helped them off with their coats, hanging them on pegs by the door. Then, just in case they hadn't seen the tall man sitting fifteen feet away, he raised his eyebrows and jerked his head in the stranger's direction. The younger of the two ladies said, "Do you have a nervous condition, Mr. Peterson? Your neck is twitching something fierce."

"I . . . I have dishes to wash." He scurried off to the kitchen.

The proprietor looked at him as he passed, then exchanged a spluttered laugh with the ladies, before heading for the kitchen herself. Soon they heard clanging of pots and shouts in German.

Middleton saw no solution but to offer seats at his table to the two ladies. He stood, his chair dragging along the floorboards, and gestured at his table. "Would you ladies care to join me? I can't guarantee the palatability of the fare, but I can assure you that the level of conversation may help to render the repast tolerable."

He saw the smile slide from the young blond woman's face. Where before there had been a dancing light in her dark eyes, he now saw sharpness. The older woman at her side held her by the elbow and steered her to a table on the other side of the room. He sighed and sat down.

It was some time before he spoke again. He had finished his meal, and it had been surprisingly toothsome. He felt a judicious comment now might help to heal the rift he had apparently caused earlier, though for the life of him he couldn't understand how a plain statement of the truth could be so offensive.

He cleared his throat and wiped his mouth with the napkin. "I had no idea such plain fare could taste so . . . truly acceptable." It wasn't really what he wanted to say. It had indeed tasted exceptional.

The young woman looked up from her plate. "And I had no idea people would travel so great a distance just to be rude."

The older lady laid a hand on the young woman's arm and murmured something, not even looking at him. But not so with the young lady. She stared at him, her blue eyes sharp and glinting.

"The truth is rarely rude, miss. And how do you know I have traveled from afar?"

"No one from these parts would ever complain about Mae's cooking."

"Exactly my point."

The sound of her rage and exasperation—a harsh growl—mixed with the sound of the door slamming open, caught them all by surprise. Mae and Harv came out from the kitchen in time to see the young lady stand up and throw her balled napkin on her half-eaten meal. Beyond her, a dark young man stood weaving in the shadows of the doorway, his face partially shadowed by his low-pulled hat.

"Hot in here, ain't it?" he said. No one said anything. He turned his head to his right as if a string were attached to his chin. Even from across the room, the smell of booze and sweat rolled in a wave off the young man. "Why, Miss Callie. . . . I didn't know you were in town." He sounded as if he had just awakened.

"Brandon," she said, barely glancing at the drunk. Then she shifted her gaze from the tall stranger, who was also standing, staring at her, his brow furrowed, a funny smile on his mouth, and looked at the swaying man. "Shouldn't you be at the ranch? Your mother's alone there, Brandon."

"Okay, okay, that's what I'm talking about. Everyone is trying to tell me what to do, like I'm a child. I'm a man now!" He thumbed his chest. "The man of the house, right? The man of the ranch now. So, everyone"—he whipped his arms wide, one hitting the door and knocking it open—"just stop calling me a child."

"Then stop acting like one," said the girl.

The young man walked toward her, and the stranger stepped from behind his table and placed a hand on the young man's shoulder. "See here, sir. You are intoxicated and in no suitable state to address a young lady. Do you hear?"

The young man's fist, despite his advanced state of inebriation, found its true mark with unerring accuracy and drove square into Middleton's cheekbone. The force of the punch, unexpected as it was, sent the broad-shouldered stranger slamming into an empty table. His head whipped backward against the wood surface; then he flopped to the floor, unconscious.

The two older women bent low over the man while the younger woman stood behind them, a hand over her mouth, hiding a smile. *He's rather handsome for a big-city dandy*, she thought. *And after all, how could he know that Brandon is harmless?* As if on cue, a belch from the young drunk interrupted her musing. She turned a sharp eye on Brandon, who smiled and wobbled in place.

Harv bolted through the door and into the street, and in minutes had retrieved a man wearing a star and carrying a half-eaten chicken leg. The lawman took one last bite before tossing it into the street. He wiped his mouth on his shirt cuff and strode into the dining room, hefting his belt and canting his head to one side.

"Brandon, what in the world have you done now?"

The young man wobbled around to stare at the speaker. "Oh, hello, Sheriff Tucker. I didn't see you standing there."

"Surprised you can see anything, the state you're in." He gestured with his chin toward the prone form on the floor. "He all right, Miss Callie?"

She nodded as the unconscious man slowly shook his head, his eyelids fluttering.

"Somebody wanna give me an explanation? I'm in the middle of a home-cooked meal and Harv here busts in to tell me this little hothead is just about killing somebody."

"Didn't think you'd come if I told you that Brandon had punched a fella in the jaw."

"You're right, Harv." He poked a finger in the hotelier's face. "Not with a meal like that and me barely set down to it." He sighed and said, "Well, I'm here now. So what happened?"

Callie stepped forward and said, "That man"—she pointed at the now awake stranger on the floor—"and I were having a, uh, verbal disagreement when Brandon barged in, drunk, as usual."

Brandon giggled and slumped into a chair at the table behind him, resting his head on his hands. They all watched him, the locals shaking their heads.

"I told Brandon that he was acting like a child and he stepped toward me, but he"—she pointed at the stranger, who had grabbed a corner of the table and was pulling himself upright—"interfered, and that's when Brandon punched him."

"Interfered?" said Middleton, shaking his head. "Why, that drunken brute was about to attack you, miss. . . ."

The sheriff and Callie snorted at the same time. "I don't reckon little ol' Brandon would ever attack Callie, mister. She's like an older sister to him. No, stranger, I guess your face was just in the wrong place at the wrong time. Best get a bit of raw beefsteak for that bruise. She's forming to lump now. I can see it. Believe me, I've seen plenty of 'em. See some more too, come Saturday night."

Harv laughed and nodded.

"Surely you don't expect I'm going to let this matter drop? I want that man arrested, Sheriff. I want him incarcerated for what he's done."

"Well, what's he really done, eh, stranger?"

"Why, he assaulted me!"

They all looked at Brandon, whose head was flat on the tabletop, and who was snoring.

"I reckon I could take him to the cell. Let him sleep it off there. Safer for him anyway." The sheriff looked at the tall man. "What with strangers on the loose and all. Harv, you wanna give me a hand with the boy?"

"Sure, sure. Let's go."

The two men left, dragging the unconscious lad between them.

"That savage should be in prison." The stranger worked a big hand over his tender cheek.

No one said anything, but the pretty young lady they'd

called Callie, the one with the sharp blue eyes, made to step toward him. The older woman with her held her by the arm and said, "No, Callie. Leave well enough alone."

The stranger shook his head and strode to the door. "Savages," he muttered. "The dime novels are correct, after all."

"You forget two things, mister." Mae stood in the middle of the room, her large white apron stained with food, fists resting on her broad waist.

"What precisely would they be, ma'am?" said Middleton, paused in the doorway.

She leaned over and snatched his derby from the chair on which it sat. "Your hat," she said, and flung it toward him. He reached for it, but it sailed past him into the dark street. The sudden movement roused a fresh wave of pain from his throbbing face. He brought his hands to his temples and rubbed gingerly.

"And your bill," she said.

"I should hardly have thought," he said in a voice little more than a raspy whisper, "that I'd be charged for being attacked in your establishment, ma'am."

"You interfered. And besides, you enjoyed your meal." She nodded at his plate, a few traces of brown gravy the only signs of the ample portions that had been piled on it a little while before.

He sighed and said, "How much?"

"One dollar."

He tossed a coin on the nearest table and walked slowly out the door and into the dark street.

"Welcome to Turnbull," shouted Callie after him. "Don't stay too long."

The laughter of the three women followed him into the street. He stretched to his full height, let out a long, slow breath with a sigh, and retrieved his battered hat from the dirt at his feet. He placed the hat on his head and rubbed his jaw and cheek as he stared at the silhouettes of the women in the window of the dining house.

Soon two of them moved away from the window, but one remained. He fancied that it was the young lady with the gold-silk hair and the fierce blue eyes. The one whose honor he had defended, no matter what the local populace might think.

Despite the throbbing in his jaw, Brian T. Middleton found himself smiling a little as he walked back to the hotel. Indeed, he thought, the West held one surprise after another.

Chapter 6

Wilf Grindle didn't so much look at his son, Junior, as take in the space around him, as if he were expecting the boy to grow larger right there before his very eyes. Finally his gaze settled on the boy's face. Eyes red again, dark smudges beneath.

By God, thought Wilf, *but I never thought I'd see the day when my own son would turn out to have bottle fever.* He pushed out cigar smoke, seeing through it the lack of success with even this, the latest in a lifetime of failed endeavors. "Did you sort out Mica's problem?"

"Well, Father, he wasn't there when I got down to the bunkhouse."

"Did you wait for him, Junior? He was probably only out back doin' his necessaries." Wilf watched his son grip the funnel brim of his brown hat, curling it more and turning it in both hands, knuckles tight. What made the boy so nervous around him? He wasn't so antsy up with the men, nor by himself; he'd often seen him relaxed and walking easy. Or riding. And the boy, by God, could sit a horse. Just as if he were part of the animal.

I guess that's just my way, thought Wilf Grindle, reflecting on the men who worked for him, people in town, people who claimed to be friends, all uncomfortable and tense around him. So much so that he'd gotten used to it over the years. *Nothing I can help.* Besides, there were few people who ever really understood him, who weren't afraid to speak their minds around him, and two of them were dead.

His dear, sweet Carla, gone now these nineteen years, and their daughter, Callie, so like her mother—though he fancied he saw a bit of himself in her too. And of course there was Mica, his near-constant companion, cantankerous range boss, and second parent to his kids since Carla passed. Though he would never tell him this to his face, mostly because he would risk buttoned eyes and a swollen jaw, but Mica was the only man of color he'd ever found to be worth a damn.

But most of all, there was Rory MacMawe, his old friend, gone the better part of two weeks. The best of friends and the only man who ever stood up to him, the only man who ever told him no, the only man to ever defy him. And look where it got them. Hadn't spoken in more than sixteen years. Not since he sent the boy away. Wilf hated that he would never again get the chance to talk with Rory.

Junior shifted from one boot to the other, gave a slight cough.

Wilf looked up. "Junior, damn it, why don't you ever sit down when you come in here?" He wagged a hand at one of the two leather wingback chairs angled in front of his massive desk. The boy sat as if he'd never used a chair before. Wilf lowered himself into his own worn old chair and said, "We need to discuss a few things more important, I daresay, than the state of Mica's supply woes. He's an old range maid. He'll figure it out—he just likes to have someone to complain to. I reckon he wants to let me know he's keeping busy. As if I didn't know it already."

"What did you want to talk about, Father?"

Wilf looked again at his son, scratched his chin, rolled the cigar ash to a point in the glass ashtray. "It's about the Dancing M."

"Mr. MacMawe's place?"

Wilf nodded. "I'm going to buy it."

Junior leaned forward in his chair. "What about Esperanza and Brandon?"

Wilf stood up fast, his chair clunking against the bookshelves behind him. "What about them, damn it? Those two are nothing more than squatters. They don't own the place. No one does, technically. Yet."

"But Brandon is old Rory's son. So that must make Esperanza his—"

The older man pointed a long finger at his son and said, "Don't you say it. Don't you ever say she's his wife, nor he's his son. Because it's not so. Bastards and housemaids do not a family make."

Junior opened his mouth, closed it again, and stared at his father, who had pushed his desk chair in and was now pacing slowly behind the desk, the width of the dark room.

"Now," said Wilf, more for himself than anyone else, "I'll admit the boy does bear a resemblance to Rory in certain respects—and while I'm on the subject, you're to refer to him as Mr. MacMawe, you hear? The woman did keep house for him and care for him in his final days, and that's good and admirable, but that's all it was. There's no proof of anything further than that. And I'd be mighty surprised if old Rory left anything in the way of a will."

He looked at his son, but the boy seemed as wary and confused as ever. Wilf leaned on the desk and said, "Of course I will pay fair market value for every one of its 2,997 acres. Pay it to who, I don't know yet." He resumed pacing. "And the woman and boy should get something . . . for their troubles. But it won't be the ranch. Not by a long shot. That was destined for us," he said, pointing the smoking cigar at Junior, "to be folded into the Driving D. Hell, that'll pretty near double the size of our spread."

"But . . . don't we have enough land already, Father?"

Wilf paused. His daughter exasperated him daily, but never like the boy. "I thought you were smarter than that, Junior. If I have to explain that, then I have failed as a father, as an example to you, son. Land is the most basic and vital thing a man can have. Without it there's no power, no influence, no . . . well, look around you, boy! No fine things! You don't know what it's like to wake up hungry and feel that way all day, then go to bed wondering if that bite of damned squirrel meat would be enough to keep you alive till morning." He stalked the worn path behind his desk, cigar smoke pluming behind him like smoke from a train engine.

He turned back to the boy, his dynamite stick of a cigar held in one hand. "Why, boy, without land there's no way a future can be built up. And while I'm thinking of you and your future . . ." He thumbed his own chest. "This chicken ain't cooked just yet, you know. And you're my son. And a grown man now. Time you had a spread of your own."

Wilf worked his way around to the front of the desk and sat on the edge, one long leg dangling, inches separating the two men. He leaned down toward his son. "Time you had a full share in the doings of this place. Carve out a life for your own family. We set you up there and you'll have your pick of the lassies. Mark my words." He winked at the boy, but Junior just sat staring at him as if he had just told him he was switching all their stock from beeves to sheep.

The jangle and clatter of a barouche out front drew Wilf to the window. "Your sister's back from town," he said, smiling at his son for the first time that day. "Let's go help her bring in the supplies. See if she remembered my bourbon. . . ." As they headed out of the room, he

patted Junior on the shoulder, who stiffened under his
father's old work-gnarled hands. Wilf lost the smile, but
it bloomed again when he opened the front door and
there was Callie, arms laden with parcels.

"My stars, girl, did you buy out Miss Gleason's entire
stock?"

"Now, Papa, you know I'm the only one in this family
who can practice any amount of restraint when it comes
to spending money."

"Ha! I doubt that very much, but I will say it doesn't
look like you bought yourself a new *ladylike* hat."

"Now, Papa...." Callie turned to her brother, who
followed their father down the steps.

"Junior, have you had to listen to this old mountain
goat the entire time I've been gone?" Into his arms she
plunked a sack of coffee beans and placed a flat, brown-
paper bundle on top of it. "That's for you," she said,
smiling at her brother. And turning to her father, she
said, "And I paid for it with my own money."

"I never begrudge family trading gifts. It's downright
civilized. Why, before you arrived we were talking of just
such a thing...."

"Nothing wrong with your hat, Callie," said Junior,
not looking at either of them.

Callie watched Wilf narrow his eyes and stare at the
boy. "Speaking of gifts," she said. "Miss Gleason insisted
on sending this for you, Papa." She handed her father a
wooden box, hinged on the side, with a carved surface. He
opened it, and nested inside was a bottle of Barr's Best,
his favorite bourbon. Wilf held it at arm's length and ad-
mired it. "Why, it's fine, just fine. But whatever for?"

"Because she's fond of you, as if you didn't know."

"We're friends, is all." He tucked the gift under his
arm, plumed more cigar smoke.

"So, Callie, anything new in the world?" Junior almost smiled at his sister.

"I should be asking you that question, Junior. That's

why I bought you that shirt." She nodded at the brown package she'd handed him. "Time you got off this place now and again—and not just to hit the saloon with the boys. Lots of nice folks in these parts. And they do hold these things called dances every so often."

He reddened. "I know, I know. That ain't what I meant, Callie—"

Wilf shook his head and stared at Junior. "I never thought any son of mine would become a drunkard."

"Papa! Junior isn't . . . and you know it." Callie turned to her brother. "I know what you meant, Junior," she said, pulling her coat down off the seat of the barouche. She stopped, eager to change the subject, and looked at her father and brother. "Matter of fact, something that happened last night was a little odd."

"How so, girl?" Wilf looked up from studying his gift. Junior stood, one step below him, but looked at her with the same look of curiosity and concern, as if they were twins separated by long years. She couldn't help smiling.

"Well, since I was staying in town with Miss Gleason last night, she and I went to Mae's for supper—my treat, Papa—and there was a stranger got there before us. It being a Tuesday, there was no one else in the place, except for Harvey Peterson." She wagged her eyebrows. Her father frowned and her brother half smiled.

"And do you know, he was downright rude," said Callie.

Her father straightened. "Harv? Rude to you?"

She shook her head. "Not Harv. The stranger was the one who was rude."

"Where is he now?" Her father looked beyond her, as if he could spot this offensive person on the horizon. He stared past the long, curving drive that led up to the house, and out over the plains that stretched for miles. His gaze took in his own vast herds of grazing cattle and pasture land interrupted only by Maligno Creek meandering through the valley.

"He's in town, Papa. And yes, he was rude to me, but he was that way with everyone. I don't think he meant it. I think he's just, well, not used to being away from a city. Anyway, Brandon put him in his place."

"Brandon? How so?" Junior was interested now.

"He was drunk, no surprise there, and the stranger thought he was protecting me, I guess." She shrugged. "Brandon up and lashed out, punched the stranger on the cheek. Dropped him and knocked him out."

"I never took a shine to that boy, and I can't say I condone his drinking ways of late, but I won't disagree with any man who defends my daughter."

"There wasn't anything to defend. It was a misunderstanding, that's all. I shouldn't have even told you."

"You ever find out who he was, what he's doing in Turnbull?"

"Mae said his name is Middleton. But I think he's from back East. Definitely a city boy." She stood, mired in thought, one hand on the barouche, her brown coat over one arm.

"Callie."

"Yes, Papa?"

"Everything all right, then? He didn't hurt you . . . ?"

"Oh no. Not at all. He's fine. A bruise on his cheek, I should think."

"You didn't answer your brother's question. What's he want here?"

"I'm sure I have no idea. But I will tell you there's something—I don't know—familiar, I suppose, about him."

"Familiar? How so?"

"That's what I've been trying to figure out. I think I finally have it. He reminds me, for some odd reason, of Mr. MacMawe, before he took sick, of course."

There was an odd silence. Then her father said, in a voice that sounded thin and brittle, "How so, Callie?"

"Well, it could well be that shocking topknot of red

hair. Or the fact that he's a fairly large man, like Old Rory. Oh, I don't know what it was. Probably just a drummer—who else would come to Turnbull? And on a Tuesday? Funny that a salesman who looks like poor Mr. MacMawe would show up in Turnbull, of all places. And just after the funeral too. It's not like you see red hair every day."

Her father turned and disappeared inside without saying another word. Seconds later, he barked for his son to follow. "Junior . . . my library. And close the door behind you."

Junior closed his eyes and sighed. His sister touched his sleeve. "Junior, whatever happened between you two? You used to get along so well—"

"Yep, when I was a kid." He took the steps two at a time. He stopped at the top step and looked down at her. "Thanks for the shirt, sis. I'll step out more often, I promise. And not just to the bars with the boys. . . ."

But the lines around his eyes were cut deep. He looked so old to her. Old and fragile.

And then their father's voice cracked the moment in two. "Junior, where in the hell are you?"

The young man sighed and turned.

The only place he'll wear that shirt, she thought, *is the saloon*. A few seconds later Callie heard the library door clunk shut.

Chapter 7

A bullet whistled, punched into the old cowhand's shoulder blade with the sound of a fist hitting a sack of cornmeal. It drove through flesh, blood, shattered wet bone, lung, and pushed out through his sagged chest. The force of the shot jerked him hard from the saddle as if yanked by ropes.

As he lay on the ground trying to get his breath back, Mitchell Farthing wondered what in the hell had just happened. Had Bullock thrown him? No, not Bullock. But then what caused the raw, hot pain in his shoulder? Had he just landed hard and broken it? Did it matter? *Mitchell*, he told himself as the pain welled in him, *none of this matters now. You have been damaged in some way and you are a long way from anywhere. And if you are now addlepated from a fall, to boot, what will you do? What can you do out here alone?*

Think, old man, he told himself. *Think*. But the only thing Mitchell could call up in his mind was that Quimby and the boys had been right. He should have quit the line at least a year back. But how do you quit something when it's the only thing you've ever done that made you feel as if you were living? How do you stop riding a horse, for God's sake? He'd lost all his money over the past few seasons, just trying to stay in the young man's game. Trying to land a choice position at a ranch somewhere. The final straw was when he'd gotten sick, had to use the last of his poke and sell off his good gear to pay for the doctoring bills. No one had wanted the horse, Bullock.

He was thankful that his old friend was as old as he was—no chance of being separated from him. Then he'd gotten what seemed a lucky break—a telegram, the first he'd ever received—from his old line-shack partner, Squirly Ross. He'd wondered about Squirly off and on over the years, and come to the decision that he'd probably made the right decision to leave the grub line and try his hand at prospecting. But the telegram seemed to say otherwise. Squirly hinted that there was ranch work, and something more, down south in New Mexico Territory. All he had to do was show up. Squirly had also mentioned he should bring his poke. Ha—if Squirly only knew that Mitchell didn't have a poke any longer. He smiled at the thought of the two of them working a ranch job together, somewhere warm. Turnbull, the telegram had said. Come to Turnbull . . . big opportunities.

These thoughts came quickly to him, followed on their heels by the knowledge that he might never get there now. *You fell off your horse, you old fool,* he thought. And he laughed, or tried to. A wet clot caught in his throat and even as he burbled up an imitation of a chuckle, Mitchell knew he'd been shot. And he also knew that he was sunk before he floated, to quote his old, long-gone Da.

For a lung-shot man is a dead-shot man.

It was the first bullet to ever pierce his old hide, which he found remarkable given the amount of time he'd spent roving the West, the saloon scuffles he'd seen, backed into a corner, not wanting to mix it up with fools too stupid to recognize a bad hand for what it was, or too drunk to take their fight outside. Or all those scrapes with ranchers opposed to free grazers, or fights with free grazers themselves—he'd been on both sides of that tiff more than a few times. And then there was the War Betwixt the States. Good God, how had he managed to slip through that one with little more than ringing ears and nightmares? *Doesn't matter now, old fool*, he told himself. *You're cooked and laid out on the hardpan floor of the Cholla Basin, miles from water and inches from rocks*.

Then he heard his horse nicker. Bullock, thought Mitchell, the steadiest old thing on four legs, standing nearby and not sure what had just happened. *Make it to the horse*, he thought. *Might stand a chance*. Mitchell's vision wavered at the edges, as if he were looking through water. Then it dimmed, lightened, dimmed. . . . And there was the sound of a horse moving, stepping closer. Bullock with a nervous chuckle. Someone else, then.

He heard that someone climb down, footsteps, and then a shadow was standing tall over him. Mitchell tried to speak, forced his eyes to move. *Come to it, you foolish old man*, he told himself. *Or this stranger will think you've expired and be tempted to drag you in a hole and cover you with rocks, or else leave you for the coyotes to sup on*.

The old man put his all into opening his mouth and felt that he'd made some sort of progress. But it was only a blood bubble; he heard it pop. All the words he would ever get to say were in that bubble. He looked up at the thin man, not too tall, and saw a low-crowned hat, black. And then the man bent low, the eyes looking down, nose twitching. *Do I smell bad?* thought Mitchell.

The man looked down and then to each side. He smiled and lifted the little sack of Bull Durham from Mitchell's pocket, then touched a finger in salute to the wide brim of his black hat.

Then the man stood, looked straight down at him,

made a kiddie's gun with his fingers. "I am going to Turnbull now," said the man. Then he smiled. "And you, my friend, are going to hell." He pulled the imaginary trigger.

The last things Mitchell wondered as he lay there on the ground looking upward was that he too had been headed to Turnbull. He could have ridden along with the stranger; they could have kept each other company. But that was not meant to be. How, he wondered, could he have wronged someone so badly—someone he didn't even recognize? He figured that the answer was that he hadn't. *Hell of a mistake*, he thought. *And I'm on the poor end of it.*

The man smiled once more; then, where before the man's fingers held nothing more than the shape of a kiddie's gun, now he held a long-barreled Smith & Wesson Army revolver. He pulled the trigger and the pistol bucked in his hand.

As hairs of smoke snaked upward from the tip of the barrel, Darturo sighed, with his eyes closed, as if he were sinking into a tub of hot water after a two-month trail drive. He breathed deeply for a few pulls, his smile widening. His slow, dry chuckle uncoiled until both horses perked their ears toward him.

"Now . . . that?" Darturo wagged his pistol at the dead man. "That was better than finding a clear stream in the middle of this dry hell." He rolled a smoke from the man's makings, and as he puffed, he rummaged in the dead man's pockets, flopping the old cowhand one way, then another. He tugged off the man's cracked boots and shook them. Only grit sprinkled out, powdering away on an unseen breeze.

He repeated his search with the man's sagged saddlebags on the old horse that had wandered but a few feet away, found nothing worthy of his interest. Darturo's top lip rose, exposing his teeth in a sneer. "Useless old man." He snatched the trailing reins and jerked the horse's head toward him. The horse blinked once as he cocked his pistol, jammed the snout of the barrel into the sunken hollow above the eyeball, and pulled the trigger. Gouts of hot breath and snot sprayed out of the horse's mouth as it collapsed, then flopped to its side and quivered.

"Come on, Picolo. We have places to be. We can make up some time while I am feeling good." He mounted the buckskin. "Of course, I would feel better, but he had nothing to give me except for this tobacco." He shook his head as they galloped southward.

Chapter 8

Callie ferried the rest of the load from her shopping trip into the house, most of it destined for the kitchen. Her thoughts dwelled half on the task at hand, half on the stranger from the night before. She couldn't seem to keep his unconscious face from her mind.

She set the packages on a worktable in the middle of the room, and noted Mica was nowhere to be seen. Probably bringing the noon meal to the men, she thought. She stored most of it on the pantry shelves, leaving a few items for Mica to attend to, knowing how particular he was about his kitchen. Then she filled the kettle and put it on to boil. *I'll bet Papa and Junior would like some tea too*, she thought, and set out her mother's teapot and three cups. When the water had boiled, she filled the pot, covered it with the cozy, and carried the tray to her father's office.

As Callie approached, she noticed the heavy door hung ajar, but no sound came from within. She set the tray on the front hall table, then peeked in the opening and saw her brother standing behind her father's desk.

"Where's Papa?"

Junior looked up, eyes red and wide. "Callie ... I didn't hear you coming. . . ." He replaced the fountain pen in its holder and slipped the page he was writing off the stack. He walked around his father's desk, resting a hand on the guest chair, running a fingertip along the carved grooves of the headrest. "He just left. Said he had to talk with someone right away." Junior looked at his sister. "But not before he told me who your redheaded stranger friend is."

"What? Who does he think the man might be?"

If Junior heard her, he ignored her question. "The old man told me to wait here for him. Can you imagine that?"

Callie saw her brother's jaw muscle working hard. "What are you up to, Junior?"

"Nothing that concerns you, Callie."

She narrowed her eyes at him. "You're not thinking of leaving, are you?"

"And why not?" He stood straighter and returned her stare.

It was the first time in a long while that she saw the fire and zest, and yes, if she had to be honest about it, there was a hint of ruthlessness there too in him that she saw every day in her father's face. But she wasn't so sure she liked it on her brother's gentle features. Once again she was reminded of how very similar the two men were. And yet so different.

"But, Junior, you're not Papa. He's—"

"What? A real man?" he shouted. "Someone who did something with his life, on his own terms, with his own hands?" Junior held up his trembling hands, their work-hardened backs to his sister. In one of them he clutched the paper on which he'd been writing. The page trembled as if in a breeze. Callie smelled the rotted-flower stink of whiskey on his breath. She saw three unfinished lines of a letter that began "Father."

Junior gritted his teeth, said quietly, "I've heard it all before, Callie. All of it." His head shook in rage. For a moment their eyes locked; then a leer spread across his face. "I may not be the old man, but I sure as hell can be my own man. And I think I know how." With precision he tore apart the letter until it was little more than ragged fragments no larger than a thumb. Then his mirthless smile widened and he let the torn bits drift from his fingertips. "Thanks, sis." He spun from her and strode with care out of the dark room, the study doors slammed back, quivering on their hinges.

"That's not what I meant, Junior!" But it was too late—even as she said it the big entry door to the house slammed hard and she heard his boots clunk down the wide front steps. Callie had never seen her brother act so strange.

So very similar, she thought, looking around her father's dark, orderly office. At the scraps of torn paper trailing across the burgundy rug. And yet so very different.

Chapter 9

Brian Middleton made it just past the southeastern sign-post of Turnbull proper when the saddled beast he rode convulsed as if pinched. The big man gripped the reins tight and wrapped his fingers around the saddle horn, his long legs, unstirruped, slamming the barrel of the horse, alarming the mount further with each bucking move.

Middleton's derby hat, now the color of sunbaked dust, popped from his head and landed upright under a thudding hoof, and his satchel, tied behind the cantle and hanging loose on one side of the horse's rump, bounced in counterpoint to his flailing legs and the horse's jumps. As the horse spun in a circle, Middleton saw a half dozen women and men watching from the end of the cursed little town's main street. And he felt his hated temper rise in him like storm water filling a too-narrow drain. His battered cheek, a sore reminder of the vicious attack he'd endured the previous evening, throbbed and pulsed with every hop the horse made.

He'd gladly be damned forever before he'd give those leering folks the satisfaction of seeing him head back to

that thief Haskell's livery for a different mount. He gritted his teeth and worked the reins left, then right, and
before he knew what had happened he was flat on the
gravel path, on his back looking up at the horse, which
stood still and stared up the sloping trail out of town, as if
in contemplation of what it might find out there beyond
the rocks and sand.

Without turning his head, Middleton shifted his eyes
back toward the people in the street. They were turned
away, he knew, not wanting to be seen by him gawping at
his calamitous descent. *Well, good*, he thought. *The less
the better*. He pulled in a great draft of air through his
nostrils and rose to his feet, smacking dust from his
clothes and looking around for his hat. It had been under
him.

The midday sun baked down, and, having no other
headgear, he picked up the flattened felt and beat the
dust from it too, then rammed an ample fist into it. By
now it looked more like a concertina than a derby, but he
set it on his thatch of wiry red hair and pulled down on
both sides of the brim. It would stay put now, by gum, or
he wasn't Brian J. Middleton. Within seconds he felt it
working its way back upward. He took in a deep breath,
placed one large hand atop the derby, snatched the
horse's reins with the other, and led the now-docile beast
in the direction he'd been headed originally, southward
out of town.

*Once we're past those trees and over that little rise, I'll
give this beast another go*. He looked at the horse. "Apparently, we have a fair distance to travel yet today. I
don't fancy spending all of it leading you. Now, you may
have been some sort of joke of a horse and Haskell, that
thief, may very well be laughing away in front of a crowd
at the saloon at my expense, but I'll tell you this one
time only: I will not be trifled with. I will not put up with
these shenanigans. This trip, this town, these people may
have been Mr. MacMawe's preference, but they are not

mine. And I will not tolerate any of this. The sooner this distasteful experience is over with, the sooner you can return to your stall and eat whatever it is you indulge in. Do you hear me?"

The brown horse flicked an ear.

"Good. That's settled, then." And they trudged on past the clump of scrub pines and up over the hill.

Chapter 10

"Esperanza! Esperanza Soles! Are you here? Is anyone about the place?" Wilf Grindle shifted in his saddle, his grand palomino gelding, Tiny Boy, fidgeting in the open space between the house and the nearest barn. Wilf looked about him again, taking in the disheartening scene before him. The bunkhouse was shut tight and shuttered, fence rails angled, leaning and unmended on the near chutes, and a rusted corner of tin on the chicken shed bounced and squawked in the light breeze that had kicked up on his way over here.

It had not been a pleasant ride, what with everything on his mind, all the things he figured he needed to do to ensure that he ended up owner of the Dancing M. And then there were the memories of happier times for all, each curve in the path, each boulder on the familiar road a reminder of the youth and blind optimism each of them had shared so long ago.

His Carla would expertly handle the reins of the gig, the same one Callie now favored, as they rode of an evening to visit Rory and Penelope, his city girl—though you'd never have known, so adaptable had she been to life on the frontier. Of all of them, Penny had been the one to truly thrive in this place. Unforgiving as the place could be at times, it was easy to tell she had become part of it. He shook his head.

All that had been a long time ago, back before children and hired help and banknotes and water rights and challenges from new settlers changed everything for them all—and he'd admit that not all of it had been for the better. But back before all that, they'd had each other and the certainties of youth, and that had been enough to see them through Indian attacks, drought, and bone-wearying labor. And then Rory and Penny had the boy, the first baby of their group.

Like its father, the baby had been born big, larger than a child should be, and Penny was no match for nature's plans. Left weakened, she died before the child reached a year. Those had been hard times, his Carla trying to help stubborn Rory to raise the boy. But between them all, they had managed to struggle through a couple more years. By then their own children came along and it was too much effort. They'd offered to take the boy in with them, anything to help. But Rory had become hard, as if his old self had been covered with horned wrappings that grew thicker and denser with time.

He'd brought in Esperanza to help him with the child, with the house, and that seemed to help, but then one day the child was gone. Rory wouldn't speak of it. They'd only gotten the story from far-off neighbors, from people in the little growing town of Turnbull. They said Rory had met strangers from the East, city folk who didn't even stay the night. They'd hired their own transport and taken the baby boy away with them.

It didn't take long after that for him and Rory to disagree about most everything, even when Wilf admitted he was wrong, or just plain gave in to Rory. Still, it wasn't enough, and Rory became more difficult than ever to deal with. He never spoke of the child, would walk away if the subject was raised. The final straw came when Carla, herself by then a doting mother, had tried a last desperate plea to get the truth from him, to reason with him. In front of Wilf, Rory had barked at her as if she were an annoying dog, and then raised an arm like a grizzly its paw, as if to strike. They never spoke again after that.

Wilf had half expected Rory to show up at Carla's funeral a couple of years later. But the bear of a Scot never did. Wilf shook his head at the memory. And Carla, to her end, regretted not doing more. It broke her heart knowing that Penelope's baby was sent away with strangers. . . .

"What is it you want, Mr. Grindle?"

The voice cracked his thoughts like morning sun rasping through the curtains in his bedroom. A squat Mexican woman stood before him, her eyes and forehead a maze of creases as she squinted up into the morning sun at him. Despite her lined face, he knew she was younger than he. She held the emotionless look so common among Mexicans and Indians of his acquaintance. Again, he wondered if it was only with him that people were cold, as if they'd stepped back and were guarding themselves whenever he was near.

"Esperanza, it's good to see you again."

She stood regarding him, one hand on her hip, one visoring the sun from her eyes. Her gaze was not hateful, nor was it that of a friend. Her clothing was the most cheerful thing about her, he decided. He'd hand it to the Mexicans; they had a way with color. Though worn, her dress was still rich in hues of brown and yellow, and the apron topping it too was neatly pressed and of the same red-flower print as the kerchief holding back her still mostly black hair.

He tried again. "It's been nearly two weeks since the funeral. I wanted to see how you are getting on here, what your plans might be. . . . May I get down?"

Still she watched him as a curious bird might watch a far-off hawk from the safety of an inner branch. Her head nodded once; then she turned toward the house. He led Tiny Boy to the rail before the house, and noted it was the same simple setup he'd helped Rory build, what was it? Twenty-four, twenty-five years back? He ran his fingers over the rusted steel band holding the end snug. They'd smithed those bands together. And gotten drunk at the same time. He remembered they had been in more danger from Penny's sharp words than from smacking their hands with the hammer.

Off to the left, backed up against a shrub-covered boulder, leaned what was left of the forge shop, now mostly a pile of warped boards and broken implements, robbed from for other projects over the years, no doubt.

"Coffee for you." A ceramic mug of steaming black coffee was held in his face. She'd caught him at it again, daydreaming of old times when he should have been pressing her with the business at hand. He cleared his throat. "Thank you, Esperanza."

Wilf offered a smile, but it didn't seem to help soften her features. She stood on the steps, blowing on her own cup of coffee. It was obvious she wasn't going to let him in. No matter, really. It'd been so long he didn't really want to go in there anyway. But he could see over her shoulder that it was neat as a pin. Plain, but neat. As was the yard and doorstep. On the floor, just inside the door and half in shadow, was a basket of brown eggs. Still warm, he'd bet.

"Esperanza, I'm curious to know what you'll be doing. You and your boy, now that Rory's, well, passed on."

"No, Mr. Grindle."

He'd been in midsip, awaiting her long-winded reply about how she didn't know what he meant, what would they do, and then the hot coffee burned his tongue.

"What?"

She shook her head and looked to the side, off in the distance, a wide, tight look set on her mouth. She shook her head fast and kept on with it while she talked. "No, Mr. Grindle. I know what you're after and it's not right. You will not run me off this place. It is my home. My son's home. It is ours. Rory told me so. I say no to you."

He stared back into her eyes for a few seconds, then said, "Well, I'll give you this: You come right to a thing, don't you, little lady?" He had to look away from her. Those dark eyes were like accusations of everything he'd ever done that he regretted. Damn the woman anyway. He dumped the rest of the coffee and shook the last drops from the cup.

"You're telling me he left the Dancing M to you all neat and legal? Got a lawyer involved too, did he?"

That same dark stare met his, but there was something there; he was sure of it. A flicker, maybe, like lightning a hundred miles off on a dark summer night, that told him a crack had opened and he, by God, was the man to drive a wedge in there and widen it, take that boulder apart all by himself. He'd own the Dancing M and make no mistake about it.

He offered her the cup, handle first. "I thank you, ma'am, for the coffee." Then he nodded and mounted up, without another look left or right. *The past is well and truly dead, Wilf*, he told himself. *Time for a bright new future*. He smiled as he rode away home, toward the Driving D. Time to talk with the boy again, get the lawyers in on this, get the situation in hand once and for all.

Chapter 11

"Well, your best bet—heck, your only bet—is the Doubloon Saloon down the street to the right. Can't miss it." Harv Peterson leaned on the ledger and winked at the swarthy stranger with the dusty black hat. "You looking to get in on a game of chance, mister?"

"The thought had occurred to me. Unless the local boys are too afraid to bring me in, that is, huh?" Mort Darturo feathered a thumb along each side of his mustaches.

For two strokes of the grandfather clock at the base of the staircase, the men stared stone-faced at each other. Then the portly hotelier grinned and smacked the counter. "Now you're funnin' me. I get you. No, no, no high rollers hereabouts, but the boys from the Driving D do play a mean hand of stud."

"You get in on those games yourself?" Mort Darturo hefted his war bag, adjusted his saddlebags on his shoulder. His coat parted.

"Not me, no. Mae would never—" Harv paused when he saw the black grips of two pistols, butt-forward in cross-draw fashion, riding low on the stranger's waist.

Darturo followed his sight line, nodded at him, and said, "They're for show. Just like my card game, huh?"

Harv nodded, not sure if he should smile.

"Four, you say?"

"Yessir, room four. Busy week. Matter of fact, it's the same room I gave to the only other stranger we've seen in the last month."

"Oh?" Darturo stopped at the end of the counter, tilted his head to the side.

"Yes, exciting too. Turns out, according to Teasdale anyway, the big stranger who came in on yesterday's train is the long-lost MacMawe boy. I remember when all that hubbub was going on. What a mess."

"What 'hubbub' was that?"

"Oh, must be pretty near twenty years back or so, one of the larger landowners, that'd be MacMawe, he lost his wife. Had a hard time with everything after that. He eventually got himself a Mexican housekeeper, if you know what I mean. But I guess it didn't matter. Seemed nothing would go right for him. So he sent his boy back East to be raised by rich relations."

"And this boy is back? He's a man now, though, huh?"

Harv nodded, eyebrows raised. "He's bigger than his father. And Rory was as big as they come."

The stranger walked to the stairs. "Well, it is no never mind to me."

"Might be, though," said Harv.

Mort smiled, said, "How so?"

"Well, if you're looking for work and if you know your nose from your tail end of a cow, then the two biggest ranches in these parts are the Dancing M, that would be the MacMawe place, and the Driving D, Wilf Grindle's spread. Course, if you're not looking for work, that's a different story."

The stranger seemed to think about this a moment. "So, this MacMawe is dead now, eh? And his land, it's good land?"

"Oh, just about as good as it gets. Toss-up, really, between Driving D and the Dancing M. Both got good minerals, plenty of grazing. But the Dancing M, that's got the best water rights. Controls the flowage of the feeder streams off the Maligno down that way."

Mort nodded as if to himself.

"Why? You got a hankering to find work out there?"

"We'll see, eh?" Mort clumped up the stairs.

Harv heard the stranger's boots pause at the top landing, then resume their slow walk toward the rear of the building. He looked down at the ledger, spun it, squinted, and frowned. The man's signature was a snaking scrawl that said nothing Harv could make out. Lawman? Bounty hunter? Certainly seemed like someone who took in a lot more information than he let out. And that accent . . . He'd bet his mama's boots it wasn't Mexican. So, where was he from? Looked Mexican, sort of dark and smallish, though there was a little bit of a dandy in him too.

Harv closed the book and wondered if he talked too much. Mae said he did. But then she'd hardly be the one to judge, since he could never get more than two words in before she rode all over his talk like a woman a-horseback.

He blew out a slow breath through the side of his mouth and looked out the window, then leaned an elbow on the counter and probed his nose with a fingertip.

"Mining for gold, eh?"

Harv spun, his finger still occupied. The new guest stood at the counter as if he'd never left. But Harv had seen him ascend the stairs, had heard the door to number 4 open and close. He wiped his finger on his trousers. "I didn't hear you. . . ."

Darturo smiled. "Which way to the saloon?"

"Oh, that way." Harv jerked a thumb behind him, in the general direction of the north end of the street.

Darturo nodded, said, "Don't wait up, eh?" And chuckled as he left.

Harv watched his shape through the gauzy lace curtains of his front windows, heard the man's boots clunking the wood boardwalk. The last of the man's low, throaty laugh seemed to echo in the lobby long after the man left. Harv watched the door and brushed at his nostrils, not liking the coldness rising in him. He had given thought to inspecting the man's traps, see what was what with him. But now something told him that might not be a good idea.

Chapter 12

Mica Bain rapped the long handle of his favorite wooden spoon on the rim of his cast-iron cook pot. "If I have to yell for them to come to dinner one more time . . ." He paused to listen, then slid the top back over the boiling orange stew. "Ungrateful family, don't know what they're missing anyway." He ambled out of the kitchen and down the carpet in the hall toward Wilf's office, mumbling and wiping his hands on his smeared apron. "One last time. Then I feed it to the hogs, and I quit. And this time I mean it."

He reached up to rap on the door of Wilf's office, but the raised voices of two men disagreeing within stayed his broad, knuckled hand. Wilf's spirited, rasping tones reached through the barely open heavy doors. So, one was Wilf; that much Mica was sure of. But the other? There was something familiar to the voice, but he couldn't place it. *Damn this getting old. Used to have hearing like a mountain cat. Now look at me. Reduced to getting right up to a door to listen in.* He leaned his head closer to the gap . . . those clipped tones. No, wasn't one of Wilf's rancher friends. *Not many of those around any-more anyways. All sellin' off and movin' out. Junior?* No, he spoke softer. *'Sides, nowadays the boy would be more likely to still be in bed.*

He noticed the familiar sharp blended smells of cherry and pine of Wilf's cigarillos. He was partial to a flake blend for his pipe himself. Then the second man spoke louder and Mica was shocked—he hadn't recognized it as Junior's voice, but it was indeed the boy. He peeked between the nearly closed doors.

"No," continued Wilf, leaning against the bookcase behind his desk. "Course, it's too much to hope for, but the best thing that could happen was if Rory's two off-spring, this newly returned prodigal and the bastard, duked it out and ended up killing each other. Solve a load of problems for us. But that's pie-in-the-sky think-ing and a sure way to attract unwanted trouble. I'll do this all legal-like and aboveboard, if it kills me."

"What about Esperanza?"

"What about her, Junior? You honestly don't think that anyone in their right mind would allow that Mexi-can mother of a drunken half-breed, and a squatting gold digger to boot, to stay around these parts, do you?"

Mica watched as Wilf smiled and thumbed a match, set flame to a cigarillo, and regarded his son through the drift-ing fog of blue smoke. He reached a hand into the wooden box on his desk and tossed one to his son. The boy re-garded it, smiled, and leaned toward a newly lit match.

Mica felt his teeth come together hard, his jaw mus-cles aching with the strain. He wanted to slam open this door and drop Wilf and the boy too, right where they stood. Drawing on their fine cigars and talking as if good, hardworking people, their own neighbors, were nothing more than a few beeves to cut out and kill off. Sacrifices for the good of the herd. He wanted to burst in, find out just what his oldest friend meant by all this.

This damn sure didn't sound like the Wilf he'd known

all these years. Calling that boy, Brandon, the "bastard"?
Everybody in these parts knew who his pappy was. And
who was this "prodigal"? Surely he didn't mean . . .
could it be? Mica stood stunned, staring at the door but
not seeing a thing. *Rory's firstborn? Back here? God in
heaven . . .* Mica leaned toward the door again.

It was as if he didn't know who these people were
anymore. Certainly not Wilf, who, to his recollection,
had never had anything bad to say about Esperanza.
Why the change of heart? And then he knew. As long as
Rory was alive, no matter that they hadn't spoken in
years, Wilf wouldn't dare broach the subject of possess-
ing the Dancing M. *But now that Rory's gone, I'll bet he's
thought about it plenty over the past few weeks.* But what
could change his plans enough to account for this nasty
new edge he'd not ever seen in Wilf?

Could it be that Rory MacMawe's son had truly come
back? If so, it would be for the ranch, no doubt. He'd
heard Wilf say often enough that though they both es-
tablished roughly the same-sized ranches when they
moved here as young men, Rory's was the better of the
two, mostly because he had better access to water, both
from a spring-fed supply, and cutting through his acreage was a vast and lush river valley fed by Maligno
Creek and several feeder braids of the main stream.

And all this over the years, Mica knew, galled Wilf
Grindle to no end. And then he stopped cold. Wilf
couldn't be trying to buy that land? It had to belong to
Esperanza and Brandon. And even the newly returned
son surely had a right to the land. Mica strained to hear
more. The way the two of them were speaking, he felt
sure that there was something bad about to happen. Perhaps it already had. Mica's thoughts turned to Espy. It
galled him that he'd only been able to offer her the small
comforts of a friend, nothing more. Maybe in time, he
thought. *But that, old man*, he told himself, *is the one
thing you don't have endless amounts of anymore.*

Mica resolved to confront his old friend about this growing fear that was fast becoming a conviction. He reached out to push open the door, and then Wilf spoke, louder this time. Mica stayed his hand again and listened.

"No, son," said Wilf, facing the window, still looking west toward the Dancing M. "Much as I'd like to say that land was ours right now, and believe me, it's worth it, we'll bide our time and play the cards as they've been dealt to us." He stood looking through the wavy glass panes, smoke curling up around his head from the cigarillo scissored in his fingers.

Junior reached under his vest and, keeping his eyes on his father, raised a small bottle to his lips. A reddish liquid bubbled up, and the boy suckled at it as if he were nursing on a teat. Mica watched in disgust as the boy's throat and jaw worked the liquid down, draining the bottle. Whiskey. So that's what was giving him his unusual courageous edge in the conversation with his father.

Junior pushed the cork back into the bottle and leaned forward, hands on his knees. He licked his lips and smiled. There was a strange glint in his eyes that Mica hadn't seen there ever before.

"But there's no saying we can't sweeten the pot a little," he said around the little cigar gripped in his teeth. "Before we make them call their play, that is."

The older man cocked his head and regarded his son as if seeing him for the first time. He drew on his cigarillo, exhaled. "Why, Junior. I'm not sure I know you at all today. You are a boy—no, a man—of constant surprises."

A quick, broad smile spread across the boy's face and he leaned back in the chair, one leg draped over the other. He puffed on the cigar.

The older man grunted and smiled as he looked out the window toward the west, toward the Dancing M.

Through the gap in the cracked door, Mica saw with

one eye something up until two days before he had long hoped to see—father and son sharing a laugh, a drink, a moment of plain, unguarded enjoyment of each other's company. But the conversation Mica had heard made him feel as if he didn't even know these men, and he was less sure than ever about what he saw. He stretched his back. *Don't want to know what might come out of their mouths next*, he thought. Not yet anyway. He rapped on the door and told them their lunch was colder than a well digger's backside. Then he went out the front door and headed for the stable. He would not break bread with them today. *Hell*, he thought, *the way I feel, I'd rather break their noses*.

Chapter 13

"Don't see how you're going to do it, Mica." The cowboy who spoke, Dilly Roberts, untied the stained apron and slipped it off over his head.

"Don't know how I'm going to do what, exactly?" Mica paused in slicing the onions.

"You know," said Dilly, balling up the apron and using it to wipe down the table.

Mica frowned, but said nothing. The boy knew that Mica would make him wash the table down properly anyway. "No, I don't know. If I did, I'd not have answered you. Now stop speaking in riddles and out with it."

The last round of hands had reluctantly departed to head into the heat of the afternoon and the rest of the day's chores. Though it was spring, the sun had already staked its claim on the season, and all the tasks that faced the men ended with each of them covered in muck, reeking to high heaven of green manure, cow belches, mud, and sweat. From branding to castrating to gathering the loose stock and newborns that emerged from a long winter, and a million other chores, it was all hot, sticky work.

Mica's meals were about the only thing the men looked forward to during the long, hard days before the drives splintered the ranch hands into several groups, some taking to the trails, some staying at the ranch to prep fences, repair corrals, lay in firewood for the coming year.

Dilly didn't respond, just kept wiping the table.

"You pumping me for information, boy?" Mica wagged his paring knife at his junior cook and sometime cowboy. Dilly had come to them halfway through the summer last year, an odd time for a hand to show up looking for work. Eventually, he reluctantly admitted that he'd just gotten out of prison. Seemed as though years before, he'd been convicted of killing a man. There had been enough doubt about the crime that though he ended up incarcerated, he had been given lax treatment. While serving his sentence, he found that he not only enjoyed working in the kitchens of the prison, but was good at it. Soon he was eligible for early release, having served four of his six years.

When he'd showed up at the Driving D, Dilly Roberts was dismissed out of hand by Wilf as a troublemaker and rabble-rouser. As a last-second plea, the thin out-of-work man said that he also had experience as a cook. "Mica does our cookin'," Wilf had said, turning away from the hopeful young man.

Luckily for them all, Mica happened to be within earshot. He'd walked over, introduced himself, and turned to Wilf. "I have been telling you since last fall that I could use a hand in the kitchen."

"You get help. All the boys pitch in."

"Wilf, you know and I know them boys mean well, but they don't know a whistle berry from a tick, nor a ladle from their elbow." He'd turned back to Dilly. "Now, tell me what all you can cook, and if you are used to cooking for groups of hungry men."

Dilly had smiled. "I reckon I have that experience." His face grew serious. "I picked it up in prison. Lots of folks to cook for there."

"I hear you. Come on back to the cook shack, see what's what. Maybe I'll take you on, a trial of sorts."

Behind Mica, Wilf had grown red-faced and shook his head. "Last time I looked, the Driving D was in my name, not yours, Mica."

"Wilf, 'less you want to spend the rest of the summer fixing your own food—and I've tasted your efforts and it isn't something I want to do again—then you ought to leave well enough alone. Let me run my kitchens, you dally with your cattle, and as long as you and your men get a full belly three times a day, well, that's all I'm going to say on the matter. Now come on to the cook shack, Dilly. Show me how you use a ladle."

They had left Wilf standing in the middle of the dooryard, shaking his head but saying nothing. And it wasn't long afterward that even Wilf had, though reluctantly, admitted that hiring Dilly Roberts was a damn good idea. He'd even tried to take credit for hiring him, until Mica smiled and stared Wilf down one midday meal when he was eating with the boys.

Now as Mica watched the young man finish wiping the table, he was secretly pleased with how well hiring him had turned out for them all. And he was not a little proud, as Dilly had learned much of what he knew about the kitchen from Mica.

"You get help with that chuck box for the short work wagon?" he said to Dilly, changing topics. "You'll need at least two other men to help lift her in there. Wilf's too cheap to let us have our own wagon for day work, but that should do you fine, while you're still close to the Driving D. You'll take the full chuck wagon for the drive."

Dilly shook the soiled apron out the door. "I guess I thought you'd know what I was talking about."

"Damn, boy, you're flopping like a banked fish. It's been some long time since I could read minds. Wait a minute. . . ." Mica poked the brim of his hat backward on his head and stared at the rafters as if in deep thought.

"That's right. It's been . . . never. Now out with it, or I'll leave all the slicing to you."

Dilly smiled. "It's just that there's talk amongst the boys that Mr. Grindle is planning on buying the Dancing M. And they're excited, but wondering if he'll bring on more men, or just make the ones who are here work longer hours for the same pay. That sort of thing."

"So that's what you bunch of mother hens are clacking and clucking about every time I leave the room. And here I thought you were going to buy me a nice birthday present."

"It's your birthday?"

"No, as it happens, it ain't. But that's not the point. Point is, no one, not even Mr. Wilf Grindle, should concern themselves with the Dancing M right now. Mr. MacMawe just passed on. I'm sure something will happen with that ranch, but it ain't nothing you cowhands need concern yourselves with. Besides, there are other people who are closer in line than Wilf Grindle for consideration where the Dancing M is concerned."

"Yeah," said Dilly. "I heard that MacMawe's long-lost son is back and looking none too like a rancher. Word is that he is looking to sell up and get back to the East as fast as next week's train will take him." He stared at Mica for a moment, but the older man showed no emotion, no sign he'd even listened to Dilly's gossip.

The two men were silent for a few minutes, each busy with his respective tasks. Then Dilly cleared his throat. Mica smiled, knew more chatter was coming, and kept slicing hunks of beef for the stew.

"So, how would you do it . . . if Mr. Grindle was to somehow buy the Dancing M? And I'm not saying he will, just making conversation, is all."

"Again, Dilly, I told you I ain't no mind reader."

"What I mean is . . . you already have your hands full with two kitchens here, let alone a third over to the Dancing M."

"You worried about work, Dilly? 'Cause I'm here to tell you that everybody likes your cooking. I'd guess your work is safe. People got to eat, right?"

"Well, I will admit I was concerned, but that sets my mind to rest. Though when you put it that way, I guess I should be worried that there might be too much work to be had."

Mica sighed. "I swear, Dilly. You'd gripe if you was hung with a new rope."

"All right, all right, but riddle me one more thing: Why maintain two kitchens here? That don't make no sense to me."

"Now, what part of it confuses you? I got a kitchen here in the cook shack, and then there's one in the main house."

"That's what I'm talking about, Mica. Why two?"

"Because a long time ago, before Mrs. Grindle, that'd be Wilf's wife, before she passed on, when Callie and Junior were just young sprouts, she did all the cooking for her family. I did the cooking for the boys. Then when she passed on, why, Wilf had his hands full with running the ranch, making sure the children were kept in line—a full-time job. If you'd seen them kids, you'd know what I mean." He shook his head at the memory. "He didn't want them to have to traipse on out here three times a day to eat around a table full of cowboys. Can you imagine the language they'd'a learned? Mr. Grindle's a wise man. He knew that the cowboys wouldn't be comfortable with such an arrangement, and he knew the kids might not benefit from it either, so he had me working double time. Just natural that I also helped out with the children. My mama raised a pile of us, and I was one of the oldest, so tending youngsters just comes natural to me."

Dilly drizzled salt into a big stewpot, said nothing. But Mica knew the young man had heard. Anything remotely sounding like gossip slipped right into that head of his.

"That give you enough information to report to the boys when I'm back at the big house, cooking tonight's supper?" Mica smiled.

Most men would blush, deny the very idea of the suggestion. But Dilly Roberts said, "Well, it's not much information, but it will have to do me, I suspect."

"Well, I'm glad I could help. I think."

"Well, in truth, Mica, you didn't tell me a whole hell of a lot that I can tell the boys."

Mica laughed as he set down his knife and wiped his hands on the towel hanging over his shoulder. "You take the cake, Dilly Roberts. I guess I know now how you got that name. You're a doozy of a dilly, no mistake."

Chapter 14

It was late afternoon before Junior Grindle, riding Spunk, his dapple gray gelding, at a steady gallop, saw his target in the distance. Junior had dismounted twice in the past three hours, and then only walking for short distances.

His horse was good and lathered by the time he saw what he hoped was the man his father had sent him out to track down. It had taken him longer than he thought to find the stranger. How the man could have made so little progress and gotten so far off the road from town was beyond him. Had to be the stranger, he thought as he galloped forward. Who else but a citified greenhorn would ride in such a manner? Even at this distance, Junior swore he could see daylight between the man's britches and his saddle. And that horse looked none too game either. One of Silver Haskell's beauties, he'd bet. Must have been a long time since the nag had seen such a poorly skilled rider.

Junior was still a few hundred yards off and coming in from the east, before the stranger, a big fellow, from what he could tell, took notice of him.

"Ho, there!" Junior yelled, a hand up in a friendly wave. He slowed as he approached and reined up within thirty feet of the stranger. For a moment, Junior could think of nothing to say, so odd did the scene strike him. Here was a man who couldn't look more odd on horseback, and who capped it off with a dandy hat that had seen better days. It looked more like a cow pie puffed with air than a topper.

And the fellow's clothes, a fine suit by the looks of it, or once had been, now sported more dust than fabric, all manner of thistle, and a few stalks of dried grasses swung with the man's movements.

"Hello."

The stranger sounded to Junior as if he would flop from the saddle if poked with a stiff finger. "You lost, mister?" Junior rested his hands atop his saddle horn and smiled.

"No, I don't believe so. That is to say, no, I am not lost. Not if this is the direction of the Dancing M Ranch."

Junior heard the sound of a carnival bell ringing in his head, telling him that he was indeed a winner. *Here's the man dear old Papa sent me to find.*

"Why, fella, you're headed in the general direction, for sure. Though if you've come from Turnbull, it appears you've strayed from the road a mite."

The big man turned in the saddle, looked about him as if he knew what he was looking for, then turned back to Junior, his brow furrowed.

"No worries. I can get you back on track. But, and if you'll pardon me for saying so, that beast of yours is played out." Junior nudged Spunk forward until he was abreast of the stranger's horse. "Uh-huh, as I thought. That's a Haskell nag. Can spot 'em a mile off. Why, fella, you're lucky you're not afoot. Or worse, carrying that thing on your back." He laughed.

"If you'll excuse me," said the stranger. Junior noticed the man's jaw muscles working as if he were chewing gristle. *Madder'n a starved billy goat*, he thought. *Plumb angry with me, and for doing nothing more than pointing out the obvious.*

The stranger drummed with his boot heels at the old brown horse. Now that it had stopped, it had no intention of moving forward. That much was plain to Junior from the locked knees and flattened ears on the thing. The stranger didn't seem to notice these signs and kicked with more resolve at the beast's gut.

With no warning, the brown nag pitched straight up in the air, and came down off-kilter enough to unseat its rider. Junior guessed this was a common occurrence, judging from the poor state of the man's suit of clothes.

As he plunked to earth, the big man's odd little hat popped off and landed beside him in the dust. *As if I needed more proof*, thought Junior. There was that red hair, sure as night followed day. And that face, now without the hat, he could see it full-on. There was the bruised and swollen cheekbone—Brandon must have taken a mighty swing to cause that one. Yes, sir, the rest of the face and the hair and the man's height all added up to one thing—this was old Rory MacMawe's long-lost son. So the old man was right. Had to be. What a guess. But then, Junior admitted, being able to put such bits of information together was probably why his father was such a successful rancher.

"No offense, mister, but as I said, that horse is plumb tuckered, and unless you want to repeat what you just did—and it looks like you've been through that procedure a few times already today—you might want to consider callin' it quits for the day. I'm fixin' to do that myself. Share a camp, if you've a mind to."

The big man stood with his arms resting on the saddle, breathing hard. "What are you doing out here?"

The question was straightforward and caught Junior

off guard. "Well . . ." He pushed his hat back on his head.
"I'm out checking herd. I'm from the Driving D. Name's
Grindle. Wilf Grindle, the second. Folks call me Junior."

The man narrowed his eyes and said, "I believe last
night I met your sister."

This was something Junior was not prepared for. The
man was quick, making connections between things he
hadn't expected. Like the old man, thought Junior. He
played along. "Why, now I think you have me at a disad-
vantage, mister. I don't even know your name, let alone
how you happen to know my sister."

The big man sighed, and said, "I am afraid I insulted her
last night at a dining establishment in Turnbull proper."
He looked up. "It wasn't my intention, I assure you." He
faced Junior fully and said, "My name is Brian J. Middleton." He nodded his head once in greeting, though he still
did not smile, nor offer his hand for a shake.

There was a quiet moment where neither man knew
what the other might do next. Junior knew he had every
right to defend his sister's honor, but that had never
ended up, so far as Junior knew, in anything but a silly
knife fight with someone going home in a box. He sucked
in a draft of air through his nose and stepped down from
his horse. "Let's make us a fire, brew up some coffee, and
you can tell me all about how you didn't mean to offend
my sister."

Junior was thankful he'd had the foresight to bring
along jerky and biscuits, coffeepot and coffee, and two
tin cups. That, plus oats, two canteens, whiskey, of course,
and a blanket made a decent enough load, for he had
expected to run into this man in just such a fashion. This
was working out well . . . so far. Now he had to make
doubly sure this was old Rory's long-lost son. And if he
was, then it was time to get to work on him.

Chapter 15

The reassuring ruffle of fanned cards, the plink of chips, and the dull clank of coins hitting others on the baize surface of the gaming table were a soothing balm to Mortimer Darturo's travel-weary mind. He should have stayed in the hotel and slept, awakened refreshed and ready for a big meal, a good bottle, and a slow game of stud. But he wasn't much for sleeping or eating. That left him with his two favorite pursuits—booze and poker. A woman could hardly be considered in a town this size, he knew. But still, he held out hope. For if he found one, then this town would surely furnish him with all he'd ever need. *No, no, Mort. Too small*, he told himself. *You will become bored in two days.* He smiled and slid another two chips, red and white, forward. "Raising, eh?"

The bartender's high red cheeks twitched, worked up and down behind the greased handlebar mustache as if he were literally chewing over the problem.

"You do not play this game often, do you?" He took another sip of his whiskey in milk, ignoring the bartender's pained expression on seeing him drink.

The bartender's slow headshake confirmed what Darturo had known since he walked in. The man was a soft touch but ran a clean place. Small and offering few opportunities, at least the Doubloon was somewhat civilized. Mort liked that. He'd never understood why so many saloons allowed their patrons to dribble their chewing tobacco on the floor, spitting at but never hitting the stained, crusted brass cuspidors.

Darturo had grown used to the finer establishments in Denver and other cities he had visited over the years. The betting could usually be counted on to pay well, and if not, the alleys never failed to yield profits from the pockets of a drunken dandy lured in with a request for help. As Darturo learned early on, good people never failed to help other good people. And most people, as it turned out, were doing their best to be good. He thought them fools, naturally, but realized that he was as necessary as were they, for he provided a balance to their efforts of kindness.

"How about we call it a game, eh? You can pour me one drink of your finest whiskey and then I'll go find a steak and that will be that. I am tired."

The big bartender looked relieved. Darturo knew he'd only agreed to play because no one else was in the place, except for the little soak at the half table by the door. He had the same near-empty glass of beer before him as when Darturo had walked in an hour before. Darturo only knew he'd been there, sitting in the shadows, from the powerful reek rising off the man's ragged buckskins.

Darturo made his way to the bar, and the bartender poured Darturo a small glass of McMurdy's Finest from a bottle he slid out from under the counter. "So," said Darturo. "What do you know about a stranger, a Mac something or other, just came into town this week?"

The bartender paused in recorking the bottle. "Why do you ask?"

Darturo sipped. It was decent whiskey. Perhaps he would have more. He would see, but first, he would play a little dumb. "No real reason. The fellow at the hotel told me something about him being a long-lost son of a . . . dancing rancher? Does that sound right?"

The bartender squinted, shook his head, and then understanding smoothed his brow. "You mean the Dancing M. Yessir, that would be old Rory MacMawe. Was a big rancher hereabouts."

"But?" said Darturo, his eyebrows raised.

"But he died a few weeks back."

"Well, that would make it difficult for him to still be a big rancher, eh?" He laughed alone at his joke and pinched it off sooner than he wished. He did not want the locals to think him insensitive. "So, the man who is his long-lost son . . . ?"

Behind Darturo, from the corner near the door, a throat cleared. "That'd be the big fella come in on yesterday's train. Rude as a log to the head, he was."

The little man shuffled out of the shadow, moved closer.

Darturo could smell him. Like a rain-wet dog, he thought. Only worse. Two wet dogs perhaps. He smiled and said, "Another beer . . . for my new friend." He winked and twitched his head toward the sullen little figure. He knew the soak had heard the generous request, because he licked his lips audibly.

The bartender sighed and filled a glass, an honest mug of it with little foam, then set it at the end of the bar and pointed at it. Faster than Darturo expected, the soiled man was at the bar, quaffing down the top half of the beer.

"Much obliged, mister. Been a long road today. Been through the mill, as they say. Hard times for an honest man, I'll tell you—"

"That's enough of that, Squirly Ross." Tom the bartender slung a fresh white towel over his shoulder and rested his meaty palms on the bar. "This man doesn't want to hear your tall tales. Drink up and go find a trough to take the edge off that sweet smell you got going."

Darturo said nothing. Of course, the bartender was right. He had no desire to hear a drunk's embarrassing thanks, the inevitable stories that dragged on with no end, always with one eye measuring the level in the glass, one eye measuring the new patron's tolerance, all the time with that begging look. Darturo half smiled and decided that if the man played that hand with him, he would gut him like a fat little river fish before he left this town. That would be repayment enough for his kindness. Surely the gift of a glass of beer deserved something. . . .

But not before he found out more about this prodigal, the Dancing M, and the Driving D. And how much money each was worth. Much, he thought. And where there is money, there is a way to take it. He wondered how much money the families would be willing to part with in return for the lives of their loved ones. Not all of them, of course. Some of them would need killing beforehand, as a matter of business. Such sacrifices he found were necessary to proving that he was a man of promise. They also helped to keep the process of negotiation moving along at a decent rate of speed. Otherwise, the families might take their time and wonder and think too much and then come to the realization that they might not love their loved ones as much as they thought they did. It had happened in the past, and he was sure it would happen again. People did very little to surprise him anymore.

Darturo turned to the smelly little buckskin-clad figure and smiled. He was about to open the ball, as the cowboys said, when the little drunk spoke first.

"So, newcomer, what say while I have your ear, I ask you a question or two?"

Mort fought the urge to close his eyes and sigh. He wanted to be the one to ask the questions, not answer them. But he held his pasted-on smile and turned to face the little smelly drunk in the rank buckskins. Had the man ever peeled them off and actually bathed? Mort doubted it. Still, he knew from experience that some of the best information he'd received in the past had come to him for the price of a few drinks, the odd full bottle of whiskey.

This he had bought and held just out of reach while the sputtering man or woman licked their lips and burbled enough coherent facts that seemed of sufficient value to warrant the proffered drink. If not, he had warned them, they would surely regret lying to him. Such threats were usually understood to have teeth. And so, the truth, in some stumbling form, had always come to him. Then he gutted them anyway. The world never mourned the passing of a gibbering drunkard.

Squirly glanced at Tom the barkeep, and, seeing the man was busy in the storeroom, he slid himself down along the bartop on one begrimed elbow, his head leaning on his bar-propped arm. "So, newcomer. Not sure I caught your name."

"I can assure you, Mr. Ross, that you did not catch my name. Because I never tossed it to you."

"Oh, uh . . . okay, then. So, what's that accent you got goin' on? I never heard of that."

Darturo stared at Squirly, said nothing.

Finally the funky-smelling little man nodded. "Okay, gotcha, then." He lifted his head from his hand and straightened his back, arching and stretching. "Ooh, but it's a hard line of work I'm in. Hard on the body and soul, I tell you, stranger. And make no mistake about it."

"What work would that be, then, Mr. Ross?"

"Well, I thank you for asking. Truth is, it's a bit of a hush-hush sort of thing. Can't really talk much about it, you know. I can tell you that it's dry work. By gum, but it's dry work."

Mort regarded the little man for a moment, then smiled. Something told him this drunken fool was smarter than the average drunken fool each little trail or rail town seemed to offer. "Mr. Ross, you began this conversation by asking if you might ask me a question. You have done that, but you have told me very little about yourself. Feel free to share your life story with me. I have all night, as I am passing through and have no plans but to perhaps play a friendly game or two of cards with anyone who might wish to do the same. And also, I might just end up drinking for the evening. That is more preferable to do with an acquaintance. Someone with whom I might share a bottle and conversation, uh?"

Mort winked at the bartender and requested a second glass and a fresh bottle. Then he motioned for Squirly to accompany him at a table.

They seated themselves and Mort poured a shot for himself and two shots in rapid succession for the little drunk. Soon Squirly's cheeks reddened enough to match the veined ball of his nose. "I wonder, I wonder," he said, staring at the ceiling. Then he shifted his gaze back to his newfound best friend and drinking companion. "Now, far as I know, you come to Turnbull from the North, am I correct?"

Mort said nothing, but stared at Squirly with a half smirk.

"So, I'll take that as a yes. Reason I am pryin' so is I have been waiting on the arrival of a friend of mine. Old trail hand from way back, so far back, we knowed each other when we were both pups, drovers on too many trail drives to mention. He'd be hard to miss, I reckon. An old cowhand riding some old bone rack of a nag, knowing him. Cheap? My word, you'll never find a man who can do more with less than ten men could. Tighter than Dick's hat band, he is."

Darturo held the questioning gaze as he stared at Squirly Ross. But his gut instincts told him that this was indeed a man to be aware of. If what the drunk said was true, the old cowboy he'd shot a few days' ride north of

here was probably the little drunk's friend. Not that anyone would miss a broken-down old cowhand. They were
everywhere. Their watery eyes and bowed legs limping
along most cow town sidewalks made for annoying ob-
stacles when one had to get from one gambling parlor to
another. He had made it a point over the years to eliminate the more scurvy-looking members of the breed. He
considered it a kindness, really, much as one would shoot
a yellow-eyed dog or a snotting cat. In the end, it made
the world a better place for all—of that he was certain.

"Reason I'm asking is, he's a couple of days overdue,
see? According to his response to my telegram—first
one I ever did send, and wouldn't you know, old Teasdale, he's the station agent, he charged me full price for
sending it! Full price, and me always down there lending
a hand, lugging bags and toting crates and keeping the
place shipshape, don't you know? Where was I?"

Mort nodded toward their glasses. "You were about
to sip to the fine weather we have been enjoying."

Squirly squinted at Darturo. "I reckon not, but I will
take you up on the sippin' part. That is, if I had something to sip. . . ." He held up the glass and winked.

Mort poured him another drink and watched the
man tipple half of it gingerly.

"Now, that's a way to wet a whistle, I say. Speakin' of
saying, I was about to tell you about Mitchell, my old
friend. We used to work on the trail drives together. Not
much call for old-timers on the trails nowadays, though.
But he's a stubborn old mule and he stuck with it. Me, I
got out of that young man's game and set myself up with
a burro, a pick and shovel, and enough supplies to go
broke quick out in the hills. That was a few years back."

"So, how came you to be here?" said Mort, mildly interested in the old drunk's tale, despite himself.

"I know what you're thinkin', Mr. City Man with the
fancy talk, but I'm here to tell you that I was nearly
skinned alive by the Apache. A more unforgiving breed

of cat you'll not find. I was out prospecting, sniffing silver ore on a light breeze, I tell you no lie. I was sure it was my day for the big strike. Bigger than old Schieffelin's Tombstone strike."

"Bigger than that, eh?"

"Oh, Lordy, stranger." Squirly paused to knock back the few drops in his glass. "Make his look like nothing more than a childish notion." He set it down on the table and looked at it as if he had just seen a kitten die. Mort refilled it.

"As I was saying, that silver ore was practically leaping out of the rocks at me. I was headed toward the rock shelf that was for certain my promised land, when out of nowheres come what amounted to a hundred and a half Apache warriors, a-howling and bawling like their heads was on fire. And they were all riding hell-for-leather right straight at me and no one else."

"What did you do?" Mort sipped his own whiskey. There were worse ways to spend an afternoon in a town without whores.

"Why, first thing I did was reach for my rifle. But it wasn't there."

"Where was it?"

"Well, it had been in its scabbard roped across the back of Agnes, my pony—"

"I thought you said it was a burro."

"Same thing, small and ornery it was, but as surefooted as a goat. Anyway, Agnes had been felled like a lightning-struck tree. Enough arrows sticking out of her she looked like a quilled-up porcupine."

"But you were not shot?"

"Now, who's telling the story? Me or you? I appreciate the whiskey and all, but I have to get one thing for certain and that's when I relate to you my adventures, I need to know that my story won't be dry-gulched by someone who wasn't even there." Squirly leaned back in his chair and crossed his arms.

So, Mort thought. *This is the sort of drunk he is—belligerent. And yet, amusing too.* He smiled and nodded. "Please continue. I will endeavor to keep my questions to a minimum."

"Well, now, yes. See that you do . . . um, endeavor to do that. Now, where was I?"

"The arrows."

"Yes, yes, I know. So, there I was, afoot and surrounded by howling savages. I was about ready to cash in my hand, call it a day, if you know what I mean. But right then, an interesting thing happened." Squirly sipped his whiskey. "You know what that is?"

Mort shook his head, tried to keep from laughing. This little drunk was indeed interesting. He'd almost forgotten that the man had been fishing for information about a man Mort had killed but a couple of days before. Almost forgotten, but not quite.

"Well, them savages didn't kill me right then. No, sir, but I am quite sure they were none too pleased that I was about to be the first white man to discover the biggest silver strike ever seen in the entire history of the land hereabouts."

"That seems plausible, to be sure." Darturo nodded as if in total agreement with the drunk man.

"You bet it do. So, next, they wrapped a dung-smellin' rag around my eyes and drug me off to their camp."

"Then what happened, Mr. Ross? I am afraid you have me at your disposal."

"If that means you need to hear the rest of the story, well, it's dry work, all this chin waggin'."

Darturo nodded. "Of course, have a drink to soothe your parched throat."

"Thanks, don't mind if I do."

"So, you were captured by hundreds of savages."

"That I was. I have a theory about why I was held."

"Oh?"

"Yeah, you see, I was younger then, and I had more

hair on my pate. Blondish it was too. I suspect them braves wanted to show off to other tribes, get themselves some blond-headed babies."

"You don't say?"

"Yes, indeed, I was held captive by them brutes for, oh, must have been a couple of years. Kept me mostly naked, used me for this and that, if you know what I mean. Tied up like a camp dog. Beat me with sticks and leather whips, and made me do all the work that women usually do. That's why I don't take kindly to the suggestion that I ought to bathe. And I will also not stoop so low as to cook. Unless I am forced to do it."

"But you are here now. So that means you must have come to some agreement with them."

"Agreement? Nah, it just took me a while to escape."

The two men were silent for a few moments. Then Mort cleared his throat. "I wonder . . . how does all this relate to the fact that you are expecting a visit from an old friend?"

"Oh well, that's easy. See, I heard from a friend of a friend of an acquaintance who come in on the train a while back that Mitchell Farthing, the very same one I knew, finally had enough of whompin' on the backsides of other folks' cattle and was out of work, sort of driftin'. And what's more, I know he had a poke that was looking for something to invest in. I also happen to know, since old Mitchell's a creature of habit, that he used to keep his coin purse lashed around his chest and sort of tucked under one wing." The little man demonstrated by patting his armpit with one hand. "Odd duck, is Mitchell, but I'd wager that's why he still has the first nickel he ever earned, and that's why I was hoping he'd been here by now."

Mort felt a tightness in his throat. So the old cowboy did have money, after all. Tied around his chest, of all places. Who in their right mind would do such a thing? In the end, it certainly didn't protect him from thieves, did it? He decided that what he suspected all along was now proved true: cowboys were a special breed of crazy men. He ran a tongue over his teeth, smoothed his black mustache with a thumb, wondering if it would be worth his time to ride back there and retrieve his rightfully earned pay from the dead man. Perhaps this old soak knew the amount. "Why do you need him so badly, Mr. Ross?"

"Because, Mr. Fancy-Talkin' Foreigner, I happen to know of a certain ranch that might soon need a couple of old cowhands to run it. I told him so in my telegram. Figured that with his grubstake, and my expertise in such affairs as running a ranch and all, why, me and him could partner up and get rich." He offered a luxuriant wink and tapped the side of his nose with a grimy finger. "Ol' Squirly heard tell that the place will go for pennies on the dollar, and right quick too." He nodded, his eyes blinking slowly.

Darturo's heart thudded for a moment. Could the old cowhand really have been carrying enough cash to purchase a ranch? No, no, it was not possible. *Keep in mind who you are listening to, Mortimer Darturo. You are listening to a drunk tell of his drunken fantasies. If there was an ounce of truth in this tale, why, this old man would surely have acted on it by now. And he would not share such information with a stranger, eh?* Still, it might pay to keep him talking, learn more. And it might pay to gut him and head back to where he'd left the dead old cowhand on the north trail. What was it . . . two days' ride back? He smiled at Squirly Ross, who he found had been scrutinizing him with a bleary-eyed intensity that he found not a little unsettling.

"That is quite a tale, sir. Was this friend of yours carrying a great amount of money? Perhaps I could help you find him."

"Who said he needs finding? And what do you mean 'was'?" Squirly leaned forward. "You know something about Mitchell Farthing that I don't, mister, you got yourself a duty to tell me."

Darturo leaned back, smiling, and raised his hands as if he were being held up. "No, no. I am merely making conversation, eh? I know nothing of this . . . this Farthing character."

Squirly nodded slowly, pooched out his lower lip. "I only wondered if'n you seen him on your way here, comin' down from up north as you did."

"No, I regret to tell you that I saw no one on the trail." Mort was silent a moment, then said, "Tell me, Mr. Ross, whatever happened to that ledge of silver?"

"Aha! Thought you'd get around to asking about that." The drunk slapped the tabletop hard enough to bounce the glasses and bottle. "I still know where it's at." He leaned over the table and in a lowered voice said, "Problem is, so do them Indians, and they keep a sharp eye out for Ol' Squirly Ross, I'll tell you."

"Even after all this time?"

"You bet, you bet. More than ever. You see, I'm what you might call a bit of a rough cob to them savages. I rub 'em the wrong way. They don't like that one bit. Can't never forgive me neither. No, sir. I still know where that old ledge of silver ore is located. Well, the general location anyways."

"By the way, how do you know which direction I came from, Mr. Ross?"

"Huh? Oh well . . ." Squirly again touched a grubby finger to the side of his bulbous red nose, the grime-ringed nail a curved claw from lack of trimming. "Squirly sees all, knows all, hears all." He closed his eyes and leaned back in his chair, a small belch working its way through his lips.

Mort watched the old man slip into a doze. In a low, even voice little more than a whisper, he said, "Be careful, Mr. Ross, that you don't see or hear or know too much. It could be a fatal habit." Darturo stood, sliding the chair quietly away from the table. He looked at the man once more, then picked up the bottle and his own glass and walked back to the bar. "Bartender, I would like another short glass of milk, sir."

"Again with the milk?"

"Yes, yes. It is for my whiskey. It soothes me."

"Right, then. Coming up."

From his seat at the table in the corner, Squirly Ross creaked open one red-rimmed eye and studied the back of the well-dressed thin man at the bar. As he drifted back to sleep, he wondered if Silver Haskell might be willing to trade a few hours of stall mucking in exchange for the loan of one of his nags for a day or two. He had a hunch if he headed on the north trail out of Turnbull, he might find sign of ol' Mitchell Farthing. He hoped, if he did track him down, that the old cowhand was just late, riding a bone rack, and grousing about the price of oats. The alternative notion did not bear thinking about.

Chapter 16

Brandon MacMawe rubbed both sides of his head as he crossed the street, and allowed himself the luxury of a long self-indulgent moan. He barely noticed that the noon sun had already begun its slow descent to mark the second half of the lengthening spring day. That whiskey of the night before had started out all right, but then he'd reached that point where any memory he'd had of the evening was at best blurred, and at worst a pitch-black night full of him snoring in the cell.

He headed toward the Doubloon Saloon, digging in his pants pocket for anything resembling a coin. All he needed was a shot of rye to dull the sharp knives trying to slice their way out of his skull. But every pocket revealed the same amount of nothing. Maybe Tom would give him one on the cuff. As he pushed through the doors, Brandon tried to stand up straighter, somehow overcome the shakes that plagued him. He didn't think he could stand much abuse today. He felt like a piece of paper trying to stay upright in a breeze.

As he closed the door softly behind himself, the bartender turned from rearranging the rows of honey-colored liquid on the shelf behind the bar. He didn't say anything to Brandon, just regarded him a moment, then went back to his task.

Brandon stood at the bar a moment longer. "Don't you know who I am? If my father were still alive, you wouldn't treat me that way. You would be buying me drinks and nodding and saying, 'Yes, Mr. MacMawe, no, Mr. MacMawe, can I get you anything else, Mr. Mac-Mawe?' So, what's changed?"

The bartender leaned on the bar, his wide shoulders framing his gleaming bald head and long, waxed mustache. "What's changed, boy, is that your father is dead and as far as I and everyone else in this little town can tell, you aren't a patch on his ass, never were, let alone someone who deserves the sort of treatment that I'd give him. That man was well liked around these parts. To be fair, so are you. Or you were before you chose the easy path in life. It don't take much effort to be a drunk, Brandon. That's like being water. You're just taking the path of least resistance. You keep this up, and there's going to be trouble, mark my words. This town is small, but it's going to grow. Now that we have the railroad stopping regular-like, instead of just whistling right past us, there will be other saloons and more chances for you to drink yourself silly."

Brandon slapped his palms on the bar in front of the man, his young face a bloodshot, shaking thing. "I am now the MacMawe man running the Dancing M." He slammed his hands down again, emphasizing each sentence with a hand slap to the bar top. "It is one of the biggest ranches around." *Slap!* "And this little pissant town better watch its step around me." *Slap!* "That ranch is mine and you would do well to keep that in mind!" *Slap!*

Quick as summer lightning, the bartender's meaty fists reached out and snatched up the thin young man's soiled shirtfront. He dragged the boy upward, over the bar top toward him, hoisting him up so that their noses nearly touched. Through gritted teeth, the big man said, "I don't care if you are the emperor of China, by God. You young ranch whelps come in here thinking you can do whatever you please with no consequences. You're worse than the other one, that Grindle boy, and you know who I mean. He may be a pain in the ass too, but at least he can pay his bills when he breaks things. You . . . you can't even afford to pay attention. You stink 'cause you don't bathe, you don't help your mother tend your dead father's ranch. Soon enough it'll fall in around your ears. All that, and you haven't got the price of a drink, but you demand that I give you a snort." He gestured with his chin toward the rear of the room. "Hell, even that old soak Squirly Ross will work for his booze. And if he's dry, at least he knows enough not to beg."

"That's right, by gum," came the old man's voice from his table in the corner.

The bartender pushed Brandon backward. The shaking young man staggered, but remained standing.

"That wasn't an invitation for you to talk, Squirly. You're still a worthless drunk."

"Yes, that's true, but at least I'm a drunk who can empty spittoons and sweep floors."

"I work, and plenty," said Brandon, not looking at either of them. He stepped back from the bar, smoothing his grimy shirt. He backed a few steps toward the door and pointed a finger at the bartender. "And you leave my mother out of this. You have no right to talk about her."

The bartender held up his hands as if Brandon had the drop on him. "You're right, Mr. MacMawe, I don't. But it's not like any of this will matter anyway."

Brandon paused, narrowed his eyes. "What's that you say? Why? Why won't it matter?"

The bartender resumed his counter wiping. "Oh, just that a stranger arrived on yesterday's train."

"What about this stranger? People come to Turnbull all the time. "

"Not on purpose, they don't," said Squirly, then laughed, a ragged, wet sound that devolved into a coughing fit.

"True," said the bartender. "And I bet this one won't be here any longer than he needs to be."

"Well, who is he and why are you telling me all this?" said Brandon.

"You really don't remember, do you? Last night . . . at Mae's? When you slugged that man in the face?"

Brandon's brow creased in thought. Finally he shook his head, said nothing, ran a shaking hand over the knuckles of the other.

"Well, from all accounts, he's Rory MacMawe's long-lost son." The bartender leaned on the bar and stared at Brandon. "You know, his firstborn. The one he always spoke of, the one he wanted to have the Dancing M. Have to say, he looks more like ol' Rory than anyone I ever did see." He leaned forward farther. "You included."

The bartender watched the boy before him tremble, his dark fists clench and unclench. Then the boy's shoulders shook, and his eyes welled wet with tears that slid down his cheeks. He turned and bolted from the bar.

The room was silent a moment. Then in a quiet voice, Squirly said, "Kinda hard on him, weren't you, Tom?"

The bartender continued to stare at the closed bar door. "Somebody needs to be." He looked at the little drunk. "That boy has a future, and he's blowing it. He's just too dumb to see it for himself. Unlike you, Squirly Ross. You're just an old pickled mess."

Squirly smiled. "Thank you, but I prefer the term 'finely aged.'"

Chapter 17

Junior watched the stranger's attempts to remove the saddle from the aged brown mare. "You might not wanna—" The saddle slipped down the horse's barrel on the beast's far side, his satchel pulled with it, and the entire mess, saddle, bunched blanket, and bag, hung there. Junior turned away and bit the inside of his cheek. This one was greener than a day-old calf. "Mr. Middleton, if I may be so bold . . ."

The tall man turned on him, his green eyes narrowed, his jaw set firm, and a big hand bunched trembling and held in front of him, knuckles white, as if to display the size of his fist. He stood like this for a moment, then turned back to prying at the cinch, now tight and twisted.

"Fine, fine. No need to get your drawers in a pinch over it. Just thought I'd offer some friendly advice, is all. . . ."

The big man paused in his fumblings with the cinch, the mare standing as if carved from stone. He put one arm on the horse's back, let out a deep breath, and turned back to Junior. "I . . . apologize. I've not had much experience in these matters . . . and I would appreciate any assistance you might care to offer."

Junior poked his hat back on his head and nodded, careful not to smile, lest he set off the man's hot temper again. With a few deft moves, he had the weighty pile of gear dragged off the horse, which, despite its calm nature—more likely exhausted, thought Junior, considering the size of this fella—stretched its back with a shudder, walked off a few paces and lowered herself to her knees, then eased down to the dusty earth and rolled.

"My God, what's the matter with it?" The stranger stared wide-eyed at the horse, then looked to Junior, his eyes begging for help. "I . . . was I too big for it?"

For a brief moment Junior thought the man was having him on. Then he saw the genuine concern on Middleton's face and he couldn't help himself. Immediate laughter forced itself right up and out of him. Angry stranger be damned, thought Junior; it had been a long time since he'd seen anything this funny. He gave over to it fully, howling until his ribs ached, his throat burned, and his eyes streamed.

He finally looked up at the tall man, convinced he was about to receive a wallop on the jaw by one of those wide pink hams the man had for hands. But instead, he saw Middleton's features soften and a half grin settle there. "I assume, by your reaction, that my alarm was unfounded." He nodded toward the horse. "And the horse appears to have recovered from its fit."

Junior choked off a fresh round of laughter and rubbed his eyes. "Oh, you are a piece of work, Middleton. Your horse is a she, an old nag mare, not an 'it'—and she's fine. Just taking a dirt bath, is all. You would too if you had to carry *you* around all day."

Junior retrieved his hat from the ground, where it fell when he'd doubled over in laughter. "Let's get a cook fire going and fix up something to eat."

"I'm afraid I don't have much with me in the way of

food." Middleton looked at his piled gear, his brow knitted. "I didn't expect to be roughing it like this."

"No worries, Middleton. When me and the boys are out here working the range, we never know if we'll be alone or bumping into another hand, so we all carry extra. Enough to keep us from chewin' our boots anyway." He winked and pulled a bottle of Milligan's Whiskey from his saddlebag. "Here," he said, tossing the bottle to Middleton. "Something to prime the pump. Make setting up camp easier."

A short while later, the horses were ground-tied and hobbled. The late afternoon sky was mellowing and shot through with streaks of gray clouds above them as the men sat before a small fire, staring into the dancing, flicking flames. The chipped coffeepot steamed slowly and the beginning gurgles of boiling coffee could be heard and smelled.

Junior splashed a slug of whiskey in each man's cup, set the bottle between them, and said, "It's not considered good form out here to pry into a man's business—and don't take this the wrong way, Middleton—but you don't seem like the sort of man who'd take it on himself to go riding across the wilds of New Mexico Territory. Lots of rough things could happen to an inexperienced fellow out here. . . ." He let the implication hang in the air like the fire's slow smoke.

Middleton said nothing, sipped his whiskey and stared at the campfire. Junior looked over at him. The man looked as if he wanted to talk, as if he'd been with himself long enough that he wanted to give over to a palaver. He hoped so anyway; otherwise this was going to be a long damn night.

One more try, thought the younger man. "I mean, it's not as though you're from here. It's different if you're born here. Then you sort of have something more, some sort of leg up on the dangers, if you know what I mean."

"No, I really don't." Middleton turned to look at Junior. "And whoever said I wasn't from here?" He waved his cup broadly about him, taking in the vast landscape now purpling and taking on a wholly different look than it had moments earlier. "Until this very moment, I'd not thought of this place as anything but a nuisance, a blighted, savage corner forsaken by civilization."

Now it was Junior's turn to bristle. "Just a minute—"

"Hear me out. I said 'until now,' for now I can detect an inherent beauty that I suppose people like you, that is to say people who are *of* this place, see every day and therefore must take for granted."

Junior nodded. "I know what you're saying, but I for one don't take it for granted." He leaned back, his shoulders resting against his saddle, and stretched his legs, crossing them. "I look at this place every day and smile. 'Cause it's that beautiful, it truly is."

Middleton grunted in understanding, then said, "You'll note I didn't answer your unspoken query." He smiled. "I was born here, actually. To a man now dead these past few weeks."

That's what I wanted to hear, thought Junior. He sipped his whiskey to hide his smile.

Middleton continued. "Perhaps you knew him—one Rory MacMawe? He owned a ranch hereabouts."

Junior laughed again, sat up, and still snorting, slid the spitting coffeepot back from the flames.

"What, may I ask, has struck you as humorous now?"

Junior lightly punched the man on his brown coat sleeve. A cloud of dust rose. "Hereabouts? Try here!" Junior laughed and with the same fist punched at the ground between them. "And there"—he pointed behind them—"and there"—he pointed southward, the direction Middleton had earlier been heading.

"I'm afraid I don't understand you."

The young man shook his head and said, "We're on MacMawe's land right now. You have been for a couple of hours, I'd say."

"What?" Middleton sat up straight. "Surely you're pulling my leg."

"No, sir. I may be a lot of things, but I ain't a fibber about land. Take my word for it, this here is Dancing M land."

They were silent a moment more while Brian Middleton looked around himself with renewed interest. "Then why were *you* out here?"

Junior narrowed his eyes and said slowly, "Because I came from over there." He thrust a finger eastward. "Other side of the town road yonder is Driving D land. D, owned by Grindle, and I'm a Grindle."

"Oh," said Middleton. "I see."

"Aw, I didn't mean to bristle, but land is everything out here. Course, you know that or you wouldn't be out here, am I right?"

"Actually, I'm not at all certain anymore what I am doing here. My grandfather, back East, in Providence, that's in Rhode Island . . ."

Junior smiled, said nothing, knowing full well where Providence was, and Rhode Island too.

Middleton continued. "My grandfather told me this was a fool's errand, but for some reason I felt it incumbent on me to return to this place of my birth, to see it for myself . . . before I sell it off to the highest bidder." He swallowed the last of his whiskey and set the tin cup on a nearby rock. It made a hollow noise.

Junior turned away, his heart hammering in his rib cage, a bold little smile tugging at his mouth corners. Here was the opportunity he needed, practically in his hands. He dug out his small skillet and gripped it tight to quell the shake of excitement in his hands. "Middleton. . . ."

The tall man looked up, eyebrows raised. *He almost looks happy*, thought Junior. *And he's definitely relaxed. Must be the booze.*

"How'd you like to get to the meat of the matter right

now?" Junior swallowed, tried to sound casual as he sliced strips of bacon into the pan.

"What do you mean?"

Junior prodded the sizzling bacon with his knife, dumped in a splash of hot coffee, and wiped his knife tip on his pants leg. "Well, what I mean is . . . I'm what you might call my father's estate agent. And I've been told to go ahead and make certain land purchases that will help us to keep this land as ranch land, if you follow me."

Middleton just stared at Junior, so the younger man pressed his point. "I am prepared to make you an offer of purchase on the Dancing M property. Right now. Then we can make it all legal and such in town." He nodded behind them to the north. "Tomorrow, in Turnbull."

He's thinking, thought Junior. *Thinking of how much money he should ask for it all, kit and kaboodle.*

Middleton regarded him, then smiled. "I think it would be best if I didn't rush into anything. I've only just arrived."

Junior couldn't help his frustration. This was not the way to go about the deal. He'd rushed into it and blown it from the get-go. Heat rose up his neck and reddened his cheeks, his ears, and he knew Middleton was still watching him.

"I've only just arrived," repeated the big man, though in a softer tone. "You understand."

Junior nodded, kept his head down as he heated a couple of Mica's split biscuits he'd brought from the cook shack. He maintained his silence as he divided the food and poured fresh coffee for both of them. He glugged a liberal dose of whiskey into his coffee and set the bottle down in the dirt.

"I tell you what, Grindle." Middleton ran a thumb across his lips. "Once I've seen what I'm facing here, I'm sure I'll still want to divest myself of this property. Send your father to find me in a day or so and we might be able to come to an agreement."

Junior looked at Brian Middleton for the first time since he'd bumbled his offer long minutes before. A dark knot of anger wrenched tight in his gut and he felt his vision blur with the force of it. So, after all, he was nothing more than a kid to this man too. *And he not much older than me*, thought Junior. He swallowed back the bile he felt rising in his gorge, and a crude plan wormed its way into his brain. If he couldn't make this work without dear old Father's help, then he'd by God make it work some other way, come hell or high water.

He poured himself another slug and, forcing a kid's half grin, nodded. "Okay with me." He poured whiskey in Brian's cup and said, "Let's drink to it, then."

They both raised their cups and clunked them together. Brian leaned back, thoughts forming in the heady whiskey vapors curling about his brain. Junior felt much the same way, though for very different reasons.

The sun was but a low ripple of light from the east when Junior rose. He intended to leave the stranger sleeping and head for home. He didn't like to leave the fool of a city boy out there alone, but he'd take care to point him in the right direction. There was no way Junior was going to wait—he had to get back and report to his father. If what the stranger said was true, the old man would have no worries. It was all coming to them. This Brian Middleton just wanted to sell up and get back East. (Though if this big goober was Rory's son, why didn't he call himself MacMawe anyway? Junior had to admit, it was not a little troubling.) And that sounded as if it would dovetail with Wilf Grindle's plans very nicely indeed.

Junior swung into the saddle, oddly anxious to see his father's face when he told him that Rory MacMawe's long-gone son had indeed returned home. He also had a sneaking hunch that, despite their chat in his father's study yesterday, even if the old man didn't doubt Ju-

nior's commitment to owning the Dancing M, Junior
knew what his father would do—he'd pay a visit to Esperanza. That would ruin everything. He wanted to be
the one to work the deal. That would surprise his father—
and impress him.

But he didn't doubt that Wilf had visited Espy, or
would soon. That'd be just like the old man—always have
a backdoor plan. It was an admirable trait, but it annoyed
the heck out of Junior too. It felt as if he would never be
trusted by his father. And that thought made Junior
nudge Spunk into a gallop. What if the old man tipped
her off that he suspected Rory's first son was back? Nah,
he wouldn't do that. That would ruin everything, including his chances for owning the Dancing M, and for proving to his father just what sort of a rancher, and more to
the point, what sort of a man, was his son. Still, he couldn't
take the chance. He had to get there, and quick.

Junior had ridden for a few minutes more when he
reined up and looked back, squinting to see sign of
smoke from the cook fire he'd kindled before he left. If
the big fella wasn't too deep of a sleeper, he thought,
then he'd awaken just about when the coffee was ready.
But that was the most he could do for him.

"I'm holding you to it, Middleton. One way or another I'm going to have your land." Junior reined Spunk
toward home, worry over his father's probable impa-
tience gnawing at him. But the idea that had sparked in
him when Callie had found him writing in their father's
study, if it worked, would prove to the old man that Junior was more of a man than he'd reckoned. And it might
just guarantee them the land his father so wanted.

Chapter 18

"I'm sorry I've not been over in a few days, Espy. What with errands in town for Papa, helping Mica with the cooking." Callie Grindle slipped out of her riding jacket and hung it on a chair back. "I promise I'll be over more often."

Esperanza Soles set the stove lid back in place with a clunk. "It does not matter. We will not be staying here."

Callie tilted her head as if she hadn't heard correctly. "What? Espy, you're not serious." She looked at her older friend and saw no sign of humor on the unreadable face. "But why, Espy? This is your home."

The squat older woman paused in sweeping the crumbs from her cutting board, opened her mouth to speak, but didn't. She resumed brushing the board, but did not meet her friend's gaze. "I have never understood why you come here and bother me. We are from two different worlds and people from yours will never understand a life like mine. Never. I have nothing and I want nothing from you or your kind."

Callie's face reddened as if she'd been slapped. She

gritted her teeth to keep from gasping. "Esperanza, I don't know what has happened, but I refuse to believe that is really how you feel. We've known each other for a long time. Years. In so many ways you've been like a mother to me."

The older woman kept her broad back to the young girl and continued to scrub hard at the worn wood of the cutting board. She said nothing.

For a few moments, no sound could be heard in the small kitchen. Callie looked at the tidy room, the oilcloth-covered table, stained but clean, the fresh-swept wooden floor, the clean glass windowpanes, and the unyielding long view of plain and mountains in the far distance.

"I'm leaving now, Espy. I guess I won't be back." Callie looked one last time at her friend and as the tears slipped down her face she set the dish towel on the table and walked out. Her horse still stood at the hitch rail, one foot canted in rest. As Callie galloped back the way she had come, back toward her own life at the Driving D, she felt hollowed, her life less sweet now that it would no longer have Espy in it. But why?

Back in the little house at the Dancing M, Esperanza paused in her work and listened as the sound of hoofbeats receded into the distance. She stopped scrubbing the counter and for the first time in a long while she let tears well up in her eyes. Knowing it was the way it had to be didn't mean it did not hurt. In its own way it was as painful as losing Rory, her big bear of a man.

Without him, her world here in this settlement of whites would no longer be her home. Nor would her son be welcome here. Though they had lived here his entire life, though he was born here, and though his father was one of the founders of the town—and one of the biggest landowners—she knew, after seeing the hatred and greed in the eyes of Wilf Grindle when he had visited earlier in the day, that it would be useless to fight him for Rory's beloved land.

The whites had their own way of behaving, making the future the most important thing in their lives, placing far more importance on it than on making sure their neighbors and friends were well cared for and happy. She knew that there were whites, some her friends, who disproved this idea, but at the moment she didn't care.

"Gringos!" She spat the word. She hadn't used it in many years and she didn't like the way it tasted in her mouth.

Esperanza turned to the little room where she had cooked and fed her family for close to twenty years. She thought of all the good times she and her son and husband had shared in this room, the laughter within these walls, and she wished her son was there with her instead of drinking himself to death in Turnbull. What would Rory think of him now?

For a time, when Brandon was a baby, Espy had begun to think Rory might get over the loss of his first son and accept Brandon as everything he had ever wanted in a boy, but had lost. In time, it had proved to be impossible. Brandon was not like other children, "not all there," as that little town bum, Squirly Ross, had once said to her when she'd gone to town with Rory years ago to shop. She had not told Rory, for she knew he would have beaten the little smelly drunk to death. But she knew he spoke the truth, as much as it pained her to hear it. In time, Espy admitted that Brandon was never going to be the sort of son who takes over a ranch, who does anything more than smile and sing and help with chores about the place. He was not stupid, but he was different from other people.

Rory loved the boy, though as one might grow fond of a favorite dog. "He's an innocent," Rory would say, calling up one of the gentle words they'd used where he came from, far away and years before.

She knew Rory liked to tip the jug himself now and again, but never too much. Brandon, though, he was different. Since his father died the boy was beyond her control. He had developed a thirst that would never be slaked. The very day Rory finally gave in to the disease that the visiting doctor had said would kill him, Brandon and she had had a fight. He had taken a drink from his father's whiskey crock. She had said nothing, figuring he was grieving. Then he took another and another.

She had tried to take the vessel from him, but he'd snatched it back from her grasp, pushing her at the same time. She struck him then, across the face, and saw the anger and hurt and dented pride staring back at her. All these things that she knew so well in her husband, she now saw on her young son's tensed, trembling, flushed features. He wasn't old enough yet to grow proper whiskers, but he was drinking like a man. And later that day, she had found him hunched up sick in a corner of the barn. She tried to help him but he pushed her away again. And that's how it had been ever since Rory's death weeks before.

The boy was a lost soul seeking solace in a bottle. He'd been good about saving his money, saving the wages Rory had paid him, and now it was all going for whiskey. She had hoped that someone in Turnbull would refuse to sell him the alcohol, grow tired of his drunken ways, or perhaps he would run out of money and have to return home to her for good. Or better yet, that he would realize how foolish he'd been and come back to her.

Maybe it was a blessing in disguise that they would have to leave the ranch. For then Brandon would be forced to come with her, and that might be enough of a shock to pull his head out of the bottle. Maybe, but what if he didn't follow her? What if this time her troubled "innocent" boy said no?

It all made her so angry. They had more right than anyone else in the world to live and be happy at the Dancing M. Her gaze fell on the deep brown wood and gentle curves of the mantel clock. She'd not wound it

since Rory died. It had been his task. Every other morning he would take the key from underneath it and crank
it a dozen times. But no more. She would leave that
clock when she left the ranch.

It would happen soon, she thought, as she stepped
outside and into the bright morning sun. Yes, it would
happen soon . . . but not today.

Chapter 19

Teasdale, the station agent, folded the newspaper into his lap and looked over the ends of his polished boots, where they sat, heel-to-toe propped on his desktop in the station house. "I hear you straight, Squirly? You want an advance on your pay?"

The little begrimed man nodded. "That's about it, Teas. I reckon I've proved up around this place, come to the point so you depend on me for luggin' and haulin' and whatnot. What do you say?"

"Why, Squirly, if I didn't know better, I'd say you have just about milked dry all the favors a man can find in this little town. You must really be desperate for a drink to expect me to pay you for work you might do one day."

"No, no, you got it all wrong, Teas. I don't want a drink. Well, leastwise not with this here money. Truth is, I need to rent a nag from Silver Haskell. Got a mission I have to take care of. Take me a day or two. He won't let me muck out stalls, nor do a thing for him. Says I'd be bad for business." He snorted and shook his head. "I can't imagine a business that could be worse off than his."

Teasdale dropped his feet to the floor. "What would you need with a mount, Squirly? I don't think you can render a horse, even one of Haskell's old glue pots, down enough to ferment it."

"Never mind, then, Teasdale. I reckon I can figure it out without your help." Squirly turned and clumped out of the office and on down the porch.

By the time he reached the stairs, he heard a voice behind him say, "All right, Squirly Ross. So help me, but you look sincere as all get out. Don't play me false, will you? Tell you what, I'll go down to Silver's with you and pay the man myself for your rental horse."

"Why, that's a kick to the head, Teas. You really don't trust me, is that it?"

"Well, Squirly, that's just about it, yes. Shouldn't surprise you any. You've played the snatch-and-run game with everyone in town."

The drunk nodded. "I reckon I have at that."

"When did you want to head out?"

"No time like the present, as someone once said."

Teasdale sighed. "Okay, just let me lock up. And, Squirly?"

"Yeah?"

"When you're out and about on your secret mission, might be you'll pass by a stream?"

"It's possible. Why?"

"Wouldn't hurt anybody's feelings if you were to shuck those buckskins and soap up. I'll spring for a bar of soap over to Gleason's store. . . ." Teasdale leaned forward in the doorway, waiting on the man's answer, a half smile on his face.

"Seems to me you'd be embarrassed, asking a question like that, Teas."

"Not half as much as you think. With a sweet stink like yours, we're way past the blushing stage, Squirly."

The little portly man scratched his whiskered chin. "Tell you what, Teas. Since you're so all-fired worked up to shine me up, just toss me the price of the soap and I'll see to it that my honest, working-man's smells don't offend your senses."

Teasdale shook his head. "No, I guess we'll let it stand as it is, Squirly Ross."

All the way down to the livery, Squirly complained louder and louder until they reached the stable, then stood by, oddly silent, while Teasdale worked to convince Silver Haskell to rent a nag to Squirly—saddle included.

Chapter 20

Brian Middleton couldn't remember ever feeling so awful. Even the train he'd ridden for the first leg of his trip out West, while unbearable, had been easier to take than this. He lay still, fully awake but unwilling to open his eyes to the harsh truth and even harsher sunlight already pushing down with an intensity he found nauseating. Then he remembered the stranger—what was his name? Junior . . . Junior Grindle. Brother of that rude young woman in town.

The sharp tang of wood smoke reached his nose and prompted him to rise on one elbow and slowly open his eyes. The sun stung and forced him to keep his lids lowered. A small fire glowed, and there was the man's coffeepot, a tin cup, and a canteen, resting by the fire as if waiting for him. He grunted upright and looked around as he stretched his big frame. No sign of the other man, nor his horse. His own horse, he noted, hadn't wandered all that far and was busy nosing a seemingly unforgiving spiny shrub. How appropriate, he thought.

He looked down to where he had lain, and there was

his hat, crushed flat once again. He must have rolled on
it in the night. A half-empty whiskey bottle poked from
under his wrinkled blanket. He resisted the urge to take
a swallow or two. Hair-of-the-dog remedies only post-
poned the inevitable. He nudged the coffeepot and offered a pleased grunt when he found that it was full—and
hot on his knuckles. A small mound of brittle sticks had
been set by the fire ring. He jammed a handful of them
onto the glowing coals of the little fire and in moments
had it breathing enough to renew the heat in the coffeepot. The brew was strong and rank, but it served to wake
him and offered a bracing edge to an otherwise bleak
morning.

I should have stayed in Providence, he thought to
himself, staring at the smoking campfire. He looked
around him and saw nothing but ridges and rises swelling and rolling far into the distance. He saw no other
living creature. "I should have stayed in Providence," he
said out loud, repeating his thought to no one but the
ornery mount he'd rented in town. The horse flicked an
ear. He repeated his oath again, but this time as a shout.
His bold bellow carried across the still morning air of
the arid landscape before him. There was no reply.

He finished the coffee in the pot, relieved himself,
helping to put out the campfire, secretly pleased with
himself for having thought of such a clever use of re-
sources. Then he packed his bag, strapped on Junior's
clanking coffeepot and cup, and readied the horse. She
was surprisingly calm. Until he tried to mount up. Shades
of the previous day's horse-chasing excursions recurred
to him and he walked around to the front of the horse,
holding the reins tight in one hand.

"If you value your life in the least, you will allow me
to climb aboard you and ride in relative comfort."

The horse stared at him. One ear flicked. Brian nodded and as he passed by the horse's head it lashed out
and bit at him, securing the sleeve of his rumpled brown

suit coat. He spun on the horse and held up a long, meaty finger, and drove it like a spike against the long shaft of skull bone between the horse's eyes. "No, horse! No!" he bellowed with such force that the horse stepped backward. He caught it up short and held it there. "We will not do this your way today! We will do this my way!"

The horse's eyes bloomed wide and stared at him. Brian shook his finger once more in the staring brown face and mounted with no hesitation. He nudged the chastened beast into a brisk trot and they were off.

Brian was annoyed with the young man for having left him alone in the savage, dusty land, though he knew roughly which way to continue his journey to the ranch. But as he rode from the rough camp, he happened to look down and saw the unmistakable mark of a boot-heel dragged to form an arrow, man-length, that Junior Grindle must have left for him, its intention clear. It pointed south. Brian Middleton followed it and soon found his trail paralleling the worn wheel grooves in the dirt track that was the road he had lost the day before.

Chapter 21

"What did you say your name was?"

"I didn't say."

"That's right." Esperanza squinted at the tall man outlined against the midday sun pinned and wavering in the western sky, the orange glow offering her nothing of the man's identity but a vast outline, so familiar, but . . . impossible. She swallowed and stood taller in the doorway of the modest little home. "So, how should I know you?"

"I beg your pardon, ma'am, but I think you know very well who I am."

The man even sounded big. But weary. And his odd way of speaking, the way he formed his words, was like none she had heard in these parts.

"I have been told since I arrived in this dusty corner of the world that I bear more than a passing resemblance to one Rory MacMawe."

So there it was. . . . "How do you know Rory?" Despite her usual slow, deliberate way of speaking, the words came out hot and sharp, sparks snapping and rising off burning logs.

For a moment the little home was filled with silence. Then the big man sighed, long and low. "I don't know him. And I'm not sure I ever did."

"Rory is dead."

"I know. I suppose that's why I am here."

"Your father is dead."

He did not respond, only stood still.

"Come in the house, then." Esperanza went back inside and slid the large coffeepot over onto the center of the cook surface, then swung open the door of the firebox, shuffled the coals, and pushed in two pieces of wood. She heard his boots on the sill, saw his shadow darken the room. She straightened up from the stove and turned to face him, to see him, really see him, for the first time in a long, long while.

There before her stood Rory. She took small pride in the fact that no matter what tricks life played on her, she always had the ability, even as a girl in Palo Cita, to keep herself calm in any situation. But this was too much, for she knew within seconds of seeing the tall, broad man that this was either the ghost of her Rory when he first came to this place as a young man, or it was her Rory's long-lost son, Brian.

He bore the same eyes, shining but dark too, like glistening river rock. And there was the thick, stiff red hair tufted at angles, the glow of it about his face, doing little yet to conceal that bootlike jaw, the edges barely softened by a day's growth of bristly whiskers, hardly the full-face beard that Rory wore the entire time she knew him. In his hands, large but soft and pink, those of a man not accustomed to physical work, he held the brim of a battered brown hat, too small and silly for such a big, fine head.

He nodded slightly and said, "I am Brian. Brian Middleton."

"We have met."

"I don't think so, ma'am. I'm from Providence, Rhode Island. A long way from here."

"I have never been there."

"I hardly thought so."

"And yet we have met."

He made no response to this, but his eyes took in the small room and she felt a creeping shame such as she'd never known flush her face. She recognized for the first time how humble and plain her life was. Judging from the expensive, though soiled, brown suit, the dusted but well-made boots, the young man was used to much finer surroundings. She did not like the way he made her feel.

"I don't understand . . ." he finally said.

"I mean that before you went away as a child, I cleaned you, taught you, cooked for you, took care of you."

He stared at her as if she were crazy, but said nothing.

Esperanza nodded toward a chair with its back to the fire, but facing the door. A large wooden chair with arms, for resting weary limbs. Rory's chair, the only place she ever saw him sit down, and then only for meals, and for an hour or so before turning in at night. The rest of the hours of his days were spent working to build up the ranch, clearing sluiceways for irrigation, milling lumber, tending stock, all with no thought to ever hiring help, other than seasonal hands. And all of it, all of those years of hard labor, for this boy, so that someday he would have something to leave him. This boy, not her boy. Not Brandon, never Brandon. Something of lasting value, as he had said so often, something on which his son, this long-lost son, could build a future.

The big stranger sat down in his father's chair and filled it much as Rory had. He set his hat on the floor by his feet. He held his hands out, palms down, as if testing the heat of a fire, before placing them on the tabletop.

She placed a tin cup in front of him, and another at

the other end of the table for herself, then returned with the coffeepot.

"So, it is true what they say."

He looked at her with eyebrows raised.

"That life is nothing more than a circle. No beginnings, no endings. Just a circle."

"I don't understand. . . ."

"That's the second time you said that. And I have the same answer for you both times." She sat down, held the cup in both hands, then looked down the length of the table at her Rory's first son. "You have returned to this place, your father's house. To this room, the very room where you were born."

He didn't hide his surprise, and again she saw much of his father there as he looked about the room, appraising, assessing.

She nodded. "Yes, it is true. And this was the entire cabin for the first few years of your parents' married life together. He didn't add the other two rooms until later."

"My mother . . . ?"

"Not me, no. But she died here, in this room. And so did your father. I moved his bed there where you see it now." She nodded to the other side of the great hearth. "To keep him warm . . . at the end."

The silence hung over them like a limp cloth. Finally she said, "And now you are here." She wanted to ask why, but she knew and she did not like the answer she felt sure she would hear.

He sipped the coffee, rubbed a large hand roughly over his features, stopping to massage his thumb and fingers deep into his eyes. "I was told of his death through Grandfather's attorney, who was contacted by Mac-Mawe's attorney. A man in Denver, Colorado. There was mention of an inheritance and I thought it was time that I attend to my affairs on my own and directly. Grandfather always says that a man must deal with all things in as direct and forthright a manner as he is capable of."

He smirked then, and the gesture warmed Esperanza lightly. Again, so like his father. Serious most of the time, then the surprise of a sudden smile. "Grandfather, however," he continued, "was not at all pleased with my plans. He insisted I reconsider this trip. It was almost as if he were fearful of what I might find out here. I am inclined to think he was correct."

"Why do you say that?"

He sighed, sipped his coffee, and regarded her over the rim of the cup. "Since arriving here I have experienced nothing but grief. Nothing but headaches and confusion. The train's accommodations were hardly that. Then on arriving I was shunted to a vile little room with no plumbing and only the crudest of amenities. Then I managed to insult the one pretty thing I'd seen on the entire trip—a young lady—before I was attacked by a drunken young man. And it has not grown better since then. The horse alone . . . oh, that beast. If it could talk . . ."

"Why did you really come, then?"

"I never thought such a savage place still existed, let alone that I would ever visit it myself. When I travel again, it shall be to Europe. Now . . ." He stood, retrieved his hat, and stretched. "I'm unsure as to what arrangements my father had with you, as his housekeeper, but I can assure you that you will be compensated for your time spent in keeping up the place since he passed on. Though I must say"—he looked about the room again, as if in disbelief—"that for all of the effort I put into getting here—weeks of travel—I would have done better to heed Grandfather's advice. He is rarely wrong. Chalk it up to the indiscretions of youth. Life, as he says, is a classroom of epic proportions."

Esperanza sat still and watched him.

"Is there a place I might freshen up? A guest room perhaps? I won't stay but the night. Then in the morning I'll head back to that quaint little hamlet of Turnbull, wire ahead to the attorney to make the necessary paper-work available for whatever sale I might be able to drum up, and you can be on your way to your homeland. I'm sure your people are expecting you?"

Esperanza looked down at the scarred, scrubbed surface of the kitchen table in front of her. At the chipped edges of the tin cup, at her own hands, thick and stiffened from the unending toil of ranch life. Sudden anger burned in her, tightened her throat, made her want to slap this boy's face. She rose, jostling the cups, and the chair stuttered backward across the floor.

She made her way outside to the chicken coop, and stood staring at nothing. The brown and black hens sounded like mocking old women as they stepped slowly around her skirts. Old women. *Ha!* Wasn't that what she was now? When did that happen? She folded her arms and closed her eyes. So this attorney must have told him he owned the place, which was about what she expected to hear at some point. She and Rory never talked about the future, especially not the future where the ranch was concerned. He had made it plain enough to her years ago that it was of no concern to her or to Brandon.

She did not doubt that Rory loved their own son, but there was never a question in Rory's mind that the ranch was being built up for this, his first son. Each year he maintained the hope that the boy would return to him, and each year, when that dream failed, Rory's disappointment grew greater and instead of growing dimmer, his urge to make it right, to leave something of lasting worth to the son he gave away, grew greater. And it kept on growing until he died.

She didn't have many complaints about Rory. Certainly he was better to her than some of the others, men from her small town across the border, had been. But that was a long time ago, and a long distance from here. She had left late one night when her father came home drunk and beat her mother. She knew it was just a short time before the same thing would happen to her, with her own husband, and in that very same village. So she left.

She had been fifteen years old then. For a time she wore large misshapen clothes and passed herself off as a traveling boy. And all the time she headed north. She never knew toward what, but she felt sure that when she arrived there she would know that it was the right place. She spent a short while tending the kitchen of a wealthy widow outside El Paso, and it was there she refined her abilities to read and write. When the woman's consumption finally killed her, Esperanza moved on, ever northward, in the same baggy clothes, but richer in her knowledge of the written word.

By then she was nearly nineteen, could no longer hide herself, and was harassed by men, it seemed, at every turn in the road. She had been forced to make what seemed at the time to be an endless series of escapes from drunken vaqueros, tinkers, salesmen, and one drunken freighter who had almost taken her. At the last possible moment, she had managed to hit him on the side of the head with a rock.

Sometimes at night she still heard that blunt smacking sound. She told herself that she did not care if he had lived, but for years after, he came to her mind, the shape of his still form in the grass, the bloodied side of his head glistening in the moonlight.

One evening not long after that, in the late fall, when she was tired and very cold, Esperanza had made camp along a river, the name of which she did not know. In the morning, she was still huddled in her blanket, sleeping but sitting upright. Before she opened her eyes she sensed somehow that someone else was there, someone was watching her. She opened her eyes but did not move. And in the swelling morning light she saw the biggest, most frightening man she had ever seen staring down at her. He was a giant with hair the color of fiery chili peppers, and as much or more hair hung from his face—a beard the likes of which she'd never seen. He was tall, yes, but most of all, he was just plain big. The distance between his shoulders seemed impossible.

And within a few seconds she knew she was in no danger, for his first question, in a voice much too soft and kind for such a large man, was, "Are you all right there, lassie?"

She nodded once, drew her knees up tighter to her body.

He turned to go. "You're on my land."

He must have seen worry on her face, because he said, "No, it's all right. Plenty of it to go around. I just mean that if you're here, then it's sort of my responsibility to see to it that you're in no trouble." He stared at her for a few moments, then said, "If you're hungry, follow me. My boy should be awake. I'll make breakfast for us. We don't get too many visitors."

She had followed him, guarded but curious about him and his strange accent. Later, after watching him burn bread and eggs and beef, she quietly stepped between him and the stove and proceeded to make a fine, unburned breakfast. They had talked, learned a bit about each other, why they were each where they were, and, of all the things he could have asked her, he wanted to know if she could read and write—for he could not. By the end of the meal, they had come to an agreement. Later that day, he fixed up a cozy place for her to stay in an old chicken coop, not far from the house.

But the thing she recalled with most fondness from that first day had been meeting the big man's son, the boy he called Brian. As big as he was, the man's entire body seemed to soften and relax when he held the boy, who was barely two years old at the time, and was a small, thin version of his father—the same eyes and the same fire-colored hair. She had never seen such hair on a person before.

Rory had eventually agreed to the demands in the unceasing river of letters from his dead wife's family back East, and sent the boy to them to attend school and be raised in what their letters called "a proper manner." Esperanza had grown so attached to little Brian that some hidden part of her heart broke forever that day. Both for the boy and his confusion, and for his quivering hulk of a father for making what he thought was the right decision. It only occurred to her later, much later, that she should have lied about what the letters said. But back then, lying wasn't something that had occurred to her.

Maybe then none of this would have happened. Maybe Brian would have grown up on the Dancing M, would have worked with his father in a way only a son can, would have prevented him from thinking he had to work himself into an early grave. Rory had joked with her, told her it wouldn't be long before he was fitted for what he called a "wooden suit"—she hated the way he could make light of his own death.

Never once had she asked him if he had accommodated for her and for Brandon, though he had mentioned many times how he hoped Brian would eventually see why he had sent him away, how he hoped his first son would come to appreciate the ranch for what it was— more than a potential fortune, more than a means to earn money. To Rory it was his entire life. That it might not be to others—even his own beloved son—was unthinkable.

But what of her Brandon? Rory had never given the boy seemingly much thought. That he loved him, Esperanza didn't doubt, but by the time she finally believed that Rory intended to leave the entire ranch to Brian, it was far too late to do anything but live, day to day, and see what might happen. Life could be a tricky game of chance sometimes; this much she knew.

"The attorney told me of you."

Brian had walked up behind her while she was daydreaming. She stiffened, and returned to the house.

He followed her and spoke again once they were back in the kitchen. "He said you were to be taken care of, per custom, as something akin to a common-law spouse of my father. I will see to it. So long as you don't expect anything more in the way of remuneration after that. To that end, I had him draw up certain documents that remove you legally from this place and any potential claim, however paltry, someone such as yourself may have on such a property. I have been led to believe that the holdings here are substantial, nearly three thousand acres. Though admittedly it seems absurd to establish ownership on such a vast tract of land, the resale value will no doubt change my mind."

"I don't doubt that, mister." The voice came from the open door behind Brian Middleton.

Middleton spun and saw a man of average height leaning in the doorframe, backlit by the setting sun.

Esperanza wanted to smile, wanted to run to her son and tell him who this stranger was, wanted this all to be so much different than it was. Instead she stood still. And she watched.

"So, you are the idiot who left Silver Haskell's horse saddled out front—that old mare looks all done in. What have you done to her?" The speaker stepped away from the door and into the room.

"It's you! The drunken ruffian who attacked me the other night in town."

"Really? I don't remember attacking much of anything."

"Except a bottle...." Esperanza surprised even herself with her spoken criticism of her son.

Brandon's soft chuckle surprised her. There was a time that he would have gritted his teeth, scowled, and run from the place. He must be growing up some. *Or he's just tired and wants me to cook for him. And I will*, she thought.

The big stranger flopped his hat on the corner of the table and turned to face the young man, his big, soft hands contracting into fists the size of a child's head. Brandon didn't move. He let his gaze trail upward from the man's flexing hands, across the broad chest, and on up to the face. As he did so his smile gave way to slow confusion, then shock. Esperanza knew then what her son was discovering. But instead of the rage that she expected of him, he stood up straight, stepped out of the shadowed doorway and into the room, and slowly removed his own hat. He filled his chest with air and stared at the big man before him. "So, you are him, eh?"

Esperanza watched Brian's face as it took in the knot of wild red hair, darker than his own, but undeniably similar. His face totted up the same emotions as Brandon's. "Who are you, boy?"

"You are in my house. I will ask the questions and you will provide the answers." Brandon's top lip curved into a menacing snarl.

Esperanza rushed between them, putting out a hand toward each. "Brandon," she said, looking at her son. "Forgive me for not introducing you. Brian Middleton, meet Brandon."

"Brandon? Brandon . . . what?" The newcomer looked straight into the eyes of the young man. "Surely you have a surname, boy." Brian's tilted head said it all—he knew what the answer would be.

"That would be MacMawe."

They stood facing each other for a full minute, Esperanza between them, her hands slowly lowering. Finally Brian half turned and plucked his battered hat from the table and said, "So, the common-law wife birthed a bastard."

Brandon gently pushed his mother aside with his left hand even while the right swung wide and caught Middleton's rangy jaw full-on. The big man grunted as if clubbed with a chair leg and pitched backward. As he landed, the stout old table creaked, something underneath cracked like a gunshot in the small room, and it slid hard three feet across the floor. Atop it, Brian slid with the table, then rolled to the edge, and off. He tried to rise once, then sagged, facedown, on the scrubbed pine floor.

"Brandon, what have you done?" Esperanza whispered, her hands covering her mouth.

"No one will talk about you that way, Ma. Not as long as I'm able to raise a fist."

She bent to the unconscious man's side. "It's not fists that need raising, but some brains. Your father would not approve of this, and you know it."

"My father is dead. And this . . . dandy . . . is the person who he lived for all those years? Bah!" He spun and left the house. Soon she heard his horse thundering away as she had so many times since his father died. To town and to the bottle, she thought. And to an early grave.

Esperanza looked with tired eyes at the stranger. She knew she would have to ask to see his documents, would have to surrender to the fact that he was now the heir to his father's fortune—in land if not in any other way—but right now all she wanted was to go to sleep. It had been a month since Rory had died, and it seemed to her that she hadn't slept, really slept, in several months. But now she was tired, well and truly tired. She felt as if she would sign anything just to be rid of this person she once knew.

Chapter 22

On his way out of Turnbull, Squirly had stopped at the sheriff's office. Tucker had been off for the morning, roofing his outhouse, something he'd promised Mrs. Tucker he would get to for months. She'd grown tired of the little structure's top being exposed to the elements. Deputy Sweazy had smiled telling Squirly this.

Of all the folks in town, Sweazy was about the only one the old drunk knew who would still treat Squirly as though he were a fellow man and not a foolish child or a lesser creature. That was perhaps why he had never hit up the younger man for the price of a drink.

"Well," Squirly said, wishing he hadn't stopped. "I'd imagine an outhouse without a roof could get a mite breezy."

Sweazy had allowed as how that could well be a reason for so many marriages ending in an angry shooting match.

"Do they really?" Despite his hurry, Squirly shuddered. "Guess I won't be marryin' any time soon, then. That sounds awful."

"So, what can I do for you, Mr. Ross?" Sweazy leaned forward in the desk chair, his brows knotted in concentration.

Squirly cleared his throat. "I would like to direct Sheriff Tucker's attention to a certain stranger who come into town lately, yesterday I'm thinking, and I think he's a murderer."

Sweazy stood up. "You mean the MacMawe boy who calls himself Middleton?"

"What? No, no, I'm talking about that odd foreigner fella. Ain't a Mex, ain't anything I know. But his tone seemed to change when I told him about my friend, Mitchell Farthing, who's coming into Turnbull any day now from up north."

"Why should that concern him? Lots of folks come to Turnbull. Well, not all that many, but it's been known to happen." Deputy Sweazy looked almost embarrassed at admitting that Turnbull was less than a destination at present.

"Well, now, I know all that. But my situation is complicated. Just tell Sheriff Tucker what I said. I know how he feels about me, so lie if you have to, but have him keep a sharp eye on that foreign fellow. There's something fishy with that one, mark my words."

"Where are you headed, Mr. Ross?"

"Why, I thought that would be plain, Deputy. I'm headed north to find my friend. If he has fallen on misfortune, I aim to gun down that foreign fellow. Savvy?"

"Just because your friend is late getting to town doesn't mean something bad has happened to him."

Squirly opened the door and looked back at the deputy. "Now, you may be right. Then again, you may just be inexperienced in the ways of the world. I, for one, have a ton of living under my belt. But the truth will all come out in the wash. Well, someone's wash anyway. I'll keep myself calm until I find out I need to do otherwise. Good day to you, Deputy Sweazy."

Chapter 23

It took all of Esperanza's strength to drag Brian's big, limp body up to a sitting position, propped against a table leg. He moaned but didn't come around right away. She felt bad for him, but her anger at what he said, at all the turmoil and pain and grief he represented to her and her son forced her work-hardened hands into fists and her mouth into a grim line. From the drawer of a sideboard, she pulled out a sheet of writing paper, tore it evenly in half, and in a precise hand wrote a brief note. She replaced the unused half sheet and the quill and ink bottle to their places in the drawer. From a larger drawer, deep in the back, she slid out a heavy, leather-covered family Bible. The corners were cracked, and the gilt edging glowed dull.

For a moment she stood, her calloused hand resting on the cover. Then she slipped the note under the front cover, half sticking out the top. She carried the Bible to the unconscious young man and set it on his lap. She stood, looked around the room, and her gaze landed on the battered bowler upside down on the floor in the corner. She retrieved it and set it atop the Bible. Then she went outside to feed her chickens.

As she ushered the last of her buff hens into their night coop, she heard the uneven rattle of horse's hooves and she knew that Brian Middleton was leaving the dooryard. It seemed to her as if her entire life was spent watching people leave, and she wondered what she did to deserve this cruelty. Maybe the next life would be filled with a dozen happy children who loved being with her. She would have liked to have more children. Perhaps there might still be grandchildren in her future. Then she thought of Brandon and knew that he was unlikely to offer her anything but grief in the future. If he even had much of a future.

Minutes before, Brian Middleton had come to on the floor of the crude little home, sitting upright against the table leg. He looked about himself and felt oddly comfortable, given his situation. For the few moments it took for his fuzzy head to clear, he thought he was home. Something more than a feeling but less than a memory of happiness and warmth swaddled him, and then it was gone. Again he took in the room, but now it seemed shabby and small, and in no way compared favorably with the many and varied rooms of his grandfather's well-appointed town house, or the family's summer estate at the shore in Newport.

He rubbed his face with a trembling hand and winced at the lumped jaw, swollen more than ever now that he'd been hit there twice—and by the same ruffian. A brute who, if the little Mexican woman's intimations were to be trusted, was his half brother. He couldn't deny the youth's red hair, doubly shocking to see it perched on the dark complexion of someone of Mexican descent. His hand dropped to his lap, cratering his abused hat. Beneath it sat a massive book with a note poking from it.

He slid out the note, the indigo script precise and orderly on unlined paper. As he read, his face settled once again into the barely tolerant, disappointed lines he'd worn since crossing the Mississippi River weeks before. He pushed to one knee, but had to steady himself on the edge of the table as a wave of dizziness washed over him, leaving him feeling cold prickliness from head to foot. Sweat broke over him, and his teeth chattered for a moment. Before long, the chill feeling ebbed.

Brian Middleton stood, plunked his hat on his head, and carrying the big Bible with him, stuffed it inside one of his carpetbags, then mounted the defeated horse and rode back in the direction from which he'd come but a short time before. He did not see the woman as he left. Nor did he want to, especially given the brutal way he'd been treated in her home. Her home. . . . *We'll see about that*, he thought as he dug his heels into the flanks of the old, tired mare.

Chapter 24

After nearly an hour in the saddle, Brian reined up, knowing he would not make town that night. Nor, did he think, would the horse. And then the angry young man's words came back to him. Idiot, he'd called him, for leaving the horse saddled. He'd said she looked all done in. He looked at the horse beneath him and knew the boy was correct.

Why did he not think of the animal's welfare before now? He'd been in such a rush to get to his father's ranch and complete the transaction that he'd neglected to attend to the animal's most basic needs—like rest. He dismounted and with a tentative hand patted the horse's shoulder. The animal looked back at him and he swore there was the stony glint of anger in her eye, though she seemed too tired to do anything about it.

It took him ten minutes to figure out how to loosen the cinch, then drag off the saddle. He tried to recall Junior's lesson from the night before, but everything seemed so muddy in his head. Finally the saddle just slipped off the horse's back. The bit and bridle looked equally as painful and the horse seemed so worn out that he doubted there was any need to tie her.

Not that there was much to tie her to. The spot he'd chosen was bereft of anything more substantial than rocks and scrubby bushes no taller than waist high, it seemed, for as far as he could see in the afternoon's softening light. He nodded in satisfaction as he slipped off the bridle. The horse walked away a few steps, then dropped to her knees and stretched out prone on her side. Within seconds her long legs were kicking in the air and she writhed in the dust as if being strangled.

And though he recalled, once again, Junior's words of assurance from the previous evening, he was certain that this time he'd lose the horse. Something was wrong; he just knew it. "Good heavens, what do I do now? She'll die because of my ignorance. She's taken a fit and I'm miles from anywhere and I should have known better."

Even as he stood there, watching in shock as the horse twisted and rolled, hooves flailing in the air, and grunts coming from her mouth, the dusty brown horse rose and shook herself, then walked a few yards, stopped, and nosed a sparse clump of spiky green grasses. Brian finally exhaled.

He set to making a camp, and as he unpacked his satchel he wondered about this trip, the people he'd met so far, the coffeepot belonging to that fellow Junior— would he even see him again? Not that he cared, but he hated the idea of being beholden to the man. He'd leave it for him in town, with a note. The boy had been kind, to an extent, though he did leave before Brian awoke, and after saying the night before that he would gladly take Brian to the Dancing M the following day. "A Western promise," he muttered, shaking out his wool blanket. "Full of holes."

Within twenty minutes, he'd conjured a successful fire, and as he fed the tiny, dancing flames he thought of the sister of the coffeepot's owner. Had Junior said her name? If he had, Brian had forgotten it. But not her face. She was a striking young lady, poised and bold in what few words he heard her speak. Back in Providence she would have been called impertinent, but out here he supposed that word was seldom used. In fact, he suspected her boldness would be highly regarded in this rough place. Then there was the ranch itself—a far cry from what he'd been led to believe from the attorney.

He supposed the value of the place was in the land—that much acreage was bound to be worth a substantial sum. He would liquidate it as handily as possible and invest the money, as his grandfather had suggested, in sureties. Though not in what his grandfather would choose for him, but rather in what he would choose for himself. It was high time he stood up to the old curmudgeon. He'd taken a first step by embarking on this trip without his approval, and despite the horrible experiences thus far, something told Brian that this trip was just the thing he'd needed to do for quite some time now.

At least he'd begun to feel that way until he met that woman at the ranch—Esperanza. Meeting her, going to that humble, tidy house, felt right in so many ways, yet also made him regret the entire trip. It was as if by walking in there he somehow willingly played into his dead father's plans, and that didn't feel good in the least. He was tired of being manipulated by everyone in his life, from his grandfather to his club friends, all the way down to the punch-throwing half brother, Brandon.

Yes, he thought, as he poked the paltry fire, *perhaps I should have taken Grandfather's advice and let Atchison take care of things. He would have called me in within a few weeks to sign over the deed, hand me a banknote for the sale amount, and I would never have been the wiser. Then why did I come out here?* He blew softly at the base of the flames. They surged higher, licking the dry, brown twigs, and he felt a small twinge of satisfaction.

A horse's low snort made him look up. Shadowed in

the dusk, a horse and rider stood not twelve feet from him. A voice cracked the space between them: "Hello there . . . brother."

So, it was the young fighter. "Don't call me that." Brian stood. "And as far as I'm concerned, we share a hair color, nothing more." He pointed a long, meaty finger at the young man. "And I shan't be convinced otherwise. And what's more, I'll not be goaded into violence. That may be *your* way, the very way of the West." He thumbed his chest. "But that is not *my* way. Not by a long shot."

Brandon shrugged, then slipped from his horse. "Suits me just fine."

Brian stood half turned toward his visitor, his hands curled into fists at his sides.

Brandon laughed. "You think I'm going to take another swing at you? Two is my limit. But I will say that for such a large man you are small on taking a punch."

Brian stared at him. He had made up his mind that he would not be struck again by this little rogue.

"Relax, Middleton. You seem tense. I wonder why that could be."

"Perhaps because I've been victimized and savaged ever since I set foot in this strange land."

The younger man looked shocked. He loosened the cinch on his saddle and said, "Now you know how I feel."

"What does that mean?"

But the young man ignored the question. "Besides, you shouldn't feel out of place, or taken advantage of here. After all"—he raised his hands up as if testing for rain, then let them drop to his sides—"we are on your land."

Brian narrowed his eyes at the lad.

Brandon laughed and said, "It's true. Everything this side of the river, for days, weeks, months, years . . . in all these directions"—he laughed and arced an arm out into the growing dark—"is the Dancing M."

They were quiet for a few moments, and then Brian jerked his head behind him. "And that side of the river?"

"That? Oh, that's the Driving D. Home of the Grindle clan. Mean as a nest of vipers. You reach in there you'll draw back a bloody stump."

"Junior Grindle?"

Brandon lugged his saddle to the fireside, flopped it down, and said, "You know him already, eh? I should have guessed. Varmints seek out their own kind. You're cut from the same cloth."

Brian backed up a step, then crossed his arms. "I found him to be cordial and generous."

"Generous? A Grindle? Ha. You're as crazy as you look."

Brian lowered his hands again, clenching them. He gritted his teeth, but Brandon only looked up from warming his hands and said, "Relax, will you? Call a truce between us for the night."

"As I recall, I didn't invite you to my camp."

Brandon didn't move. "That's true. But the way I figure it, you have questions you might like answered, and I have questions I would like answered, and we each might have the answers the other wants. Then after a night's rest we can both go our own ways and never have to see each other again."

He didn't look up from the fire, but Brian saw the young man's jaw muscles working, as if he were chewing tough steak.

"What information could you possibly have that I might find useful?"

Brandon stared into the flames. Finally he shook his head and said, "Forget it, Middleton. You're a tough nut to crack. Too tough for me. I'm just tired. And I wish I had a drink. You got any whiskey?"

Brian nearly dismissed the question, then remembered the half-full bottle of booze that Junior Grindle had left at the camp that morning—possibly because it was half-wedged under Brian when he awoke. Brian had stuffed it in his bag before riding off in search of the ranch.

"As a matter of fact, I do indeed have whiskey. I can't vouch for its veracity, but then again, I doubt your palate is sophisticated enough to discern the difference between something refined and something that will put you over the edge in short order."

"Believe it or not, I understood what you just said. And you're probably right. But I'm not looking for anything more than a cheap way to vanish for a time."

Brian stared at the flames a moment longer, then bent to his satchel. He pulled out the Bible and the note poking from beneath the cover, and reached for the bottle.

"Hey! That's my mother's Bible. Did she give that to you?" Brandon snatched the note before Brian could stop him.

"In a manner of speaking, yes." Brian popped the deep-set cork from the bottle with a *tunk* sound that brought Brandon's gaze up from the paper. He smiled and involuntarily licked his bottom lip. Brian splashed some of the dark liquid into his tin cup. The other man handed him his own tin cup of chipped blue-black enamel. Brian tipped whiskey into the cup and watched the young man.

He gulped it down and held his cup toward Brian, a smile and raised eyebrows doing the talking for him. Brian splashed more into the cup. The boy frowned, looked at the chipped blue-black enamel, then looked up at Brian, wagging the cup. Middleton sighed and drizzled more into the cup.

"Now, what did dear old mother hen write to you that was so important?" He held the note toward the fire to read it better, and Brian snatched it from his grip. "Hey!"

The bigger man regarded him for a moment, took a healthy swig from his cup, then said, "If it's that important, then I'll read it to you."

"Why? Don't think a savage like me can read?"

"You've not exactly proven yourself to be a shining example of the benefits of a solid education, now, have you?"

Brandon just stared at Brian, eyes narrowed. Brian looked at the paper and said, "She does have exemplary handwriting."

"Does that surprise you?"

Brian lowered the note and looked at the young man. "Why are you so thin-skinned?"

"I was going to ask you the same thing."

"Is it because you're . . ." He nodded at the young man. "You know. . . ."

"Nope, I guess I don't know what you mean." He almost smiled.

Brian sighed. "Forget it."

"No, no. I think I know. It's because I'm half Mexican and half Scottish and a whole lot of nobody."

"What does that mean?"

"It means just what I said. You try it sometime. When I say hello, women put their hands to their throats and pull their children to the other side of the street. Even in Turnbull, where everybody has known me my entire life."

"I apologize. I didn't mean to—"

"Keep your sorrow for someone who will need it. Like your future wife, God bless her, whoever she may be. What a trial she's in for."

"What makes you say that?" Brian was intrigued more than angry by the comment.

The boy drained the whiskey in his cup and held it out. Brian downed his own, then half filled each cup.

"Because," continued Brandon, "you have a bad way of conducting yourself."

Brian began to protest, but Brandon held up a hand. "No, no, no, you asked me and I'm going to provide you with an answer." He sipped again. "In town, then with my mother"—he nodded at the note—"then again with me, you are rude. You act as if everyone you meet here is stupid and of such low character that it's taking all the effort you can muster just to hold a conversation before you can get away from here and return to the perfect East, where you belong."

They were quiet for some time. Finally Brian said, "I didn't realize it was that apparent."

"I'm not wrong."

Brian shook his head. "No, you're not wrong. I should never have come."

"Then why did you?"

Brian laughed, a short, clipped sound that could have been mistaken for a sign of disgust. "I thought I knew. I thought it would be a way to show my grandfather that I am a man capable of handling my own affairs without his help."

"But it's not turning out to be the case, is it?"

Brian sipped from his cup, then looked at the young man across the fire. "No. For someone who's little more than a boy, how did you become so astute?"

"You see? That's what I'm talking about." He waved a hand at Middleton. "You just insulted me and you didn't even know it." He smiled and shook his head. "Go ahead, read my mother's note to me."

Brian regarded him for a moment, then said, "Okay. But just remember that you asked." He cleared his throat, held out the note toward the fire. "'Brian—Though we do not know each other now, we once did, and you were a dear boy, the center of your father's life, and the reason for all he did in his too-short life. I knew this day would come and I hoped, for your father's sake, that you would love the Dancing M as he did. But that has not happened. So here are the only things I have of your father's that I trust one day you will find comfort in. I hope you find peace.'"

He straightened and stared at the fire. He opened the

Bible, intending to slide in the note. But the book opened to reveal other folded papers. "What's this?"

Brandon prodded the fire and added a few sticks, saying nothing.

Brian slid out the papers and unfolded the topmost. The firelight revealed a sheet of parchment, its creases worn limp from much folding and unfolding. The calligraphy told Brian that it was a marriage license between one Penelope Regina Middleton and one Rory Mac-Mawe. His throat tightened. His mother and father. To actually see their names together ... something his grandfather never spoke of.

"They were married twenty-six years ago, in Providence, Rhode Island. At Our Lady of Salvation Church." He looked up at Brandon. "I know where that is. I have passed that very church more times than I can count." He looked back to the sheet, but there was little other information there. Then, as if he were a man begging water after a crawl through a desert, Brian Middleton clawed open the next paper. He recognized the precise, clipped hand—that of his grandfather, Horatio T. Middleton. It was dated the day before the marriage certificate, and it too had seen much opening and folding. Unlike the grandeur of the previous sheet, this was a plain, personal letter.

He read it quickly, and halfway through, a groan escaped his mouth.

"What does it say, Brian?"

The larger man looked up from the letter, sipped from his cup, and nodded. " 'My dearest Penelope, light of my life, I will cut to the quick and state plainly my wishes and the subsequent results of disobeying them. I plead with you not to wed this Scottish ruffian. He is a hoodlum with a head covered in fire and a heart full of treachery and woe. His kind only bring ill luck and can only produce more of the same, even if tempered with the fine stock of your proud and noble upbringing, Penelope Regina Middleton. If you insist on wedding this brute, I shall have no choice but to disown and disinherit you, and disavow any knowledge of you from here on. Your heartbroken but loving father, Horatio T. Middleton the Third.'"

For several minutes the only sound was the soft crackle of the small fire. Then Brandon shifted position and poured another drink. "He sounds like a bad person. Bad to the core."

"What do you know about him? What do you know about anything in my life?" Brian waved him off as if dispelling a fly. "Let's see what else is in here." He lifted from the folds of the Bible a last tri-folded sheet, with smudges and blotted words.

"This looks as if it's written by a child." He held up the sheet, as if Brandon could see it in the dull firelight, then resumed reading. "The spelling's atrocious, even for a child, and some of the letters are backward."

"What does it say?"

"I'm getting to that," said Brian, irritated at the interruption. "Let's see. . . . 'I want to take you up on your offer which you have put to me for years now to give my son—'" Brian slowed his reading, then recommenced, "'The good Eastern education his dear mother would have wanted for him. I would not allow him to be taken from me without your promise that he will be sent to me for a time each year until he is growed.'"

Despite his advancing inebriation and the waning light, Brian read the note twice out loud, slowly, carefully.

"Well, what do you know?" said Brandon, smiling. "So that's the letter that started the ball rolling, eh?"

"What do you mean by that?"

"Aha! So Mama didn't share with you the stack of letters she wrote for Papa. Well, they were really for you." He stood and stretched his back, motioned with a hand toward the letters in Brian's lap. "You can see for yourself how poor his own writing skills were. He had none at all before Mama taught him that much. But Mama, now, she has a way with words. She wrote all those letters, and even after I came along she continued to write letters for him. Of course, by then he was obsessed with getting you back. He nearly lost the ranch in lawyers' fees trying to get you back from that tender old man you call 'grandfather.'"

"How do you know all this?" said Brian, still smarting from all these revelations.

"Some from my mother, some from rummaging in the sideboard where all the letters that came back unread were kept. We all knew, even him, that they were rejected by your grandfather. So it's really no surprise to me or Mama how you come to be here now, not knowing a thing about our lives."

Brian said nothing, just stared at the fire as the younger man spoke.

"If your dear grandfather had given you the letters, you would know that mostly they were full of Papa's descriptions of life here at the Dancing M. News of Mama and even me. He didn't want there to be any secrets; that much I knew. I always wondered what happened to the presents he sent you. Special things—toys, books, knives, even a fine hand-tooled holster and six-gun once, not too many years ago. We never had much here, but he made sure to send you fine things. I always thought he was trying to lure you back here. But I guess you never got his gifts."

Brian shook his head. "I never received any gifts, nor information about him or my mother from my grandfather other than that I was better off not knowing him, as he was, and I quote, 'an unschooled ruffian.'"

"Well, that unschooled ruffian, as you call him, owned one of the most promising ranches in this part of the state."

Brian stared at the young man standing over him, his

back to the fire. "I had no idea of any of this, Brandon. No idea."

"That doesn't make how you've been behaving right."

"I know." Brian looked at his hands holding the aged sheets of paper. It was too dark now to read, and the little pile of wood was nearly spent. He'd read most of what he needed to anyway. For tonight. He knew that tomorrow he'd reread the pages. And for days after. "I'd like to see those other letters."

"You'll have to ask her. I'm sure she didn't share them because she was afraid of hurting you." Brandon stretched out on the ground again. "That's just how my mother is." He settled back and tipped his hat over his face. "She's a saint to put up with him and then me." He lifted the hat slightly and stared at Brian. "But make no mistake, Brian Middleton," said the young man, his square, tan jaw reflecting light from the fire, a finger pointed straight as an arrow at Brian. "I will punch you on the nose if you upset my mother again like you did today." Then he settled his head against his saddle once more.

Brian nodded slowly, only half hearing what the boy had said. Tomorrow he would return to his father's ranch and talk with Esperanza, ask to read the letters that she wrote to his grandfather on his father's behalf. Letters that were returned unopened. He folded the papers into their familiar creases and slid them between pages in the heavy Bible and closed it.

After he too had settled back and the night noises became less worrisome, he thought back on the day. What a mess he'd made of things by coming out here. If only he had stayed in Providence. . . . But was not knowing something any better than knowing it?

"Middleton, you still awake?"

"Yes."

"Answer me this: Why don't you still have the name MacMawe? Is it so bad to you?"

There was a pause, and then Brian said, "I had no

choice in the matter. I was raised by my grandfather as a Middleton. As far as he was concerned, everything about me was Middleton and there was no such thing as Mac-Mawe in his eyes in the world."

"But legally, are you a MacMawe or a Middleton? What does it say in the court documents?"

Brian sighed. "I have no brother. I have no father. I have no mother. I have no one but an old grandfather. And that's just the way I like it. Now go to sleep."

There was no response. Brian lay awake for a long while wondering about what he was going to do next, the whiskey dulling the edges of his thoughts with a warm glow, despite the harsh words he had just spoken to the one person in years with whom he'd let down his guard.

Chapter 25

Junior Grindle sat on the hard boulder until long after he'd heard the last snatches of talk drift away from the meager camp. Though there was nothing more than a slight breeze tonight, he sat downwind of the two men, and made sure to stay that way. Horses were mighty sensitive creatures. Fortunately Middleton had no idea how to pay attention to his mount, the perk of the ears, the low, throaty whinny, the attentive stance. But that Brandon MacMawe, now, he was one person Junior knew in these parts—or anywhere, for that matter—who could practically tell what a horse was thinking just by looking at or hearing the beast nicker.

He couldn't take any chances. Drunk or no, that half-breed MacMawe would be the one to watch. He almost giggled aloud. Drunk. . . . That's where he was at himself. Or nearly so. It had taken a mighty effort to put down that last glass and bid the boys a good evening. Including that foreign gambler fellow, an odd one, to be sure—friendly but something about him seemed a little oily too. Probably just a damn cardsharp coming around to skin the boys out of a week's wages. He'd seen 'em before, and they'd no doubt show up in Turnbull again.

He surely wanted to stay on at the table, at least for another hand or two. But when the idea hit him, well, Junior knew it was now or never. All he had to do was track down the big greenhorn. In his hazy whiskey glow, this seemed like an easy task. And halfway home, on the ranch road south out of town, he heard the big greenhorn making far too much noise out in the open and he knew that his plan was meant to be.

Junior shifted on the rock, slid down, and glanced back behind him toward Spunk. Still nibbling unseen grass and not having to walk too far had put the horse in a relaxed, quiet state. He still wasn't sure how he felt about Brandon MacMawe's presence at Middleton's campsite. But heck, the more he thought about it, the more he realized that having Brandon there too could work in his favor.

He'd waited long enough. Now that it was dark, Junior breathed deeply and started off toward the campsite with slow, deliberate steps, keeping the faint ember glow of the men's fire roughly in front of him. He knew what he felt needed to be done. He also knew that his sister, Callie, would surely disagree with him, but there was no other way. He'd been over it in his head and he knew sure as a prairie dog digs holes that Middleton thought he was just a kid. Heck, he saw the man's face when he proposed buying the Dancing M from him. Eastern dude just wanted to laugh at him as if he were a child.

That ranch would be sold off, hacked up, covered with a hundred settlers, and ruined forever. And because it was right next door, he was sure that the Driving D would struggle to keep from being a ruined wasteland too. No, he could not—would not—let that happen. Finally, tonight he understood what his father had been talking about. And if he could make this thing happen, then his father would give him the Dancing M and he could make a heck of a success of it, he just knew. Then one day he would run both ranches as one.

There would be the matter of coming up with a dowry to buy off Callie and her husband, whoever that might be down the road. All he knew right now was that she was a girl, and there was no way he was giving up any land to her. But he'd worry about that later. Right now he wanted to make sure that he accomplished what he was sure his father meant. He'd have to hand it to his old man, saying what needed to be said without actually saying it. The mark of a true businessman.

Now, you take Rory MacMawe. He'd been a good fellow. Junior would freely admit that, but there was no way he was a businessman. Just look at the ranch, the state of the buildings. Sure, the house was solid enough, but it wasn't even a quarter the size of the Grindle home. That was the mark of a man who didn't have his priorities in order.

Junior was still a few hundred yards from the camp when he checked his pistol, the .36 Remington model, the same one that Brandon MacMawe owned. Another reason his plan would work. It was easy enough when you looked at it like that—eliminate one problem and shift the blame of it on the other problem. Two problems gone and done for. He planned on gunning down the big, sappy stranger. Then with any luck, Brandon would be blamed. Made sense, as the kid had the motive and the pistol. Having him here was just plain lucky. The good fortune was enough that Junior almost giggled.

He stepped slow and low now, for he was but a few yards from the two humped forms of the sleeping men. And judging from the heavy breathing rising from each, this would be easier than he guessed it might be. Brandon first, then the damned interloper. Maybe it would look as if they did each other in. Junior grinned in the dark. He had a head for such thinking; he was convinced of it.

MacMawe or no, neither of them was worthy of owning the Dancing M. His father wouldn't be around forever and Junior knew that he could do the job as good as his old man, maybe even better. Far as he was concerned, he was the only one capable of doing that ranch justice, just as he'd told that little foreigner at the bar.

Junior bent low and squinted at the sprawled form to his right. Had to be Brandon—it was a foot shorter than the other and about half as wide. He was on the small side, as was Junior, but Brandon was scrappy, as Junior well knew. Though the boy was a few years younger, he had whipped Junior in a couple of wrestling matches, horsing around at the river on hot summer days. But that was before things changed, before life required them to be men, not kids playing at being men.

The breathing from both sleepers came in ragged counterpoint, like a pair of pulling mules after a steep grade. The fire was little more than dulled, orange embers, and the crescent moon a fingernail offering little help. Junior bent low, now two feet from Brandon's head. He saw the faint outline of the boy's cheek, nose, chin, one closed eye, his hat tipped to the side. This would be the easiest and the most difficult part of the entire night.

Though he held no great hate for Brandon, Junior knew that there was nothing about to happen for which the boy would truly be guilty. But sometimes being born into the wrong family is the biggest crime of all. At least that's what Junior imagined his father might say about the matter. It warmed him to know that he was thinking like his old man.

Junior drew in a lungful of cool night air and held it. He drew his pistol and wrapped his hand around the barrel, raised it high over Brandon's head, but a grunted shout from behind him stilled his pose.

"What's that? Who's there? Who . . . ?" Junior spun, and there was Middleton, raised on one elbow and leaning toward him, trying to see through the night air. Beneath him Brandon MacMawe stirred, squinted up just as Junior looked down at him. No thought at all came to Junior as he drove downward with the pistol's clublike handle at the boy's temple. MacMawe was stilled with the single blow—it felt to Junior like a death blow—and he turned back to who he hoped was the lesser of the two adversaries.

"Say, what's the matter here?"

As Junior spun, he swung the pistol low and hard and connected with nothing but chill night air. The force of his swing spun him backward and over Brandon's unmoving legs. The big stranger was nearly on his feet now, and Junior managed to rise to his knees. He grabbed the pistol with his left hand and spun it in his palm, the deadly end pointing at the dark hulking mass in front of him.

"What is the matter, Brandon? I thought we agreed . . . for tonight . . . but if you take another swing at me, so help me . . ."

Junior's mind flashed on the idea handed him. "You just keep away," he said, hoping in the frenzy that he sounded somewhat like Brandon.

"Or what? You little fool. I've had enough of your games. Pretend you're asleep, then attack me when I'm sleeping!" The big man lunged forward.

"No!" Junior thumbed back the hammer and before thought could play a role, he squeezed a shot straight at the big man. The boom filled the night air for what seemed miles. Brian Middleton groaned, a long, gasping sound, like air leaving a train engine's boiler, then slumped to his knees and fell to the ground, faceup, inches from the nearly dead campfire.

Young Grindle froze, smoke curling from the short barrel of his pistol. He'd only really meant to make it look as if one man attacked the other—maybe sully their reputations a bit. Enough perhaps to have them both driven from the area, forced to sell up. But not this, not gunfire. Not a shooting. Or was this what he had wanted all along? Why bring the gun, then? He shivered at the thought. No! Now that he was faced with his foul act, he realized he did not want a shooting, not a death. He stiffened as if seized, and stumbled backward to land, seated, on a wind-smooth rock, and the lousiness of his plan pressed down on him like a wagonload of boulders. The booze, good God, but he had let it get the better of him again. Up to now it had only been money lost at cards. Up to now. . . .

Snatches of words flew at him like bats in the night, and in them he heard his father's voice as if the old man were sitting beside him. "No son of mine would act that way. . . . Land is all . . . Where have you been, boy? What have you been up to?"

Junior spun, shouting, "No!" and swinging his fists in the dark. No one was there. "Get a hold of yourself, Junior," he muttered, clenching his teeth and shaking his head to dispel the lingering blurring feeling of the damnable whiskey. The old man was home in bed and could never, would never find out about this.

He sat still for a moment more, breathing deep and thinking. He knew he'd been lying to himself. He'd meant exactly what had happened. In fact, it couldn't have played out better. The one stranger, the interloper, shot dead by Brandon MacMawe, the man who had the most to lose should the stranger invoke his rightful claims to the Dancing M.

Now with the one man surely dead, the other, if he too wasn't dead, was sure to swing for his murder. And what of Esperanza, the mother of a killer, the grieving widow—no, not even that!— the mistress of a man who left his estate in ruins. Why, Junior and his father, as the most logical, not to mention the most law-abiding, well-respected ranch owners in the region, were sure to find the path to ownership of the Dancing M a smooth and unchallenged one.

After all, who else in the valley could afford the price of such a ranch, even at the reduced rate it was sure to bring?

Junior shook himself out of his daze and took stock of the situation. He had shot a man who was even now bleeding out into the grit and soil of this hard plain. The boy, Brandon, would need to be dealt with. Check him first to see if he was dead, then . . . the gun!

Junior crouched down over the boy and fumbled at his waist. Nothing. Then by his side, then the saddle horn by his head, where a man might coil a gun belt with the grip of his pistol at the ready. But there was no gun. He groaned, forcing his rising panic down. Of all the times for MacMawe to leave his gun at home. He squeezed tight his chattering jaws and paused, his hands gripping nothing but dirt.

What would it matter? He knew the boy carried a pistol, just like half the men in the territory. And who would believe the boy anyway? Everyone who knew him knew he had been an unreliable pup since Mac-Mawe died. And everyone also knew—or soon would, if Junior had any say in the matter—that this boy had every reason to kill the stranger, especially if the boy had assumed he was the sole heir to the ranch. So, thought Junior, it was possible that Brandon threw away the pistol after shooting his half brother.

He leaned closer, to within inches of the boy's face, and even through his own boozy breath, he smelled the rank curdle of whiskey on the boy's ragged exhalations. Brandon was still unconscious, out cold. Junior knew it had been but a few minutes since he'd shot the big stranger, but still it felt as if half his life had passed by.

He clenched his fists and looked into the darkness to orient himself, then strode with purpose back toward the snag of brush where he'd left his mount. Within him, the stone-cold feeling of guilt at having forever altered other people's lives sat heavy and deep in his guts and warred with a cautious anticipation of pride in knowing that his father would be pleased with the outcome. At least he hoped the old man would approve.

Junior scissored his legs wider, eager now to reach his horse and be away from the scene. The odds of anyone out and about were slim to none, but with each passing month newcomers were making their way into the region, squatting for a time on any land that suited them, until they were driven off. No telling if any around these parts heard the shot. It wouldn't do to be seen, for even on a half-lit night like this, eyes were everywhere. He pulled his hat brim down low over his forehead and picked up the pace.

Chapter 26

"Picolo, are you as tired of riding as I am? Still, I had to follow that loudmouth boy rancher. 'My father this' and 'my father that.' What an idiot. Doesn't he know I will gut him and his entire family like fishes? Hey, Picolo, are you listening?"

The horse nickered and Darturo smiled, nodded once. "I am impressed, my friend. All these years and I thought you were ignoring me. Besides, a decent bed in town is no match for the firm bosom of Mother Earth, eh? Oh, who am I kidding? Give me the bed any night. But still, it pays in the end to learn more about this young wealthy boy and his family. He might be a way to the money." Mort watched the roan's ears perk as he spoke. He reined up short at the same time and leaned low on the horse's neck. "I heard it too," he whispered, his eyes scanning left and right. "You see? We are close to something, eh?"

Ahead, just over a rise between his route and the road south, he heard a man's voice, deep, bellowing about something. Ah yes, there was another voice, softer and younger, but also a man. Could there be more than one? And more importantly, thought Darturo, would they have anything of value about them? Of course, he knew that everyone carried something of value, but since Denver he felt he could afford to be choosier, and perhaps only take those things that would be of personal interest to him. Like a fine watch or a good knife. One could always use a good knife. Small items such as these might also be useful should he feel forced to buy his way in or out of a situation.

He slipped from his horse's back and ground-tied the beast. Crouching low and taking care not to raise dust or sound from the graveled rise to his left, Mort made his way to just below the top of the low ridgeline. It would be full dark in less than an hour. *If I want to see who these men are*, thought Mort, *I will have to peek now or wait for morning.*

He removed his hat and set it beside him; then as slow as he dared, he raised his head. He knew that people rarely paused to consider anything that was motionless or nearly so. But something that moved invariably attracted the eye. The descending dusk should conceal him from them. And there they were, a big man wearing what looked as if at one time it had been a bowler hat. The other wore his own hat low. But there was something about the two that seemed familiar. He took in what other details he might, while the light allowed, then eased himself back down to a sitting position and listened.

Mort had planned on making a small fire, just enough flame for coffee, and making do with jerky and biscuits he'd bought in town. But that could wait. Long ago he'd trained himself to take advantage of that fickle lady known as Fortune when and where she smiled on him. He sensed she was maybe planning to grin.

He leaned back against the hill and listened to the two men arguing. It was more interesting than he expected it to be and soon his eyebrows rose in recognition of the drama playing below as having something to do with the reason he intended for this scouting visit to the Dancing M ranch. Mort smiled in the near dark and played with the curled ends of buckskin tassel that swung from his right holster. Forgoing hot coffee and jerky for a few hours was a small price to pay considering the maudlin saga that floated up to his ears from the two men below. So, these must be two brothers, judging from their conversation. And what's more, they must be the heirs to the Dancing M, the inheritors of all that land. The pity of it, from what he could hear, was that neither of them sounded particularly competent or even interested in such a rich holding. He smiled again and settled back, enjoying more with each minute what he heard, several possible plans forming, curling in his mind like tendrils of smoke twisting together, drifting apart.

Some time later, Picolo raised his head and nickered low, his ears perked forward. Mort roused from his half doze and waved a hand toward the horse somewhere below him in the dark, not that it mattered, for he knew that the receding peal of the gunshot would cover the reactions of ten horses. Mort could scarcely believe what he saw—a new man, who looked to be that idiot kid from the bar, had stumbled into the camp less than an hour after the two men had finally dozed off. The small campfire, with each passing minute, had lost more of its vital glow.

Mort was left squinting into the dark, desperate to see the intruder's face, to verify that it was indeed that foolish ranch boy. But even with the heavy moon, he could not. And he dared not climb down closer. From the look of the intruder, his staggering gait, his shouts like those of a man crazy in the head, and his wild arm-swinging actions, it was obvious the fool was drunk—drunker than when he had left the bar. All the more impressive, thought Mort, considering he'd bested two men. Though he knew that they too had hit the whiskey bottle themselves before turning in, and had been asleep when he crept upon them.

In the rolling silence that followed the gunshot, Mort heard the uneven clopping of two horses running hard in different directions. He had seen no other men around and he wondered if they were the horses of the sleeping men. Not hobbled, then, and probably headed for their home corrals, he thought.

Finally the man stumbled off into the dark, mumbling and shouting low oaths. Mort was able to only pick out a few words. Among them he heard "old man" and "land." These meant nothing to him. But he chose to keep them and not to forget them, for he might have use of them yet. At the very least, if all else failed him, Mort knew he could blackmail this rich boy about what he had just witnessed. Surely the young fool would not want anyone to know he had just attacked, perhaps even killed, two sleeping men. Yes, Picolo, thought Mort. Skipping the soft bed in town tonight had proved to be a wise move, eh?

With each passing minute, the small campfire withered. Mort waited long minutes before he slid up and over the gravel ridge he'd hunkered behind, just above the camp. He descended, sliding and scraping, step by slow step, until he was less than twenty feet from the wounded men. Here was a mess. He smiled and bent low, keeping his right hand poised above his gun, his legs well back from any arms that might belong to a man playing at death, biding his time to grab and trip Mort. This and more he had seen in the past, and he had no intention of giving in to such pathetic, wounded fools.

He approached the smaller of the two men and pushed his forehead aside with the toe of his boot. Even in the dim firelight and half-clouded moon, he saw the dark, matted mess of the man's hair, the pooled blood beneath the man's head. He pushed with the bottom of his boot and moved the man's head back and forth as if he were disagreeing with Mort. But the man made no sound. If this one wasn't dead, he soon would be.

He turned to the other, bigger man and toed him in the side. The man spasmed and groaned, which surprised Mort, since the man's light-colored shirt glistened with blood from his gut wound. Perhaps the shot hadn't been as bad as it might have been.

"I'm no doctor, eh?" Mort toed the man again, heard the groan, and smiled. "But I do know that you will probably die if no help comes." He sighed and looked around the meager little camp. "Besides, from what I heard you saying, it might not be so bad if you did die. For you deserve to if you are complaining about money and ranches and land and mothers. Ah, if these are your problems, then you have no right to complain, eh?" Mort headed back up the gravel bank. "I don't really care. There is other money in this for me. And perhaps more if I leave you to your fates, much as I would like to speed you along your probable journeys. We'll leave you be, for now. *Arrivederci*!"

Mort slid down the opposite side of the ridge and mounted his horse. "It's time we move in some other direction, Picolo. Someone will find these fellows, dead or alive." One of them was a local; that much Mort was sure of, given the content of the conversation he'd heard earlier between the two men. "You know these small-town people . . . always thinking the worst of strangers. Come on, Picolo. We will head back to town, slip in quietly. After all, who would have thought that young loud-mouth rancher boy would do our work for us, eh? We can keep from being bitten if we are in the nest, right, my friend?"

The horse, barely a shadow in the dark, tossed its head as Mort guided him northward. He was silent for a mile, thinking of the possibilities of all he had seen and heard in the last few hours—from the fool boy in the bar to the fools dying at the campsite. He concluded that he would

think about these three men some more as he rode. A lot
of land such as they all were talking of, he thought, surely
would be worth a lot of money. Perhaps his blackmail
should include more than money. Perhaps land would be
wiser. Perhaps it was time to settle down. He wasn't getting any younger, after all. It was worth considering,
surely. Slowly a smile spread on Mortimer Darturo's face
and he urged the horse into a trot.

Chapter 27

Junior doubted there would be anyone awake at this time of the night. The Driving D men worked, and they worked hard. And at night, they slept as hard as they worked — one ear cocked toward the bunkhouse when it was full would verify the fact — the snoring sounded as if a forest of trees were crashing down at a constant rate. There hadn't been Apache attacks in years, not since Junior and Callie were young children, so the need for night guards had gradually diminished, then disappeared altogether.

Besides, he thought, much of the crew was out on range duty, shuffling stock from one range to another. They wouldn't be back to the main ranch proper for weeks yet. Still, as Junior led his horse into the long, low stable, a cold sweat stippled his skin. What if he had been seen? His hands trembled as he loosened the cinch on the horse's girth.

He'd just scooped an ample bait of oats in the trough when a low, rasping voice said, "Hey there, Mr. Junior. How's the daily battle treating you?"

Junior swung tight and fast, his pistol already in his

hand as if it had been a live thing with a mind of its own.
His mouth pulled wide and his lips stuck to his teeth.

"Whoa, whoa there, boy! It's me, Mica." The large
man stood a full eight inches taller than Junior and half
again as wide, and his dark skin shone like burnished
cherry wood in the glow of the low oil lamp. *I may be a
large man*, thought Mica, *but I am no match for a drawn
six-gun.*

Junior didn't move, kept the pistol aimed at the mid-
section of the ranch cook, his father's oldest confidant.
Could be a trick, thought the boy. Why was Mica here?
And at this hour?

"Junior, is this any way to treat a friend?"

Junior eased the hammer down and holstered his
sidearm. "I'm sorry, Mica. It being so late, I guess I'm
just rabbity."

"You don't say." Mica stood in the doorway, his hands
on his narrow hips, his bald head tilted. "Since when did
you get so speedy with that silly thing anyway?"

He stared at the young man long enough that Junior
fidgeted and finally turned back to his horse, running a
wad of sacking over the sweat-stained withers. "I said I
was sorry."

The man didn't leave. Junior knew he would want
more of an explanation than that. It had felt at times
growing up as though he had two fathers. And now Mica
would probably tell his father of this incident too. Without turning around, Junior said, "What are you doing up
anyway, Mica? It's late."

"Early, you mean. My morning to get up before the
roosters. Me and Dilly split the duty. Someone's gotta
make the biscuits, get the gravy and whistle berries pop-
pin' in the pans. They don't do it by themselves, now, do
they?"

Junior half turned and smiled, sighed deeply for the
first time in hours, and said, "No, I reckon not."

"You reckon right, sonny." Mica returned the smile,

turned to go, and said, "Everything working all right with you, Junior?"

Junior's teeth immediately came together. He turned back to the horse, who munched his feed, oblivious of the tensions around him. Junior smoothed at the coat with the sacking and said, "Would be if people would just leave me be."

Mica regarded him a moment longer, then said, "Suit yourself, boy. Suit yourself." He walked from the stable and Junior heard the old man's muttering mingle with the crunch of gravel under his boots on the path outside. He stood still until he heard the cook shack door clunk back into place. What was wrong with him lately? He'd snapped at everyone who meant anything to him, and all for what?

Then as if he had been slugged hard in the gut, the jagged memory of what he'd done earlier that night overwhelmed him and he sagged against his horse. He'd killed a man, maybe even two. One of them he'd known his entire life. So this was what it felt like to know there was no returning to the way things had been. He couldn't let tonight's risk and danger and violence happen for nothing. He'd gone too far to change course. Was it worth it? Yes, he had to believe it was. His father always said that a man must make up his mind, believe in himself, and then bull ahead. He had to do everything he could to gain ownership of the Dancing M. Everything. And he must let nothing stop him.

Junior rubbed down his horse mechanically, long after the sun's first rays glinted over the far hills east of the Driving D. It was a day he knew would be filled with worry and questions. Questions he was not yet ready to answer.

Chapter 28

The cool of the early morning was ideal for a brisk ride, though Callie preferred the danger and thrill of a full-out gallop in the moonlight. But that was a thrill for which she'd been reprimanded by her father and Mica more than a few times over the years. Wilf had one day finally shouted at her in a red-faced rage such as she'd never known, asked her how she'd like it if Butter broke a leg in a chuck hole. That had finally forced her to see the folly of such undertakings. But Callie had never really understood what Wilf had been so incensed about. At least not until Mica explained that it had been such a misstep years before by her mother's filly that had caused the death of both her mother, Carla Grindle, and her prized filly.

Mica also said that anyone who had ever known her mother was instantly reminded of her when they met Callie. She imagined it was most difficult of all on her father, who saw her every day. She couldn't imagine such a constant ache.

Callie pushed all that from her mind on this morning.

She felt as if they were racing the sun. She was sure Butter felt it, the beast's breath chuffing a steady rhythm as they covered mile after mile.

If there was one thing she could use lately, it was a chance to get away from everything odd that had happened since Rory MacMawe died. It was as if a poison had wormed its way into their lives. Everything was coming to some sort of snapping point and she didn't like it. It felt off, somehow, and other than Mica, no one else seemed aware of it or if they did they weren't willing to talk about it.

Everyone—her father, her brother, Esperanza, Brandon—all the people closest to her were acting strange. What she saw the day before in her brother's eyes had shaken her to her roots. This wasn't the Junior she knew. And then came Espy's unfounded rejection. She'd wanted to talk with Mica about it all, but he was nowhere to be found. So after a sleepless night she'd slipped out of the house, saddled up before light, and hit the trail. She'd never failed to find some measure of solace alone with her horse.

Callie reined up at the big old boulder that marked the junction of their road with that of the Dancing M. The massive gray rock always pulled a comment from her father whenever they passed it in the barouche on their way to town. Her mare, Butter, blew through her nose and wagged her head to let Callie know she had no intention of stopping for long. Callie laughed and said, "Let's go, then!" and rapped heels to the horse's barrel. She'd almost, though not quite, let Butter choose the route. And that just happened to be the Dancing M road. She knew then that the real purpose of her ride had been to see Espy. She had to try. Something had been very wrong with her old friend and she had to get to the bottom of it. Surely there was a bolder reason for the older woman's anger of the other day.

As she rode, her thoughts returned to her brother.

Though he was but a year younger, they were practically twins. She knew how gentle a soul he was, that he craved their father's attention in a way that she supposed only young men felt about their fathers. From the time he became, in their father's eyes, a "young man," Junior had spent every hour of his days trying to impress the old taskmaster. But she knew that Junior didn't particularly like ranch work. He spent so much of his time second-guessing their father's wishes that Callie suspected Junior never really explored exactly what he wanted to do with his own life. What did he do with himself in his own quiet hours?

It had been a couple of years since she'd been in his room. Did he still read? What did he think about when he was alone? Did he harbor a love for one of the local girls? He used to be such a fun friend growing up—and now he was nothing more than an obsessed shell of the person she used to know.

And then there was Esperanza. She had made it plain that she thought Callie was just another Grindle. At the memory of their odd meeting, Callie's jaw muscles tightened. It could only mean that her father had visited Esperanza, had made her an offer for the Dancing M. She wouldn't put it past him. If he had a fault, it was a lust for land. He never seemed to have enough. She had tried to tell him once that she didn't want it, and she doubted that Junior did. "Can you take it with you?" she'd asked. His response was a red-faced rage such as she'd never seen come over him before. Had her father paid a visit to the widow? She knew he wanted the entire Dancing M, and in her experience he never left the table hungry.

The sight of a horse walking along the road not far ahead snapped Callie from her reverie. For a moment, her horse chomped and shook her head, fighting the interruption. The unexpected sight pulled Callie up short, and she patted her horse's neck to quiet her. "*Shhh,*

shhh, Butter," she whispered. "There's a good girl. Now, whose horse could that be . . . ?"

Dead ahead, the strange horse came to a standstill. Even from this distance Callie noticed it favoring a foreleg, saw scratches and streaks of blood caked on its flanks. They caught up to it and she recognized the distinctive Dancing M brand. As they walked closer, she felt sure it was Brandon's gelding. The horse stood tired and quivering. Her horse nosed the other, and Brandon's horse lowered its head in a passive stance.

"What's the matter, boy? Huh?" Callie dismounted and walked around in front of both horses. She held the reins of her mare and knew something was wrong when Brandon's horse didn't so much as twitch. "You've run straight through mesquite, torn yourself to pieces." She slid a hand down the horse's neck, stroking and patting, talking softly. "Where's Brandon, boy?"

Callie looked northward, but saw nothing. It seemed the horse had probably traveled from town, the most likely place for Brandon to have been. Perhaps something had happened to him, and the horse had wandered through the night, heading for its home stable. But that didn't explain why the horse was unsaddled. Since his father's death, Brandon had spent all his time in the saloon in town, or holed up somewhere with his hands wrapped around a whiskey bottle. But he was a fine horseman, one of the best in the area. Her father had even said so.

Brandon must be camped somewhere, sleeping off a drunk. His horse probably spooked at something in the night, or just wandered off. Maybe, she thought. But it didn't quite sit right with her. *What's Brandon running from? What's in store for him?*

Unbidden came the memory of a saying Mica had told them when she and Junior sat in his kitchen one afternoon many years before: "You got to watch out for a man who's running from something. 'Cause that's a sign that something bad has happened—or will soon."

The old man had leaned against the carving board, drying his hands on his smeared apron, then said, as much to the ceiling rafters as to them, "Now, I can think of three things a man ought to run *to*." Then he'd smiled.

"What are they, Mica?" she and Junior had said in tandem.

"Well, let's see. Firstly, I guess the loving arms of a fine wife. Nextly, someone wanting to give him all kind of money."

"What's third, Mica?" Callie had asked.

"Third, you see, is the most important." He'd leaned in close to them, over the table, and said, "Third thing is a man ought to always run fast and hard straight toward a hot meal. Now we're talking!" Mica's laugh boomed in the warm kitchen.

The memory brought a brief smile to her face. She mounted up and said, "We'd better get to Espy's, see if she's missing a horse." She felt sure that she'd not find Brandon at the ranch. Why else would his horse be in such a state? The horse led easily enough, though she didn't dare move any faster than a walk. She was thankful they were about a half mile from the ranch house, but if it had been any longer, she would have left the horse there and ridden on ahead.

By the time they arrived at the dooryard, the sun had cracked open the day. *Looks like you won the race*, thought Callie as she looked up at the orange glow. She was still a hundred yards from the little ranch house when she shouted, "Esperanza! Esperanza!"

It didn't take long for the squat woman to emerge from the house, wiping her hands on her apron. It seemed to Callie as if that was how she'd always seen her answer the door. Except she used to wear a smile for her. But like everything else in this crazy life now, those days seemed to be gone forever.

"Espy!" Callie slid from the horse.

"What is it, Callie?" Esperanza rushed up to grab the

horse's reins from the girl. "What are you doing with Brandon's horse?" Her look was more of concern than suspicion.

"I found him like this. I think we should hitch your team, Espy. Brandon would never let his horse wander off—not unless something's wrong."

"That stranger," said Espy in a low voice.

"Which stranger, Espy?"

"Middleton. He was here. They fought—Brandon hit him." Espy turned to Callie. "Do you think he did something to Brandon . . . out of anger?"

"I don't know, Espy." Callie squeezed her friend's shoulder. As she rushed to the barn, where the draped tack hung on the rail of an empty stall, she thought about Middleton. *He's certainly rude enough—and big enough—to hurt Brandon.*

Espy stood stroking the blowing gelding's nose, looking over the beast's cocked leg and bloodied flanks, then led him to the water trough and tied him there. She turned to the barn.

"Our team is in the close pasture. There, you see them?" She paused, a hand on Callie's sleeve, and said, "Do you think Brandon is . . . ?"

Callie looked into those eyes she'd come to regard as those of a second mother. "I don't know. But he wouldn't leave his horse like this—" They both looked at the drinking horse.

As Espy hustled to the house for water and medical supplies, just in case, Callie heard her say, "That drunk boy will be the death of me."

Callie turned her attention back to calling in the horses. Within a minute of banging a dented pail against the fence rail by the barn, just as she'd seen Rory do a hundred times over the years, the cantankerous Scot's old, graying matched team were at the barn, nosing for a feed.

Espy soon emerged with blankets, a satchel laden

with her own herbs, liniments, and tinctures—all accumulated and put into heavy use over the years by Esperanza in her role as family doctor. Her kind face was set hard as if carved, determined and steadfast in her new mission.

She tossed these items in the worn work wagon and helped Callie coax the horses into the traces and buckle on the harnesses. Despite the years of practice they each had at such tasks, their hands wouldn't work fast enough to suit them. Callie uttered oaths of anger that she normally wouldn't dare to give voice to in front of Espy, and Espy just gritted her teeth and worked through the harnesses, buckle by buckle. Callie was relieved that Espy, while not smiling at her, didn't let their harsh conversation of the day before interfere with Callie's concern for Brandon.

Callie finished buckling Nan's rig as Espy did the same with Dan's. "You finish rigging up the wagon, Espy. I'll go on ahead and start on the back trail, see what spooked him." Callie headed toward her horse. "It seems like his horse would have come from town."

The older woman didn't look up, merely nodded as she tossed the blankets in the wagon.

Callie swung into the saddle and headed back the way she'd come, forcing down the growing fear that she'd find something very wrong with Brandon. They'd all known it would be a matter of time before his drinking hurt himself or someone else. Now that it was just her and her horse, they made it back to the crossroads within minutes. Callie bent low in the saddle and nudged the horse forward at a walk, urging it to meander along the narrow road from side to side.

After the better part of an hour of searching in vain to find where the tracks began or ended—she still wasn't sure which she was looking for—Butter perked her ears forward and snorted at something off to the left of the road. Callie reined up and they stood still, horse and rider, heads canted in the same direction. There was a noise. Callie leaned that way. What was it? And where? It sounded like wind through ancient rocks from a far-off place. . . . Or a groan? There it was again. And it *was* a groan.

Though the morning was warming, a chill trailed up her spine. Whatever made the noise didn't sound earthly. She urged the horse from the road to step cautiously through snarls of brush and clumps of boulders. Then she heard it again, closer now and to her right, from the north. Not much farther, she slipped down from the saddle and slid her Winchester from its boot.

She had never had to draw it save for that one time when the coyote came out of nowhere, snarling and flashing its teeth in broad daylight. But that was a year or more ago. She'd dispatched the slavering beast with three rapid shots, one to the head, dead between the eyes, and two more to its chest. Her father had taught them early on of the dangers of hydrophobia.

She tugged the reins and led the horse a few yards more before stopping. There was the groan again—and what sounded like someone speaking. Callie tied off her horse around a thick branch of a spidery bush and carried the rifle high across her chest, gripped in both hands. It would not do to be too surprised by this unknown situation. Could be someone was hurt, could be they were drunk; she didn't know. She walked forward another few feet and smelled the faintest whisper of wood smoke. She made her slow way up a small rise and there, just below her, a man's legs poked out from behind a knob of rock. Brown leather ankle boots, brass buckled, and brown wool pants, but a fine cloth, not the coarse weave of a rancher. The boots and legs were far too big to be Brandon. Whoever it might be was lying facedown.

Her first thought was that she had stumbled into the camp of a sleeping man, and just as quickly dismissed it as a foolish notion. Of course it was Brandon's camp—

but doubt nagged her. With as much care as she could muster, Callie backed in the direction from which she'd come. A groan, the same as those she'd heard from the road, sounded just to the right of the prone man and stopped her in her tracks. And again words followed the shapeless sound. She crouched and reached out with the rifle in her trembling hands. Her barrel tip nudged the leather sole. Nothing.

She swallowed. "Who's there?" No answer. Callie felt her heart knock hard in her chest. She repeated her question and heard in response a small voice say, "Hey . . ."

"Brandon?"

She scrambled around the prone man toward the noise, saying, "Who is it?" in little more than a tight whisper.

"Help. . . ."

There before her lay Brandon, on his back, his head flopped to one side, his eyes half-open, though unfocused, the lids fluttering as if he were playing a game, acting coquettish. In his hair she saw something wet and thick, and then in a flash she knew it for what it was: blood.

She set down the rifle, looked from the large prone man behind her back to Brandon. She leaned close. "What happened, Brandon?"

"Callie?"

"Yes, it's okay. I'm here. Tell me where you're hurt and I'll help you."

"A . . . fight . . . hit me in the head, then . . . shot him."

"Who hit you, Brandon? Did you shoot him?"

"No, no . . . he's dead. Brian . . . my brother."

Callie looked back to the other man. His face was turned away, but could it be the stranger from Mae's restaurant, Brian Middleton? There was the unruly red hair, the same brown coat lay balled up off to the side, that horrible hat dented and wedged under scattered firewood. It was the missing MacMawe boy they'd all been speaking of.

But what did this mean? Had Brandon and Brian Middleton fought? Did Brandon shoot him? Was that what he was trying to tell her? She couldn't imagine Brandon shooting anyone. But then, up until a few weeks ago, she never would have guessed she'd see him drunk either. But all the proof she needed lay before her—the handsome stranger, facedown in the dirt, unmoving.

Chapter 29

Callie's first reaction was to ride for home, for Mica and her father. But there was no time, and Espy would be along soon with the wagon. For all of a moment, Callie didn't know which of the two men to attend first. Brandon was moving, alive, and badly hurt. The other, Brian Middleton, she didn't know about, though she had seen two dead men in recent years, one an old miner in town who had pitched out of his wagon while waiting for his wife to finish her shopping at Gleason's, the other a Driving D hand, who had died a slow, painful death after a bucker landed on him. Middleton didn't look any more alive to her than they had.

She felt along the length of the large man's prone body and found that he lay across the jagged hunks of rock from a cold campfire.

She pushed against his shoulder and by wedging her boots against a larger, solid rock, she was able to roll the big man onto his back. Then she winced as she saw his head flop back onto another rock from the fire ring. He did not react; he was well and truly unconscious—or worse.

It was but a moment's work to lift from under him the rocks that held him up, and then she dragged toward him what must have been his own blankets. She left him close to the fire ring and covered him with the blanket for now. Though faint, the stale scent of whiskey clouded up from him much as it had with Brandon, who, she thankfully noted, still groaned where she'd left him.

She had to get this man out of the way so she could make a fire. Then, if he was alive, she'd need to make him comfortable. By the time the feeble fire engulfed bits of small branches and twigs and begged for more, she had dragged closer the remnants of a small stack of firewood the men must have gathered the previous night. She quickly fed the greedy flames, then turned to see the extent of the wounds the large man had received. Her gasp was loud enough to force a slurred "What?" from Brandon.

Brian Middleton had been what her father would call gut-shot. She hadn't seen a wound on his back, so either the bullet must have gone through somewhere she hadn't noticed, or worse—the bullet might still be in him. She bent low over his face, turned a cheek to his mouth to feel for even the slightest breath. Her left hand rested on his chest, well above the bullet wound that left his shirt a sticky, matted smear against his stomach, and she thought she detected a faint heartbeat, maybe even the slightest of breaths. . . . A strand of her long, dark honey hair slipped free and lay across his face.

His eyes shot open and he gasped air, pulling it in as if it were soon to fall out of favor. She shrieked and jumped backward.

"I'm sorry," she said, smoothing her hair back and staring into the man's eyes. His skin had a glassy, unhealthy sheen that contrasted with the man's shocking red hair.

"Where . . ."

"Shhh." Callie leaned in close and said, "Lie still now and try to relax."

"What has . . . happened to me?"

Callie hesitated. She didn't know how to break the news to him, or if she should at all. But a direct, nononsense approach had always been her favored way of conducting herself, and she saw no reason to change just now. "You've been shot."

But if he heard, she wasn't sure. His head lolled to the side and she leaned in close again and checked him. Still breathing. She didn't think he could hear, but she said out loud, "I need to go for help as soon as I know Brandon's going to make it."

"Don't worry . . . strength of a bull." Brandon tried to rise and it was as if his elbows were yanked from under him—he groaned and flopped back against the saddle she'd dragged over for a pillow.

She knew she would have to try to stop the bleeding that had begun anew when she'd moved them. She spied a large satchel but didn't want to waste more time rummaging. She gripped her blouse's sleeve up high where it joined the shoulder and yanked until she heard threads pop. Within minutes she was sleeveless and had dressed Middleton as best she could, wadding up a fist-sized clump of shirt fabric and gingerly placing it atop the wound, then securing it in place with a tied strip from her shirt.

Next, she ripped the other sleeve into strips and swaddled Brandon's head. While she worked she listened for Esperanza. She should have been here by now. Callie cursed herself aloud for not thinking to leave more of a trail for Espy to follow, though she had dismounted now and again and gouged an arrow into the dirt of the road. And she hadn't been that far ahead of her.

Callie knew she would have to leave the two men here, with her rifle and firewood. Then ride back toward the Dancing M. She was sure to meet up with Espy. And as she worked she fought down a growing suspicion that arose from her memory of the conversation between her father and brother of the day before. *Lord, forgive me*, she thought, but she didn't trust her own family. She hated the very idea that had formed in her mind, but neither could she discount it.

She rose and checked her rifle. It was loaded.

"Brandon, can you hear me?"

"Yes, yes, Callie. Is Brian alive? He's been shot."

"Yes, I know. But he's alive, Brandon." She leaned close to him and tried to get him to focus on her. "Look, Brandon. I have to leave, but I'll be back soon. I have to find your mother—she's on her way. Your mother will know what to do, more than anyone I know."

No answer greeted her ears. She tried again, and this time Brandon said, "Yes . . . yes."

Callie nodded and turned toward the road. Where was Espy with the wagon? Callie knew the woman would be able to follow her trail well enough. As if in response to her thoughts, she heard the clank and groan of the old work wagon followed by Espy's shouts, from nearby where Callie had left her horse.

"Callie! Callie! Where are you?"

"Over here, Espy!" No sense trying to soften the shock of the scene—she'd know soon enough what she faced.

Callie knew that, like many women, Espy possessed the enviable ability in a tense situation of remaining calm and clearheaded when others panicked.

Callie hefted her Winchester and headed to meet Espy and guide her to the gruesome campsite. She prayed under her breath that this mess would end well, though she doubted there was any way that it could. No one was yet dead, but two men lay wounded. Did they do this to each other? It was possible and yet something told her it didn't seem likely. If that were the case, whoever did it might still be close at hand. *Oh, please*, she thought, *don't let it be Junior*.

Chapter 30

"You look like hell, son." Wilf Grindle set down his coffee mug and dragged his chair closer to the table. "Like you been rode hard and put up wet."

Junior directed a pinched look at Mica. "Didn't take you long to butt into my business, did it?" But Mica stared him down, shaking his head.

Wilf dropped his fork on his china plate. The sound brought the other two men's heads around as if they were attached to strings. Mica left the room and headed for the kitchen, shaking his head and mumbling to himself.

Wilf shot out a forefinger at his son that looked to Junior like the ridgepole of a new barn. His voice uncoiled and lashed out like a whip. "You ever dare to show your ill manners again here and you will feel the toe of my boot, boy. I will not stand for such rank looks, nor such snide talk. Not to your sister, certainly not to me, and never, ever to Mica. And for what, I don't know. Why, that man's been like a second father to you."

Junior's anger with Mica was replaced with shame.

He knew that Mica could hear every word the old man was saying, and was probably rankled by this forced flattery. He'd bet Mica wanted more than anything to protest, but felt it wasn't his place to interfere in affairs between the father and the boy, though Junior knew that there had been many times that Mica had wanted to say something.

Junior closed his eyes and nodded. When he opened them he was looking at his own plate, heaped with a breakfast he did not deserve, especially considering how he'd treated Mica. And despite that, Mica had made a plateful of Junior's favorites: corn bread, scrapple, and a mound of eggs, brown gravy pooling over it all. Still, much as he knew he should, much as part of him wanted to, Junior could not bring himself to apologize. Mica had, after all, unwittingly almost forced him to reveal last night's activities.

He wanted to tell his father in his own way, in his own time, and without anyone else butting in. But he had to choose the best time. Still, he wasn't so sure his father would understand, would applaud him for his actions. He thought the old man had been telling him how he wanted the situation handled, but now Junior wondered if he had gone too far.

"Now, what is all this about?"

"What?" Junior stabbed a forkful of egg, smeared it around the plate. His father didn't reply, just stared at Junior, his coffee mug held close to his face. The urge to punch his father boiled up inside him. "Why, what did Mica say to you?"

"Say to me? About what?"

Junior stared at his father.

"You know we hardly say a thing to each other until noon. It's how we are. Your mother used to call us the Bear Brothers, because we're both so blasted grumpy in the mornings."

Junior knew that his father was telling the truth. Mica

truly hadn't said anything to him about Junior coming in so late. About anything at all. Junior forced a smile and said, "Two peas in a pod, that's what you and Mica are."

His father almost smiled, resumed his breakfast. God, thought Junior, but that man could be so infuriating. He wished he could be free of him, of this place. But at the same time he wanted to be just like the man. At that moment he wanted to tell him everything, wanted to tell him how he'd grabbed the Dancing M for them, single-handed, with no help from anyone—least of all his father. But he also knew that would tip his hand too early. No, it was better to let the events unspool of their own accord. Somebody would find the men, one or both of them dead. But no one would ever suspect Junior. No, sir, thought Junior as he sipped his coffee, he'd taken care of that, confidence growing in him with each restorative bite of food, each swig of black coffee. Best leave well enough alone. Junior smiled and stabbed a big fork-ful of gravy-soaked egg, jammed it in his mouth.

"Where's Miss Callie, Wilf?" Mica ambled in carrying the coffeepot.

"I assumed she's already been up and out." Wilf leaned back in his chair and tossed his napkin on the table.

"Mmm. Could be, but I ain't seen her since last night at supper."

Wilf sipped the last from his cup, rose from his seat, and stretched. "Well, Junior, go knock on her door. Maybe she overslept. I'm headed to the stable, so I'll see if her horse is there."

Junior nodded automatically, and halfway up the stairs he slowed. *I'm doing it again*, he thought—*jumping first and thinking second whenever the old man tells me to do something*. The familiar bile of self-disgust rose in his throat. *Not for long, Junior, old boy*, he told himself as he trudged up the rest of the stairs.

His hard knuckle-rap on the door produced no shouts

from within, so he pushed open the door and said, "Cal? Hey, Cal, you in here?"

The curtain wasn't drawn and the room was filled with morning light. The bed was made, as if she'd been up and out early, which she often was. Orderly and with no clue about the person who slept there, that's what he would say were he a stranger looking in. But he knew her better than that. And he knew that it was all show. Her wardrobe was jammed full of clothes, unfolded and balled up, and the space under the bed was stacked with books and shoes and boots and Lord knew what else.

He smiled, knowing that her forceful and tidy outward appearance belied the zesty, too-curious, slightly scattered person she really was. Looking into her room, he missed the old days when they talked more, explored the surrounding countryside together, camped within easy range of the ranch house. All gone, he thought. Gone and traded for adult lives with adult responsibilities. He closed Callie's bedroom door and in that moment, everything he'd done the night before flooded back to him all over again. A core of ice filled him and he stood in the dark-paneled upstairs hallway, his hand on the doorknob, staring at nothing.

"Junior . . . is Callie up there?"

The boy shook his head and said, "Uh, no, no. Looks like she got up and out early."

"Let's hope so. Just the same, saddle up, see if you can find out where she's gone to."

Junior descended the stairs one step at a time as his father spoke. Mica stood at the bottom of the staircase, leaning on the banister.

"I'm off to the east range, see if I can find out why the boys ain't driven the young stock back this way yet. Should've been done by now."

Mica smiled. "Shoot. You're headed on into Turnbull, see if Miss Gleason is up for a carriage ride."

Wilf looked at his old friend as if he might draw on

him, then inclined his head and said, "Hmm. Could be I'll take your suggestion, Mica. After all, it is turning out to be a fair day at that."

When Junior passed his father at the bottom of the stairs, he could not suppress his scowl.

"Boy," said Wilf again. "You look like hell. You sure you weren't up all night?"

Junior pushed past him and snatched his hat from the coat tree beside the door. He had to get outside, away from his father, from Mica, acting like a couple of clucking old hens. He had to get away from anything that reminded him of ranching and land and his father and this place. After all, it was those things and more that had landed him in the predicament he was in.

Chapter 31

It was well into Squirly's second day out of Turnbull along the north road that he saw the buzzards. And he wasn't even surprised. It was as if he'd been expecting to see them. "Hell, old Methuselah." He leaned forward and patted the plodding mare on the neck. "Been a long time since I spent so much time on my backside in the saddle. Can't say as I miss it. No offense, dearie. But it looks to me we won't have far to go, sad to say. I'd wager them death birds are swoopin' in on something I don't want to see." He regarded them a moment more, then reached back and unslung the canvas sack tied behind the cantle.

He was pleased that Teasdale had forced him to go with him to Gleason's to buy some jerky and hardtack, and Silver Haskell, that old rascal, had even lent him two canteens. Kept mumbling something about how he didn't want Squirly's death from stupidity to be on his conscience. And then the biggest surprise of all was the bottle of whiskey Teasdale had bought him at Gleason's store. Stuffed it into Squirly's sack and said, "Man in your condition, without a bit of this inside you, why, you'll shiver and shake yourself to death before you can get back to Turnbull and pay off this debt. You hear?"

"Old Teas," said Squirly to the horse as he took a measured pull on the bottle. He eyed the level, still above half-full. In a way he hoped that if Mitchell Farthing was done for, the buzzards marked the spot. It wouldn't do to run out of tanglefoot before he got back.

Another hour brought him to within sight of the scene. He saw the great-winged birds in two close bunches, their bobbing heads and raised wings giving the groupings the freakish look of dying creatures. He heard them too, their guttural squawks shivering him and causing the old horse to blow and falter and hesitate in her steps.

Squirly suspected the horse's eyesight wasn't all it should be. *So long as her legs are*, he thought. *I got the eyes of a twelve-year-old boy*, he told himself, *and the legs of a drunk*.

Next came the stench. It wafted to him on an unfelt breeze and nearly turned his stomach. He prayed it wouldn't, as that might waste some of the effects of the whiskey, and that was one thing he couldn't afford to lose out on, being that it was in such short supply.

The toes of the dead man's boot stuck up, facing the sky, and waggling side to side as if he were fidgeting. But Squirly knew it was from the digging, snatching curved backs of the buzzards, hunks of ragged flesh dangling from their great hooked beaks. Had to be Mitchell, he thought. *Ain't no other thing it could be*. And nearby, he saw the gleaming wet bones of the man's horse, the curve of its ribs still pink with blood and gristle. One of the buzzards tried to claw its way up the slick bones, but slid backward, disturbing two others, who hopped about the mess, their nasty bald heads bucking and squawking.

Squirly had a wide-bladed sheath knife, but no side-arm or rifle. He didn't feel the need for protection, for he didn't much care, so he told himself, what happened to himself. But as he dismounted and tied the horse's reins to a mesquite bush, he wished he had a scattergun. He knew the buzzards and probably the coyotes too who had feasted on this poor old cowhand were just going about their lives, making their living as they could, but that didn't mean he had to like it. He slid the great knife out of its sheath and shouting as if he had just found religion, Squirly Ross barked and howled and ran at the teeming mass of flapping birds. He got within kicking distance of a few and let loose with a fresh round of whoops, when he recognized the profile of his old friend, Mitchell. The man's cheeks were pocked with fresh wounds from the birds' claws and beaks, but there was no mistaking that high, narrow face, downturned mouth, as if he himself smelled what had become of his body and didn't much like it. The man's hat hadn't rolled all that far, fetched up as it had on a tumble of rocks.

Despite his best efforts, Squirly Ross cried then for his old friend, for the times they had had years before, for the times they would never have in the future. He'd been more excited about Farthing's visit than he had been for anything about his life in Turnbull for years. But no more.

It took all his vigilance to keep the buzzards away from him and the long, prone body of his friend while he knelt beside the body and scrabbled in the dirt with his bare hands and with his big knife. It took the better part of two hours to dig a trench long and deep enough to roll in the body of the man who was perhaps his only friend in the world, a man who got himself killed because he'd been summoned by Squirly.

Again, sobs bucked his old shoulders. He did grope the body where he could, just in case the poke was still about somewhere, though he'd doubted he'd find it. He felt certain that the little foreigner had taken it all after he'd killed Mitchell. Trick was to prove that the little well-dressed foreigner had done the vile deed. And as near as Squirly could figure, there was little way he could prove it.

Finally, he rolled Mitchell's body into the shallow grave, but had to rejigger it, as half of the man faced down, while the other had been disjointed somehow and faced nearly skyward. It was then that Squirly saw the bullet wound on the man's upper back. The front, where the shot would have exited, had been chewed away by varmints. He got him righted around, facing skyward, and laid the man's hat on his face, and mumbled a few nearly silent words. It was harder than he expected it would be. Finally he said good-bye.

By the time he'd finished mounding rocks on his friend's grave, enough he figured to keep the birds and digging varmints out of it, the buzzards had really set to on the corpse of the horse. He shooed them away. Most of them hopped hissing a few feet back, their wings held open as if they were great hooded snake heads ready to strike. But they kept their distance enough for him to search the pecked-at saddlebags. He turned up nothing of value, save for a small cameo rimmed in gold, picturing a young woman. It looked to be a painted photograph. She was a looker, for sure, and Squirly wondered who she was, what she meant to Mitchell, and where she might be now. He nibbled at his bottom lip, then returned to Mitchell's grave. Immediately, the shiny black birds crawled back onto the carcass of the horse, jabbing at it in their feeding frenzy. The picked-over thing rocked and moved as if shaking in its sleep.

Squirly removed a goodly little pile of rocks from the grave and pushed the cameo brooch down as far as he could in the crevices between the remainder of the rocks covering his friend's head, then mounded up the rocks again.

He had no way of making a marker, so he decided to just leave it be as it was. He mounted the old horse, wanting to put some distance between himself and the

sad scene before he had to make that night's camp in a
few hours. As they walked away, he took a pull from the
bottle and saluted his dead friend with a silent toast.
"Should be easier, somehow, especially considering I
ain't seen him in so long." *Should be*, he told himself, *but
it ain't.*

Chapter 32

"He took a nasty knock to the head. I think he'll pull through, but the Middleton man . . . he's been shot, Espy." Callie slid Espy's medicine bag to the rear of the wagon and hefted it.

Despite her firmness and usual lack of emotion, Esperanza's eyes widened and a hand covered her mouth. "Is he . . . ?"

The two women hurried toward the wreckage of the little camp.

"Did Brandon do it?"

"I don't know, Espy. I don't think so. Let's worry about that later. We're closer to the Dancing M than we are to town, but we have to get them back to the ranch soon."

Espy nodded once and, bunching her skirts and apron in one brown hand, hurried ahead of Callie. "Brandon. Brandon, my baby boy!" The boy's mother slapped his cheeks lightly, and his eyelids fluttered open.

"Ma? Why are you . . . here?"

Before she could answer, the other man moaned and

Callie hastened to him, trailing a bundle of cloth for bandages and clutching the tin coffeepot full of water.

Esperanza did not leave her son's side, but pointed at Middleton. "You can see he is on fire with fever, Callie. Wet his head and mouth with water, quickly!"

The young woman swabbed his forehead and his eyes almost opened. She squeezed water on his lips, and his tongue worked to catch the drops. The effort, it seemed, was too much for him, and soon he grew still.

Esperanza set her son's head down on a wadded horse blanket and turned her attention to Brian Middleton's wound. She peeled away the sopping, gritted shirt that had matted into the wound. Callie saw that it was worse than she expected—the ground beneath him was nearly black with his drained blood. It looked as though he was bleeding out right before their eyes.

"Callie! Listen to me, girl. Pay attention. . . ."

Callie did as Espy bade her and within minutes they had the unconscious man's wound bound.

Espy grunted. "I do know that he still has blood left in him. Probably enough for a lifetime of rude comments. . . ." She winked at Callie and that one simple gesture made Callie's heart sing, and she marveled at the woman's fortitude in the face of this situation.

The two women soon managed to carry the big man to the wagon. His feet hung out the back, so Callie bent his legs at the knees enough to slide the tailgate back in place. Brandon's eyes would not focus, though he was now awake and mumbling, nothing of which made sense to Callie as she tossed into the wagon the last of the camp's gear.

As Esperanza made ready to leave, she mentioned that Middleton had been riding a rental mare from the livery. Callie scanned around them quickly, but if it had been there it was now gone from sight. She knew that someone would have to pay Silver Haskell for her—for Callie was sure she would end up as coyote bait—but the old nag's fate was the least of her concerns right now.

Callie tied her horse behind the wagon. She climbed aboard and snapped the reins hard on the old work team's backs. Esperanza reached back to steady Brandon as he swayed, seated beside the prone form of his older half brother. Callie worked the buggy whip, tickling the backs of the now-churning team, the steel-rimmed wheels of the work wagon cutting into the mealy, dry earth.

The first few minutes of the journey back to the Dancing M were quiet, with Esperanza steadying her son's sagging body against the jarring wagon ride. The older woman gritted her teeth each time the wheels clunked into yet another road rut, all the while keeping a sharp glance on the jostling, bouncing body of the little boy she used to know, aware she could well be looking at a dead man.

Finally Callie broke the silence. "Will he make it, Espy?"

The older woman looked up at Callie and saw she'd been near tears. A long silence followed, and then Espy spoke. "We will see what we will see. I can do nothing until we get home. Except to apologize to you for the way I spoke the other day." Espy frowned and squeezed Callie's arm, then continued. "You're a good girl, a good friend. I was afraid you might get in trouble with your father by talking with me. Now that Rory is gone, I am not wanted in these parts—that is plain enough. We will move on soon."

"No, Espy. Don't say that. Who will run the ranch?"

"The ranch belongs to Mr. Middleton now."

Then it occurred to Callie that Brandon had referred to the stranger as his "brother." But until now she'd not given herself time to think about it. "Is Middleton . . ."

Espy nodded. "Yes, he is Rory's son by his wife of long ago. She died and the boy was sent back to the East, to a place called Providence, where his mother's family was from." She sighed and rubbed her eyes with thick fingers. "But now he is grown and he has come back to claim the land that has been left to him."

"But what about you and Brandon? Surely you two should have the land, as Mr. MacMawe's wife and son." They exchanged glances then, and in that flash of a moment Callie knew all she had never before learned about her friend's life. "You never married?"

Esperanza looked out at the muted greens and shoe-leather brown and dusty red of the landscape as they passed through it, the horses running hard, their great sides heaving with each unaccustomed lunge down the road. Esperanza saw all this, but all she could do was shake her head once, twice.

There had been no wedding. Not that she'd ever expected one from Rory, but it would have been nice. Something simple there at the ranch. They could have invited friends, she would have made much food, tended her flowers, and kept the chickens in the coop for the day so they wouldn't be underfoot. Perhaps she could have coaxed Brandon to play the fiddle that his father had bought him so long ago. That would have been nice.

A jutting rock in the hard-packed surface of the road jolted her from her daydream. *Silly woman*, she thought. *There is no time for such thoughts. Nor will there ever be again.* The world was an uncertain place, and lately she felt that that was about the only thing she had really learned for certain in her life.

Chapter 33

His morning chores complete, Mica had saddled his horse with the precision of a man who has done so more times than he can count. He'd thought about Callie for the past couple of hours and where she might be. Her father didn't seem too worried, and the boy was off in his own head, saying and doing things that made no sense to Mica.

He had a thought that the girl might be visiting her friend Espy. He'd wanted to pay her a visit himself, especially since Rory passed on. He murmured a soft grunt of encouragement to the horse and nudged the big gray gelding into a steady trot.

As he passed under the arch leading to the Driving D's ranch buildings, Mica wondered, not for the last time, what people might think of him should he take up with someone ten or so years his junior. He snorted at himself and said aloud, "Old man, ain't nobody going to want to spend more time with you than they have to. Just a plain fact." He smirked and continued on his way anyway, confident that at the very least he'd have himself a fine morning ride, and maybe at the end of it, a cup of coffee with an old friend. "What more can a man ask of life?"

The horse, as if in response, tossed his head and worked its nose up as if it smelled something unpleasant.

"Oh, hush, you. Ain't nobody asked for your opinion."

The horse repeated its head toss, then settled down to a slow lope along the trail leading southwest to the Maligno, then northwest for a couple of miles to the Dancing M. Within minutes, from far off up the road to the north, town way, he heard a wagon's creaking rumble. It drew closer, each squeak and creak more distinct.

"Moving fast," he said, turning his horse to face the rising dust cloud. As it drew closer, Mica visored his eyes with a calloused hand. He recognized it as a work wagon with two people on the bench and a horse snugged close behind. The closer they drew, the more Mica felt he might know one of them—that fawn hat, the gold hair bouncing, and was that a split riding skirt? Callie? *It is Callie*, he thought. *But what's she doing? And going that fast?*

Long before the wagon drew abreast of Mica as he sat his horse beside the dirt track, waiting to see what this commotion was all about, Callie recognized the large black man, astride his distinctive gray, and stood in the wagon, swaying and gripping the steel armrest with one hand. "Mica! Mica!"

She was frantic, that much he knew, and beside her, huddled low and looking into the back of the wagon, was Esperanza.

"What's the matter?" he shouted, though they were moving too fast to have heard him.

Espy rarely ventured this far from the ranch—hadn't in months, not since Rory became ill. Except for the few times she'd had to retrieve Brandon from the jail, sleeping off another round.

He heeled his mount into a lope and shouted, but the wagon shot past and kept on going, headed toward the Dancing M, Callie waving to him, beckoning him. He nudged the horse harder and came up alongside.

There in the work box, he saw Brandon huddled at the front of the wagon, just behind the seat, his mother's ample arms holding his head and shoulders. And stretched on the floor, his legs bent because of his obvious height, was a tall, rugged young man with thick red hair that looked the spitting image of Old Rory, back quite a few years when they were all three, Mica, Wilf, and Rory, good friends and full of themselves. Long before grayness and age had nibbled at their edges.

Mica looked down at the tall boy and knew then that what he'd overheard was true, that it was Rory's first son, come home. But judging from the wad of red clotted cloth bound to his midsection, he didn't know if the boy was alive.

Mica kept up with the wagon, and shouted over the rumbling din, "What's happened, Callie?"

Only then did Esperanza look up, seeing him for the first time. Her face was a pale, cracked thing, an eggshell ready to collapse. Mica had never seen her look so delicate. Even so, her eyes were sharp and taking in everything about her. Mica thought the boy, Brandon, looked poorly too, though not as bad off as the big fellow. Espy's son raised an arm, swatting at nothing, before letting it fall fatigued to his lap.

"Mica!"

He followed Callie's shout to her worried face. "They've been hurt bad. Ride ahead and get the fire going. Clear the front room."

He took all this in and nodded once, then sank spur and headed for the little house at the Dancing M. The entire road there, the haunted look in Espy's eyes plagued him. Brandon didn't look right. He must have taken quite a knock on the head. And the other one, the

big fellow—what did she call him? Brian? He'd looked
more dead than alive as he lay there jostling in the
wagon.

Mica made it to the little house at the Dancing M and
knew he didn't have much time—but there were still
glowing amber coals when he swung open the stove's
squawking door. The coals stirred bright when he blew
on them, sparked to flame the brittle twigs he layered on
from the battered wooden box.

The fire well in hand, Mica snatched up the large
scorched kettle and another enamel bowl and grabbed
the wire bail on a bucket on his way out the door, headed
for the well.

He was halfway to the well when he heard the familiar creak and rumble of the buckboard roll closer with
each passing second. He filled the vessels as the wagon,
swirling in a great cloud of dust, rolled to a stop.

The horses' muzzles were flecked with foam and their
heaving hides bore the white lather of hard use. Callie
circled to the back of the wagon and Mica hurried the
buckets of water inside, setting them on the stove top,
before rushing back out to lend a hand.

Leaning heavily on his mother, young Brandon, head
lolling and eyes nearly closed, stumbled his way to the
house, and Mica and Callie hefted the big young man,
Rory's oldest. Mica didn't think there was much point—
the young man looked to him to be gone. He'd seen
enough men in such shape from his time as a buffalo
soldier in the war. As they slid him from the wagon,
Mica was shocked to hear a moan, low and thin like
steam leaving a far-off train. He looked at Callie, but her
pinched features were unreadable.

By the time they lurched across the dooryard with
him sagging between them, Esperanza had dragged the
table to the far wall and had prepped space enough for
the two injured men to lie before the fireplace, on the
wall opposite the cook stove.

The fireplace had been the house's first heat and cooking source, and only years later had Rory added the second chimney for the cook stove. It was a concession he'd gladly made for Esperanza, since she was such a fine cook. It showed too, after time, on Rory's big frame. The man had thickened, though he was as active as he had ever been. Mica used to tease him on his visits to the couple.

Visits that, on occasion, he'd arrange to coincide with mealtime. He made no apologies—the woman was an amazing cook. And as a man who'd spent years of his life in the kitchen and squinting through smoke over a Dutch oven on the trail, well, he knew food and fancied that he appreciated the work of a culinary master more than most. Galled him to no end to see a cowhand bolt down a wedge of mock apple pie with nary a thought, other than to gargle it back with a mouthful of hot coffee before climbing back into the saddle.

He'd visited her but once since Rory passed. He was afraid of giving people the wrong idea, and Espy seemed to have her hands full with the boy. He'd offered to help her with him, but she would have none of it. Now he shot a quick glance her way. Aged was how he'd describe her. She looked mighty tired and old. *Guess we all are*, he thought, as he eased the big man to the tabletop. He hoped like heck that the newcomer would live to feel the same.

Callie leaned over to remove the bandages wadded up on Brian's gut, but Mica's big hand stopped her.

"You can't just take that off, Callie."

She looked up at him. "We have to know how bad this is."

"First things first. I saw plenty of this sort of thing in the war. Now, even if there was time to ride to town for the doc, the only thing Turnbull's got is Durkee the barber. He's a savage with a pliers on teeth and he's even worse with a head of hair, let alone a gunshot wound.

And that roving Doc What's-his-name ain't due back around these parts for weeks yet."

"What are we going to do? He's in a bad way, Mica."

"I know, I know, but getting worked up about it ain't going to help matters none. We need hot water and clean cloth for bandages. And I'll need a sharp knife, and a few other things."

Despite the dire situation, Mica felt solid. He liked being in control of a situation and he knew he was at his best when a problem arose. Oftentimes other men would go weak in the knees at the thought of having to fish out a bullet from a man's gut, but Mica knew he could do it. He had no choice. The boy might die in the process, but he was darn sure going to die if no one did anything.

Mica unbuttoned his shirt cuffs and set to work, delegating tasks to the two women, though he knew that Espy needed no prompting. He cut his eyes over to Callie and yes, no mistaking it, there was a gleam there, of concern and maybe something more. Too early to tell, but all the more reason to make sure this big red-haired boy didn't up and die on him.

Chapter 34

After a leisurely sleep-in and a late breakfast, Mortimer Darturo had checked on Picolo, then crossed the street and headed for the saloon. And all the while, even before he rose and dressed for the day, he decided he had made a mistake in making sure that he knew the identity of the shooter in last night's campsite raid halfway to the Dancing M. He was almost positive that it was the foolish young ranch boy, Junior Grindle. And while it did not bother him too terribly much to pin the blame on the boy, it was always preferable to make sure you had the right person in your sights before you pulled the trigger. Or not. Still, the odds were that it was the boy. And never had he been handed a more promising blackmail victim.

Darturo was still smiling when he heard the sheriff's voice addressing him. He looked up to find he was being addressed by a man wearing a badge.

"You're new here, Mr. . . . ? Any particular reason you came to Turnbull?" Sheriff Tucker had been about to pass the swarthy little man on the sidewalk.

Darturo nodded and smiled. "Yes, yes, a fine town you have here. I am on my way somewhere. As are we all in this life—merely going from one place to another, eh?"

Tucker thrust out his bottom lip, considered the small, slender man standing before him. He was white, but something about him seemed dark, more a feeling than anything specific. "You don't sound Mexican.... Where you from?"

"Now, that, Sheriff, is a question I am still trying to answer, eh?"

Tucker stared at him, waiting.

"As a boy I came from Italia."

The sheriff's eyebrows rose. "Italy? Now, that is a far piece ... Mr. ... uh ..."

"You know Italy, then?"

"I know of it. Does that surprise you, Mr. ... ?"

"Oh, it is no surprise. In my travels, I have found that people are from everywhere and nowhere, all at once."

Sheriff Tucker shifted the matchstick to the other side of his mouth. "That so? Where have your travels taken you, then?"

"Your questions are interesting to me, Sheriff. Very interesting, eh?"

Tucker slid the match from his lips, said, "Why?"

The little man laughed, said, "I was told a long time ago that it's not polite to ask questions of people out West." He rested a hand atop the batwings of the Doubloon Saloon and stood like that, a half smile on his mouth and his eyes narrowed as if he were looking at the sun.

Sheriff Tucker stared at him a moment more, then flicked his splintered matchstick into the dirt street. "Good day to you, then." And he headed for Silver Haskell's livery.

"I don't know any more'n you do, Tucker. Seems harmless. And his money spends same as the next man's." Sil-

ver Haskell stabbed his hay fork into the half-loaded
wheelbarrow and ran a forearm across his face. "You're
welcome to search his traps—though he didn't leave
much with me. I expect it's all at his room over to the
hotel. Go ahead, look at his horse. It's that feisty buckskin over there in the last stall before the door. But there
ain't no brand. And his saddle's got no markings neither."

"Why, Silver, it seems that you've anticipated my
visit." The sheriff plucked a fresh match from the same
shirt pocket on which his star was pinned.

"Nope," said Haskell, retrieving his fork and disap-
pearing into the open stall behind him. "I'm just nosy, is
all." A few seconds passed, and then Haskell said, "Why?
Is there paper on him? What's he done?"

But there was no answer. The sheriff had moved on.
Haskell thought briefly that maybe he should have mentioned that he thought the stranger had been out awfully late. But by the time he brought the horse in, Silver
had been in his rooms off the stable, curled around a
near-empty bottle of rye whiskey. And he didn't feel like
listening to Tucker's superior tone about the dangers of
too much drink.

Haskell went back to forking the sullied hay. He was
a grown man, by God, and there wasn't nobody alive
who could claim to be the boss of him. He wasn't about
to change that now.

"Harv."

"Well. . . ." The man behind the counter smiled, then
closed his accounts book and drew his eyebrows together. "Hello, Sheriff Tucker."

"Knock it off, Harv. Or should I say, 'Hotel Owner
Harvey Peterson'?"

"Bee in your bonnet, Tuck? Would a cup of coffee
help?"

"Nah. Got a pot of sludge on the stove at the office.
Just wanted to ask you what you know of the new fella."

"MacMawe's prodigal? He's—"

Sheriff Tucker shook his head and said, "Naw, that other one, the short, dark-looking rig, looks like a Mexican."

"Oh yeah." Harv ran a hand through his fringe of hair and scratched behind his ear. "That one." He leaned over the counter toward Sheriff Tucker. "He's a mite strange. Don't know how to take him. Something about him doesn't sit right with me. Don't know what it is. . . ."

Tucker thought for a moment, then said, "Notice anything odd about him?"

"Odd how? Other than the way he talks, the way he dresses, sneaks around like he's some sort of snake man. Odd like that?"

Tucker smiled. "Yeah, I guess that would cover it. How do you mean 'sneaks around'?"

"Day he checked in, I saw him go upstairs, heard him trompin' around up there. I turn around for a minute, next thing I know he's right there behind me. Gave me the shivers, I tell ya."

"Okay, thanks, Harv. I better get back."

"Is there paper on him?"

"Seems like there ought to be, what with everyone thinkin' there is. We'll find out." He rapped the countertop once with an open hand, then headed out the front door.

Chapter 35

Callie rode back slowly to the Driving D, stars glinting in the cool night sky. Mica had returned to the Driving D hours before to get supper cooking for the crew, but before he left, he'd made her promise to come home soon from Esperanza's, said her father would be worried. That had made her smile—Mica was the biggest worrier at the Driving D. But the time had crept away from her and now it was full dark.

Fortunately, she and her horse knew the route well enough that they loped along, her head filled with conflicting, confusing thoughts. Try as she might, she couldn't stop thinking about the big stranger, Brian Middleton. After that first night in the café, she'd been prepared to hate him. But seeing him so helpless today, so reliant on them—on her—had made her see him in a new light. Several times she found herself studying his face, wondering what sort of man he really was, what his childhood away from his father had been like. For a pompous Easterner, he was handsome; that was obvious to her. But there was something else that had kept her staring at him, until she'd been interrupted by Mica and Espy both, her face reddening red each time.

The larger issue, of course, was the identity of whoever had committed the foul act against the two brothers, for she, like Espy, didn't believe that Brandon had attacked Brian. She failed to detect any justification behind the savage attack. Who would have a good enough reason to want them dead? And if someone did really wish them dead, wouldn't that someone have finished the job? Who would be so blatantly spineless, so indecisive?

Then, with the force of a bullet, the strongest possibility of all hit Callie, and she had her answer. It pulled the breath from her throat as if yanked, and she reined up without knowing it.

Her sudden conviction felt all too true. There were only two people who could have such reason to want the brothers dead, no matter how wrong and twisted that reasoning seemed to her. She rubbed her temples. It was too horrible to think about. But there it was, in black and white in her mind. Her father and brother were plotting to take control of the Dancing M. And apparently they were prepared to take it no matter the cost.

She shook her head. "It can't be," she said aloud. For despite what her head told her, her heart told her no, she had to be wrong.

Callie sat up in the saddle and shook her head as if doused with cold water. This sort of thinking would not do. She had to find out the truth. She nudged her horse into a trot and ten minutes later found herself back at the Driving D and confiding in the one person she felt she could tell—without fear of shame.

"Now, right here's where I have to stop you, Miss Callie." Mica regarded the young woman with an unintentional scowl. He softened his features and tried to smile. It was difficult, especially considering what she'd just told him. Like it or not, the girl's notions had the ring of truth about them. "I can't be any other way but blunt, so I'm just going to say it. . . . Way you feel for Brian Middleton might be clouding your thinking, making you say things you might not mean, or that might not be true."

Callie set her jaw and straightened. "I certainly don't know what you mean, Mica, but I promise you, I have no feelings for—"

The big man smiled and shook his head. "Ain't no way you can convince me otherwise, girl. I've known you too long. So let's cut to the chase, okay? I saw you today, tending to the boy, staring at him when you thought no one was looking, asking Espy questions about him. . . ." Mica's raised eyebrows said it all.

Callie's shoulders relaxed and she closed her eyes. She was too tired and confused to argue the point, even though she wasn't so sure Mica was right. "But, Mica, you know what my father is like where land is concerned. And you should have seen Junior's face. It's as if I saw in his eyes that he will do anything at all to please my father."

Mica held up a hand and shook his head. "I've known your father pretty near as long as anybody, I guess. And as hard as Rory MacMawe's death was on all his friends, me included, it was hardest on your papa. They might not have talked in years, but there was still a mighty bond between them. There are some things that even time can't erode, if you know what I mean."

"But—"

"Girl, let me finish my piece. Now, you think your papa and your brother are hatching some sort of scheme to get hold of the Dancing M. I will admit that I have heard your father, on more than one occasion, speaking covetously of that ranch, of all that land and water, and what he could do with it if only he had it." Mica held up a long finger, like a stick of dynamite, between them. "But that's just dreaming, girl. He's got the Driving D, a ranch any man would envy."

"Mica—"

"Callie, your father's a good man and I don't believe for one minute that he would try to corral your brother into doing anything like plotting to steal the Dancing M from Esperanza or her son, let alone cause them any harm."

But inside, Mica knew different. Those plans of theirs he'd overheard as they smoked their cigarillos gnawed at him. *The boy's been a tough one to figure for a couple of years now*, thought Mica. *Wilf has ridden him too hard, always trying to make him into the way he was, or worse—the way he always wanted to be.* And Mica knew it was that rough treatment more than anything else that bent the boy inward, made him crooked.

No, sir, he wouldn't put it past Junior to have savaged the Dancing M boys on his own. He had to confront the boy. But should he talk with Wilf first? Knowing how the man felt about his son—proud and angry all at once—he was afraid there'd be a fight, and that wouldn't help any of them. Especially not now that all this had happened.

Callie shook her head and folded her arms, and sighed. "It's all so confusing, Mica." Her voice trembled and she covered her eyes with her hand as if she were playing hide-and-seek with her brother.

Where did those innocent children go? thought Mica. Surely it wasn't so long ago that they played harmless games. *And now look at things. A world of hurt, that's what his mama used to call this.* Mica knew that if Callie's suspicions turned out to be true, then they were all in a world of hurt. And he wasn't sure he knew of a way to get out of it.

"I didn't want to believe it, Mica." Callie wiped her eyes.

"Believe what?"

"I don't want to think this, Mica. But what if it was . . . Junior who attacked Brian and Brandon?"

"Now, girl. That's a big thing to be saying." But she seemed so adult, so determined in what she suspected. Admitting this suspicion to Mica seemed to have taken the air right out of her thin body. He knew just how much her brother meant to her. She was devoted to her brother, to be sure. But he wondered if she might also be confused by her new feelings for the stranger, Brian Middleton. He also knew she was nearly all done in by her need for sleep.

At that moment, she looked just like her mother, her concern for others seeming to ride over all her other worries. She was Carla's twin in nearly every way, and for that they had all been thankful. But it seemed as if the boy was fast showing he'd inherited only the hard side of his father's personality, and none of Wilf's kind ways. The peculiar mood Junior had been in that night of the attack when he turned up late at the stable, plus Callie's suspicions, made Mica think that Junior could well be behind the entire thing.

"You should get some sleep, Callie. And come morning, I'll fix you a nice, big breakfast. You'll see, the world will be a brighter place."

"I should leave early. Espy needs me. . . ."

He grasped her shoulders and gently turned her toward the house. "Espy's a grown woman and knows more about taking care of people than everybody in this valley put together. I think those boys will be just fine with her until you've rested up."

Looking back over her shoulder, for the first time in what seemed like weeks, Callie smiled. "When are you going to ask her to marry you, Mica?"

The big man felt as if someone had sucker punched him square in the breadbox. For a moment he could not speak.

Callie giggled, and that broke his spell.

"You get off to bed now," he said in a low, husky voice, trying to sound menacing. "Or there will be hell to pay, mark my words." He watched her run to the big house and mount the front steps, turn and wave once, then disappear inside. "Nosy little upstart," he said, smiling as he turned back to the stable.

He loosened her horse's cinch, still smiling, and hummed a tuneless tune. *Girl might have a point at that*, he thought. He snatched a handful of straw to rub down the horse, and heard footsteps behind him.

"So, that's how it is, eh, old man?"

Mica spun, the golden straw clutched in his hand, a smile fading from his mouth.

Junior stood in the doorway. And his right hand held a cocked Remington revolver.

Chapter 36

Junior looked at Mica as if he'd just stepped in something rancid. Mica stared back, his heart ringing blows in his chest like a hammer on an anvil. He swallowed, dry and thick.

"Sure, I'm old," said Mica, straightening, letting a hand slide back behind him.

Junior shook his head. "You don't keep from moving that hand, old man, and I'm going to shoot the other one."

Mica held still and didn't take his gaze from the boy's face. He'd seen that look once before, and it was not something he ever thought he'd see again. Not until the other night in this very stable. And now here it was again, same stable, same boy, same situation. Only this time Mica didn't see that haze of doubt in Junior's eyes. Now he only saw the crazy, all-or-nothing, convinced look and Mica wasn't so sure this time he could talk his way out of a confrontation.

And especially not when the boy had the drop on him with a cocked six-shooter. How much of his conversation with Callie had the boy heard? Judging from the way his nostrils flared and his teeth gritted in a grim smile, he heard more than Mica would have wished. *Got to protect Callie*, he thought. *Can't trust that Junior won't turn on her too. Because now it's plain to me it was Junior and no other who savaged Brandon and Brian.*

"You and Callie have been talking, Mica. And I don't believe it's polite to talk about people when they're not around. Am I right? Isn't that what you and dear old Papa always told us? Not that you had any right to butt in on private family matters. You weren't any more family to me or Callie than a damned goat or the old black cook stove. Leastwise you have something in common with that."

Despite the tense situation and the gun pointed at his body, Mica felt a knot of anger rise in him. He stepped forward, a frown pulling down his mouth at the sides, his eyes glinting like cold, hard jewels. "Who do you think you are, you young whelp? I spent the best years of my life being a nursemaid to you, to your sister, and to your father, all after your mother died. Your father was a drifting ship and I pulled him to shore and kept this family from floating off in separate directions. Prevented distant relatives from snatching you and your sister up, cutting you and her out of the herd, taking you off to live elsewhere."

Mica stepped forward again, until he was within arm's reach of the pistol. If the young crazy fool was going to kill him, by God, he was going to go down scrapping. "And what do I get in return? A tongue-lashing from a spoiled, know-it-all boy who will never be a man as long as he spends time sneaking around in the shadows and doing things that hurt other people."

He saw that he'd taken the boy by surprise, and as soon as he was within reach, he lashed up with a spade-like backhand. The work-scarred knuckles connected with the young man's stubbled cheek, snapping Junior's head backward as if jerked by a string. At the same instant, Mica grabbed the boy's gun hand by the wrist and squeezed hard. The fingers went limp and the pistol dropped to the straw without a sound.

The slap to his face did little more than anger Junior, who shook it off as a wet dog shakes off water. Then he growled, lowered his head like a battering ram, and drove himself straight into Mica's gut. The older man pitched forward, air rushing from him like a flattened bellows, his grip on the young man's wrist now lost. Junior dug in hard and pushed Mica backward. Mica lost his footing and slammed into the tethered horses. In the stable and outside, horses danced and nickered in agitation as the battling men slammed, growled, and grunted.

In the flared honey glow of the lamplight, fists rose and fell, finding purchase on chins, arms, backs, cheeks, eyes. Both men felt teeth loosen as the other's fists connected with a shot to the mouth, where teeth cut knuckles and split the skin. When they fell apart, minutes later, each man sagged, Mica against a barrel half-filled with scraps of metal, old hames, and broken tools, and Junior to the floor, backed against a timber upright holding the loft in place.

For a full minute, nothing but heaving breaths could be heard. The horses had stilled and the two closest to the fighting stood fidgeting, barely uttering a throaty snicker.

"You . . . damned fool kid . . ." Mica heaved out the words. "What do you . . . hope to gain . . . by killing me? What do you hope to gain by . . . anything you're doing?"

Junior pushed up to his feet and pulled in drafts of air, calming his breathing sooner than Mica. "You just don't understand, do you, old man?" Junior smiled and dragged a torn sleeve across his bleeding mouth. His eye caught something in the straw a stride away from his feet. He stepped over to it, keeping his eyes on Mica the

entire time. "Seems to me you'd have been better off
keeping your mouth shut and your nose into your own
business." He bent, retrieved what Mica saw was the
Remington, still cocked. The boy blew bits of chaff from
the steel and hefted the gun flat on his palm as if com-
paring its weight with something unseen.

"Shooting me will only point the finger of blame
straight at you, Junior. You're a young man, a good
young man. I've known you your entire life. What would
your father think of how you're acting?" Mica watched
the boy's face darken, cloud as if presaging a storm front
blowing in hard and fast from the north. *That was either
a big mistake*, thought Mica, *or the best thing I could
have said.*

"You bring my father into this? I've spent years—yes,
all those years you've known me—trying to live up to his
idea of what I should be." Junior's voice rose higher,
veins framing his forehead bulged with each word he
spat.

"I know that, Junior. I know. I was there too. You forget the times we sneaked some cookies and took off for
our secret spot on the bench behind the house—just to
talk?" Mica stood full height and stretched, rubbed his
shoulder. He was more confident now. He'd cracked the
shell of craziness that Junior had let harden over him.
Now the Junior he knew might get a chance to breathe
again.

As if reading his thoughts, Junior eased off the Remington's hammer, but still held it, not quite pointing, not
quite at ease. The boy was staring beyond Mica, into the
gloom of the stable, when boots sounded behind him,
crunching in the barn doorway.

Chaz Ganzolo, one of the newer hands and one of the
few left behind at the ranch while the others were out
gathering, peeked in the doorframe, no hat and one side
of his red braces flapping loose, his trouser cuffs bunched

about his boots. "What's the problem here, guys? You havin' a party in here?"

Despite the situation, Mica smiled at the young man's half-serious, half-asleep tone. *Some party*, he thought. "No, Chaz, you go on back to bed."

But the young cowboy had seen the pistol in Junior's hand. His eyes lost the last of their sleepy glaze and traveled from the pistol to Mica, then back to Junior.

Mica was about to repeat his gentle order to Chaz, but he caught sight of Junior's face and knew that any progress he'd made at getting through to the Junior hidden away was lost—but only for now, he hoped.

"I'm just teaching this one here—" Junior wagged the pistol in Mica's direction—"that he should mind his own business and remember his place." He shifted his gaze to the Mexican cowboy. "Seems to me you could learn something from this." He stretched his lips wide and tight over his teeth, the leer in no way resembling a smile. "A word of this and you'll be draggin' your saddle across the Llano looking for work, you *comprende*?"

Chaz stood still, one hand resting on the door's edge, the other hanging limp.

"Go back to bed, Chaz. It's all right."

"Shut it, old man." Junior once again ratcheted back the hammer. His eyes narrowed and returned to their glinting, frenzied state.

A sound like a nervous dog might make squeaked out of Chaz, but he didn't move. He stared first at Junior, but the young man was looking hard at Mica. Mica cut his eyes to Chaz and thrust up his chin once. The young cowhand seemed to understand and he disappeared, walking away from danger. Mica was relieved and not a little envious. A quiet bunk sounded good right about now.

"You don't want this, Junior. Just let each of us agree to disagree on whatever it is you're so bent out of shape about. I'll go to bed and come tomorrow I won't mention a thing to anybody, and you do the same." Mica stood, hands lank by his sides, angry and, more than anything else, tired.

Shots, Mica knew, would bring the other few hands still at the ranch racing to the scene. He also knew that those boys were already awake and perched on the edge of their bunks, taking in Chaz's story, unsure if they should rush to Mica's aid or steer clear of the strange young man they all thought they knew—but now realized they didn't.

Junior's face held, taut and grim, as he mulled over his next step. From a stall in the dark behind Mica, one of the horses blew hard out its nostrils. Another rattled a gate as it circled in its stall, still agitated by the commotion. Junior's features sagged into exhaustion for the second time that night and as Mica watched, it seemed to him that the boy gained twenty years on his life, so gray-faced and haggard did he appear.

He eased back the hammer, holstered the pistol, and walked out of the stable without a further word to the man who had been like a second father to him. And that man sagged back against the old barrel and rubbed his thumbs hard into his eyes for a long time, too tired to wonder just what was happening to his adopted family.

Chapter 37

"You're movin' stiff today, you old dog. Visiting with that chiquita down to the Dancing M's getting to you, huh?" Wilf winked at Mica, looked up at him as Mica set down a platter of hotcakes. "What in God's name happened to your face?"

"Horse threw me." He let the words trail as he limped back to the kitchen. Mica nearly poked Wilf in the nose, making a comment like that. He pushed the bacon to the back of the griddle and stared at the two brown eggs in his hand. He turned his hand over and appraised his knuckles. Cut all to hell from the boy's teeth. He ran his tongue over his own teeth, poked at the loose one on the side. Then he set down the eggs, stripped off his apron, and plunked his hat down on his head as he headed out the back door of the kitchen. People thinking something, by God, he'd give them something to justify their suspicions. Might be Espy'd welcome him with a cup of coffee this morning. He didn't know her as well as he'd like to, but he was beginning to think he knew her a damn sight better than he did this family.

Wilf heard the door clunk shut, then silence from the kitchen. He sighed and looked around at the empty table. As he speared a stack of cakes, he wondered what in the hell was happening to his family.

Mica raised his hat, nodded. "Good morning, Esperanza. I was just . . . passing. Thought I'd check on the boys."

Espy nodded, and regarded her old friend, Mica Bain, as he swung down from his horse. He had been in a fight. One cheek was knotted, the other eye reddened. Why did men do these things to each other? To everyone? She slipped her towel over her shoulder. "Have you eaten?"

Mica pulled off his hat and for the span of a few quiet breaths, their eyes met. He half smiled, shook his head, and followed her inside.

"Good morning, all," he whispered. "How are we today?"

Brandon walked over to Mica, his hand outstretched, but he veered too far to the side.

"Boy, boy, you better sit yourself back down. No call to be shaking my hand." Mica steered the dizzy young man to a chair, exchanged a look with Espy.

"Time," said Mica. "You just need a little time to get your head mended." But he knew that sometimes that wasn't enough. After a blow like that, sometimes people were off their bean forever. Esperanza pushed sausage and sliced chilies around her pan with a wooden spoon. But he saw that her face was tight, as much worry as she would allow herself to show.

Mica patted the boy's shoulder softly and looked at the tall man stretched out on the bed to the side of the fireplace, the same bed the boys' father had died in. Espy was far too practical to move him from it, but it gave Mica the worries anyway. Might be foolish, but it also might be something in what some folks called superstition. Way he looked at it, there was a reason for everything. Even superstitions started somewhere, somehow.

The big fellow, Middleton, looked better than Mica thought he had a right to. It had been a blessing that the bullet had passed right on through the boy without hitting any vitals. Cleared a path sure enough, though. He'd drizzled half a bottle of medicinal whiskey right into that boy. Mica had hoped Middleton would have stayed unconscious, but the searing pain, he knew, was enough to raise a dead man. And that nearly dead man screamed blue hell. Great bellowing howls as that whiskey tore through him. Scared them all to blazes. And then he'd slept, and for that they'd all been grateful.

Middleton's hoarse half whisper pulled Mica out of his reverie. The boy had opened his eyes and looked up at him, and the deep voice suited his size. "I understand I have you to thank."

Mica stood by the bed, shook his head. "No, you have Miss Callie and Miss Esperanza here to thank. I was just lending a hand, is all."

"But you—"

"Hush up now, you'll need your strength." Mica smiled at him and took a seat at the table. Espy set two places, two cups of steaming coffee, two plates of food, the smells of which forced him to close his eyes and inhale. "Esperanza," he said, rubbing his big, work-thick hands together. "You are a cook's cook."

She almost smiled.

Chapter 38

"Where've you been, boy?"

Junior spun at the sound of his father's voice behind him, from the gloom of his office. The wide double doors were half-open and Junior saw his father's silvered hair in a drifting haze of cigarillo smoke. He spun to continue past and trot up the wide, dark stairwell. But he checked himself. Why not talk with the old man? Could be the perfect time to throw any suspicion off him like a dirty shirt being shucked on laundry day.

"Hey, Pop." Junior pushed the doors open, let them swing wide behind him. One of them clunked a chair. "What can I do for you today?" He knew he should rein in his tone, but the whiskey he'd finished off on his ride back from town was just now flowering full and warm in his gut and he liked the feeling. Liked it a lot. Maybe that little soak Brandon wasn't such a sap after all. *Too bad we may never know*, he thought.

"What you can do for me is tell me where you been." Wilf set down his cigarillo in a big black ashtray, the last of the gray smoke curling out of his mouth, chasing the words out the front door.

Junior shook his head, smiled, and plunked down in the guest chair. "You see, that's just what I've been talking about with the boys down at the Doubloon. You still seem to think I'm just a pup."

Wilf regarded the boy for a moment, then leaned back and said, "So you've been to the saloon. With the boys."

"Yep." Junior nodded, closing his lids for a moment.

"Junior!"

The boy's eyes snapped open.

"Least you can do is stay awake when I'm talking with you. You want to be treated like a man, then don't go running off to the bar when there's work to be done."

Junior knew that somewhere along the line he'd stepped in a big ol' cow pie. He kept his mouth shut and tried to focus on his father's scowl.

Wilf leaned back in his chair, shaking his head and running his fingertips through the carved wood on the armrests. "I'll take your silence to mean that you know nothing of the events of the past couple of days."

Junior let his father's comments sink in. Sure, he'd left in a huff, ticked off Mica and his father at the same time. But . . . then he remembered what he'd done, remembered clubbing Brandon, shooting Middleton, then his heart hammering hard in his rib cage to get out of there. He blinked hard. This whiskey was starting to play tricks on him, making him forget things that he knew just five minutes before.

When he left the saloon he'd gotten his story straight, finally headed home, knowing he couldn't stay away forever, just long enough to establish what seemed to him to be a likely alibi. No one would remember how long he'd been whoopin' it up if he stayed there for a few days; at least that's what he hoped. And all had been fine—felt fine—until his father started in with the questions.

A hard knob of fear knotted in his gut and he stood, squawking the chair backward on the wood floor. "No time for jawin', Pop. Got work to do."

He forced himself to focus on his father's face.

"Sit down, boy. I'm not through with you."

Despite his best intentions, Junior felt himself dropping back into the chair, just like old times. *Get up, get up*, he told himself. But it didn't work. The old man glared at him just like the portrait of Grandfather at the top of the stairs.

Wilf leaned over his desk, seeming to balance his entire body on his fingertips. "Now, you will sit there and shut your drunken mouth for a minute. Then you can drag your sorry self upstairs and sleep off what's left of your spree and waste the rest of the day in the bargain. By God, I'll not have you slopping around with the men and have them think that's how a Grindle conducts himself. And in the middle of the afternoon too."

Junior felt tired and try as he might he knew he wasn't about to raise himself from the chair. *Let the old man yell*, he thought. *I'll just sit right here and sleep through it all*. He half smiled and closed his eyes.

Wilf stared at his boy. He had been about to tell the drunken sot that they'd found Callie safe and sound, no thanks to him, but that the other young drunk of the region, Brandon, had attacked his half brother and now they were both near dead. He'd been about to tell the young fool all this—and then Junior dozed off right there in front of him. It was more than Wilf could stand.

He grabbed the corner of the desk and propelled himself at the boy. The fire in his veins was a feeling of rage such as he hadn't known in years. He reached out and smacked the young fool hard across the mouth with a sharp, stout hand. The lad's eyes flew open and for a moment Wilf thought he might have to hit him again—

harder, this time. But Junior just sat there, shaking his head, trying to focus on the situation before him.

"What . . . happened?"

"I hit you, you little fool. And I'll do it again if need be." Wilf growled and rubbed his reddened hand as if polishing a fine knife blade. He breathed a rapid cadence through his nose, like a small bull with its blood up.

The boy rose from the chair, his right fist windmilling wide and high, clearing Wilf's head. The rancher raised his left arm out of reflex and blocked the wayward swing, then pumped two short, tight punches into his son's gut. The boy half spun backward and dropped to his knees, coughing and gagging, snot and blood spooling to the carpet.

"I'll . . . kill you . . . for that!"

Wilf snorted. "Pack yourself a meal, boy. Killin' me will take you all day. Better men than you have tried to get the drop on Wilfred Grindle!" He grasped the boy's belt from behind and heaved him to his feet, then bum-rushed him to the stairwell. "Now get up there and sleep it off, damn you!" He stood at the base of the stairs. His hands, trembling in shock and rage, hung tight at his sides in half fists, ready for another round. Up out of view, the boy's door slammed hard. Wilf sighed, ran a thumb and forefinger hard into his eyes, then turned back to his wide-open office doors.

He was nearly through when movement from the doorway's shadow pulled Wilf's gaze. Mica leaned there, watching him. "Mica—how long . . ."

"No worries from me, Wilf." The tall black man straightened. "No worries. Just wanted to tell you I'll be heading on over to the Dancing M for the day. Espy—Esperanza—could use a hand, what with the boys stoved up an' all."

Wilf worked his teeth together tight and turned from the door. "And I suppose Callie has practically moved in there with that . . . that Mexican and her damned brood!

What makes everyone think they can just up and leave the Driving D?"

Wilf turned around and flicked an accusing finger at his oldest living friend. "I haven't paid you all these years so you can work someone else's ranch! I deserve—no, no—I demand to be treated with more respect by you and these ungrateful offspring of mine. One's a drunk, one's a flirting thing just shy of a floozy . . . and you! Look at you . . . all dolled up like it's Sunday-Go-to-Meeting Day!" He stared at his friend standing in the doorway.

"You wanna know what's wrong with the boy, Wilf? Look at yourself." Mica paused. Wilf tried to speak, but Mica cut him off and kept right on talking. "Ever since Carla died, you got hard. Hard and mean, mostly where the boy's concerned. All he ever does is try to please you, but it's never enough. Never. And now look at him. Kid's a mess."

Wilf opened his mouth, but said nothing. Their eyes met. Mica held the gaze for a moment, then shook his head and walked out the front door.

Wilf gritted his teeth hard and stared at the closed door long after he heard Mica's horse drum its way down the lane westward. His shoulders slumped as he turned back to the dark, paneled room. He slopped whiskey into a tumbler. The first glassful burned going down.

Chapter 39

Mortimer Darturo sat his horse, one hand atop the other resting on the pommel, waiting. Someone would come out soon enough. They always did. He'd found that people were nothing if not curious. *Ah*, he thought as a shadow grew in the doorway. *Here we are*, and a stout little Mexican woman in an apron appeared.

"Good morning to you, ma'am. I am seeking ranch work. I was told to look for a Mr. Rory MacMawe. I am good with cattle and horses. And people too."

She regarded him, one eye squinted shut against the morning light. Finally she spoke. "We don't need help here." But she made no movement to go back inside.

This could prove interesting, thought Mort, sizing up the woman, even as she regarded him with the same hard stare.

"No offense, ma'am, but you do not seem to be the type to tell me what to do. In fact, no one is. It has been a long time since I took any orders from a woman." He laughed, a short, sharp bark. "Maybe never, eh?"

The woman turned back to him, stood a little taller, and now her hands were on her hips. He continued to smile.

"I own this ranch."

"As I said, I was told that a man by the name of Rory MacMawe owned it. Now, you don't look like someone of that name. Let me speak with Mr. MacMawe and I won't mention this little show to him. How does that sound to you, eh?"

To his left chickens scattered as if dried leaves in a sudden stiff breeze as a young man, head wrapped high in a bright white bandage, staggered out of a leaning coop, the door wagging open behind him. "Dead, dead, dead. He's dead. We are all dead. . . . And I have done this. . . ." The boy tried to focus on Mort, then pitched too far to one side and flopped to the hard-packed yard, dust rising.

This could not be more fun, thought Darturo, as he steadied Picolo with his heels, his hands tight on the reins.

The short woman ran down the two steps and bent low over the boy, but he pushed at her to no effect. "What does it matter now?" said the boy. "We won't be staying and you know it." The boy turned to face her. "And you are to blame, old woman!" With her help, he rose again to his feet, then pushed at her, missing her with his flailing hands, and staggered off toward the barn.

I know that voice, thought Darturo. *So this is the home of at least one of the savaged men from the other night*. And as if to set the idea with a final hammer blow, a deadweight thump and then a moan drifted out to them from inside the house.

The old woman met Darturo's gaze. His eyebrows rose and he nodded, still smiling, toward the house. "Sounds like you got yourself another problem in there, eh?"

She stared at him hard, but he waited her out. A few seconds, no more, and she was gone into the little house.

Darturo smiled. He knew she had been itching to get in there, tend to the other man, the one who was shot. *Must be him*, he thought. *A tough bunch. We'll see how tough.* He turned his horse and together they sauntered out of the yard.

Chapter 40

"You foolish boy." That was all she said. But it was enough to make him feel like a child. He had tried to rise off the floor and get back to the bed before she could help him. Brian had only managed to grip the edge of the old wooden table before stiffening as if he'd been shot again. Pain coursed upward like a lightning strike through his gut and into his head, blurring his vision. He felt her strong hands lifting him under the elbows and together they got him back to the edge of the bed. He sat there heavily, panting and drained of all strength.

Once she was sure he could sit upright without help, Esperanza left him leaning and padded back to the big black cook stove. From the snatches of moments he'd come around during the past few days, it seemed she was always standing at the stove, her back to the room, strong, spiced smells rising from her steaming pots.

"These boys will be the death of me."

He tried to speak, but had no strength for it. "I'm sorry . . . for this." When he finally opened his eyes, she stood in front of him, her hands on her waist.

"You should be. Bad things happened before you came here. But since you come, even worse things. Why is that?"

Before he could respond, she'd grasped his shoulders with strength that surprised him and eased him backward. "Look what you've done. Your wound has opened."

He looked down and a dark red patch flowered on the white bandage wrapping his middle. "I heard voices, saw Brandon fall. . . . Was there trouble?"

"Nothing of your concern."

They were silent for a few minutes as she eased the old bandage off him, reapplied the soft, folded wad of fabric to absorb the blood, then rewrapped his middle, easing the bandages under him, tying them off.

"How is Brandon?"

"His head will heal. His mind won't." Then she looked at him and her eyes softened and she looked so much older.

"I must have done it, but that means he must have . . ."

"No." She shook her head. "No, no. You did not hit him like that and he did not shoot you."

"How can you be so sure? We fought the first two times we met." He tried to raise himself on an elbow, but fell back to the pillow.

She put a hand flat against his broad chest. "Brothers would not do this, even with the horrible power of too much drink in their bellies." He reddened but she continued. "And besides, Brandon no longer has a gun. He does not think I know, but he sold his father's old pistol for liquor money weeks ago."

Brian's brows met in question.

"Callie saw it for sale at Miss Gleason's store and bought it back for me. I have it here, along with Rory's old shotgun."

He was silent a moment, working to take in what she was saying. "I read the letters in the Bible. I don't know what to say, other than I'm sorry."

She smiled. "You were a good boy, Brian. I hated to give you up. But you were not my boy, no matter how hard I wished otherwise. And your father . . ."

She looked up at the stones of the fireplace, and above, the mantel, all crowned by a deer skull. "Your father was a good man, but also a difficult man to understand." She stood, smoothed the little towel that always seemed to be draped over her shoulder. "You have much of your father in you, Brian. I only hope you will find peace here with his ghost."

From the front door, a soft knock interrupted their silence. Brian's eyebrows rose as she crossed the room toward the door.

"I'm not staying here," he said. "I just can't. This is no place for the likes of me. I have a life elsewhere. . . ."

She nodded in agreement, but her eyes told him she thought she knew better. "If you are the result of the way they raise children back East, Mr. Brian Middleton, then when you get back there, do all of New Mexico Territory a favor and tell your friends to stay put. We have enough rude children of our own. We don't need any more, thank you."

Esperanza turned to the door. "Hello, Callie." Espy waved the girl into the kitchen and set out two cups for coffee.

Brian and Callie exchanged glances. He looked away, tired and confused, and chewed the inside of his lip. He felt his face redden like a struck thumb, but there was little he could do. He couldn't even care for himself, couldn't stand, couldn't sit, nothing, at least not without assistance. And as much as it pained him to admit it, the woman had every right to feel as she did, bitter with him for being rude. Since he arrived in this backwater, enough people had told him he'd been acting that way that he supposed they were right.

The devil of it was, this "backwater" was beginning to grow on him. The beauty of it, which he'd finally realized, the beauty that Junior had seen on that first night of camping out under it, the vastness of the night sky, with nothing but the great arching dome of heaven above, beset with the jewels of that sky flashing down just for him . . . No, he'd not easily forget that. Even before they'd been attacked, he had lain awake for a few minutes, staring up at the same sky. Wondering about the possibility of making a life out here in this wilderness. But no, he'd decided, that would be impossible. His life lay in the East. There were a few young ladies, and one in particular, who awaited his return. And more importantly, his grandfather awaited his return. His grandfather! That man was destined for an earful on Brian's return.

To have denied him at the very least the knowledge of his father and yes, if he had to admit it, his father's love, plus this home place, all these years. And the presence in his life of this strange woman, Esperanza, and so, his half brother, Brandon. That was galling him, especially in light of the fact that he'd probably been the one to hit Brandon hard enough to have caused him permanent damage.

He hoped that wasn't the case. But despite what Esperanza said, he felt certain it was he and Brandon and no one else who had inflicted these wounds on each other. It stood to reason, as they'd been at odds since they first met. They also had good cause to dislike each other, even to the point, dare he think of it, of killing each other. And if all that weren't enough, they had been drinking whiskey.

"I just don't know what to think about Junior anymore, Espy. . . ."

Brian heard Callie Grindle's voice crack as she spoke, low and in private conversation with Esperanza. He looked at her, her gold hair, a few strands of which had slipped down over her face from the loose gather she'd made at the back of her neck. Her profile was . . . perfect, and he knew in that moment there wasn't a woman in all of Providence, or Boston, or in all of the East, for that matter, who could compare with her pretty face, sharp mind, steellike resolve. She looked at him, stiffened, and the soft look in her eyes was replaced with the fierce glint it seemed she reserved especially for him. Still, he did not look away. In truth, he knew he could not, such was the power of her gaze over him.

To his surprise the softness made its way back into her eyes. They stared at each other a moment more, and then she rose from her seat at the table. Espy carried their cups to the dry sink, picked up her egg basket, and went outdoors.

Callie stood over him, her arms folded. "Espy told me you got out of bed, opened your wound because you thought Brandon was in trouble."

"I heard the stranger—"

"Don't do that again. It was foolish of you."

"That's what she said."

"She's right."

He looked away, toward the smooth gray stone of the fireplace, and felt the heat of early anger rise in him. This woman would never give him the time of day, so why did he bother feeling anything at all toward her? It was a waste of energy that he could put toward healing. And the sooner he did that, the faster he could get out of this backwater. And then he looked back to her. There was no hard glint in her gaze, still the softness. What could that mean?

"Miss Grindle?"

"Callie. My name is Callista, but people call me Callie."

"Callie, then. I want to thank you for helping me. I don't know how I can repay you, but I'd like to. Somehow."

She sighed. "You think I did this for payment, Middleton? Is that all you care about? Money?"

He tried to protest, to tell her that what he meant to

say was thank you, nothing more. But the formality of the phrase, the way he was brought up to say things, blocked the way. It always would, especially with someone as thin-skinned as Callie Grindle.

"I don't understand you or your kind, Mr. Brian Middleton. And I don't think I ever will." She walked to the door as she said this, but paused at the threshold, stopped by his words.

"Fortunately for me and *my kind*, Miss Grindle, you need not worry your pretty head over it. I will take my leave of this place as soon as my injuries permit. Then you will be free of me forever."

She shook her head, looked at him as if he would never understand anything she said. "Whether you like it or not, Mr. Middleton, you are *from* here. You are of this place as much as any of us. Yes, you were forced to leave as a child, but if you hadn't been, you would still be here, no different than the rest of us, the very people you seem to despise." She looked at the floor, seemed about to say something else, but walked outside instead.

Brian shook his head again. When would he learn? Never, it seemed. Never.

Esperanza looked up from wiping out the chickens' water trough. "What's the matter, Callie?"

The girl said nothing as she let the cracked corn sift through her fingers.

"Let me guess—you've had an argument with Brian Middleton."

Callie nodded, looked up. "Why are you smiling, Espy? It's not funny in the least. He's such an . . . ass."

"Yes, he is, but I think that ass is in love with you."

Callie stiffened, corn dribbling from her hand.

"Yes," said Espy. "And I know you think he is special too."

Callie looked at her, her face hot and her throat tight. "Did he . . ."

"No, Callie." Espy stood up straight, held a hand to her back. "He said nothing to me. But Espy has learned a few things. Oh, I know things."

"But, Espy, he's—"

"No, no more names, Callie." She chuckled. "Take your mind to other things. Help me find Brandon." She lost her smile. "Before he wanders too far."

Chapter 41

"I tell you, Sheriff, that stranger is the man you want to be looking for." Squirly stood before the sheriff's desk, his buckskin-clad arms crossed on his chest.

Sheriff Tucker sat staring at him. He wasn't sure he could trust that what he was seeing was truthful. There stood the town's worst drunk, still smelly, but not wobbly and slurring his speech. No, this had to be some sort of trick. "Now, just hold on there a minute, Squirly. You say you just got back to town? From a trip up north? And on a horse?"

"Yessir, I did. And—"

"Hold on there." Tucker held up a hand and shook his head. "First off, should I be worried about you being a horse thief? 'Cause last time I looked, you didn't have enough money to buy a horse, a saddle, or even a handful of oats."

"My good friend, Station Agent Teasdale, staked me. I'm going to pay him back, work off what I owe him for the rental of the horse from Haskell's, the groceries he sent me with."

Tucker closed his eyes. He felt sure a headache would soon be on its way. The world was changing, and he wasn't sure he wanted to be part of it. "So, you're telling me that the stranger, Rory MacMawe's son, murdered your old friend, the cowboy?"

"What?" Squirly regarded the sheriff as if he'd just eaten a live tarantula spider. "No, no, no. The other stranger. That little foreign fellow."

"Well, now, that would make a bit more sense. But where's your proof, Squirly?"

"Proof! Well, by gum, I guess to hell I know my own old friend's face if'n I see it. I spent a few winters with old Mitchell Farthing in a line shack far north of here."

"I understand, Squirly. But the law operates on things like evidence, proof, motives, you see? Without them, we'd be in a world of hurt. And no offense, 'cause it seems like you're not all that drunk, but you're not known for being overly coherent most of the time, let alone truthful. So if I go question this man because you say he killed someone who may or may not exist, and without proof, well, I'd be a fool. You see?"

Squirly let his arms drop. After all that riding, all that work burying Farthing, all those miles with nary a drop to his name. And that's all he could expect from the sheriff? He snorted and shook his head. "I wasn't asking you to hang the man, nor arrest him, nor even accuse him. Just wanted to see if you'd keep an eye on him, is all. Long time ago, Mitchell Farthing saved my hide a time or two. Figured it's the least I can do. But I reckon you're a busy man and I been a burr under your saddle for far too long to expect you'd listen much to what I have to say." He left the office. Tucker stood up and watched out the window as Squirly crossed the street, head hanging low, and headed for the saloon.

Chapter 42

"Where were you today, girl?"

"Oh, hi, Papa. Didn't see you in there in your gloomy cave." Callie sat on the foyer bench and pulled off her boots. She stayed seated, holding the second boot and staring at the flagged floor.

"Callie?"

"Oh yes. Sorry. I was at Espy's."

"I knew it," said Wilf. "Off playing in that nest of fools and rogues. For the life of me, girl, I don't know why you associate with them."

She looked up at him as if she'd just awakened. Her jaw was set hard, her teeth clenched. "I see now why Junior feels as he does toward you."

"Just what do you mean by that?"

"I mean that you ought not to ride Junior so hard. He's not right lately. I think he's in some sort of trouble...."

"He's weak, nothing more, nothing less. I'm beginning to think he always will be."

Callie shook her head as if he'd disappointed her. "You are insufferable."

She had made for the stairs when he spoke again, stopping her in her tracks.

"Insufferable, eh? Fancy two-dollar word. Now I know you've been hanging around that back-East city fellow. I've heard all about him from the folks in town. I'd appreciate it if you'd stay home. At least for the time being. No sense you traipsing off over there every day. I expect that Mexican housemaid of Rory's knows how to heal him up enough to send him on his way back to wherever it is he came from."

"He came from here, Papa. And maybe he wants to stay."

"What makes you say that?" He came out of his office, drink in hand and eyes narrowed.

"Because . . . because he's in love." She blurted the words, then turned away.

"Ha. From what I hear he can barely sit up. And everybody talks about how rude he is. Who'd love that fool?"

She stayed standing at the bottom of the staircase, her hand atop the newel post.

"Oh no, Callie. Don't tell me . . ."

She spun on him, her blue eyes glinting in the warm glow of the oil lamps. "Would that be such a bad thing, then?"

"Yes, by God, it would." He knocked back the last slug in his glass and stood shaking his head.

"And why is that?"

He stared at her and barked. "Because you're my daughter!" He looked down again and said in a quieter voice, "No one is good enough for you." He looked down at his hands, his mouth trembling. "Not even Rory's son," he said as he walked back to his office and pushed the door closed behind him.

Out in the hallway Callie stood with her hand over

her mouth, her throat tight with laughing and crying. She was a fool to even think such things, she knew. But it shut her father up. She walked up the stairs and lay back on her bed, replaying this strange day over and over again in her mind. She wondered if Brian Middleton was doing the same.

Wilf stared out his library window into the dark of the night. He sipped his drink and said, "Callie and the missing MacMawe boy, eh? Well . . . I suppose that's one way to get the Dancing M into Grindle hands." He leaned back in his chair, a bitter smile on his face as he sipped a fresh glass of whiskey.

Chapter 43

Esperanza looked out the little window that faced the dooryard. "Sheriff Tucker," she said.

Callie joined her at the window. "How do you suppose . . . ?"

But both women knew that in a close-knit town such as Turnbull, it wouldn't take much for word of a shooting to get around. The who didn't matter so much as the fact that the sheriff could not be let in. Once he had proof that there was a shooting, he would insist on answers, and they had none to give him. For even though they were convinced that the boys didn't do this to each other, it would be obvious to the sheriff that they had indeed savaged each other. Arrests would be made, and none of this would end well for any of them.

Espy came outside the door, pulling it nearly closed behind her. She pulled her shawl tighter about her shoulders.

"G'morning, Esperanza. I hope you are well on this fine spring day."

"Thank you, Sheriff. And the same to you."

"Brandon wouldn't be around, would he?"

Esperanza looked briefly at the paunchy man standing before her. It was not like her not to offer a visitor—especially an old friend of her Rory's—a cup of coffee. Maybe another time. "Brandon . . . is not here. He is out. I don't know where he is or when he will be back."

"Now, look, Esperanza. We've known each other a long time—ain't that right?"

"Yes, Sheriff."

"Haven't I always looked out for that boy of yours, even when he's filled himself to the gills with drink?"

"Yes, Sheriff."

The paunchy man regarded her a moment, saw that he wasn't getting anywhere at all, and pushed his fawn hat up high on his forehead. "Look, Esperanza. I've been told that a man's been shot. Don't that mean a thing to you? Hiding such a thing is a crime. Why, it's wrong and . . . and unlawful not to report it. You understand me?"

"Yes, Sheriff."

"Well, good. Then, can I come in?"

"No, not today, Sheriff."

He dropped his hands to his side. "Well, why forever not?"

Esperanza stared at him, but said nothing. From behind her, Callie Grindle emerged in the doorway, pulled it partially closed behind herself.

"Why, Miss Callie. I didn't know you were here." He looked round the yard, half expecting to see her horse tied nearby.

"Hello, Sheriff Tucker. It's good to see you."

"Well, I suppose you've heard this entire long and frustrating conversation, eh?"

She smiled, nodded. "Yes, I have."

"Well, then you know by now that I aim to come in, have myself a look around."

"I'm sorry, Sheriff. But I'm afraid that won't be possible today."

"What?" He swung his ham fists at his sides, looked askance at the chickens picking at the grit of the yard. "Will you mind telling me why forever not? Don't you think I wouldn't get wind of such a thing as a shooting? I am, after all, the sheriff in these parts. And as I say, I have it on good authority that a man has been shot."

"I don't doubt you, Sheriff Tucker, but such hearsay doesn't mean you can just barge in on people."

"I ain't bargin' in anywhere. I'm the sheriff."

Callie sighed and leaned against the doorframe. "Sheriff, if you must know . . ." She glanced behind herself, into the dark interior of the room. "We're busy in here, Sheriff . . . with womanly things. I don't think you really want to force me to say what that might be, do you?"

The sheriff's eyes widened. For a moment, he felt as if he had just woken up to find he was in the midst of sleepwalking down Main Street Turnbull with nothing on but his hat and gun belt. He had no idea what she meant, but he did know he had no intention of finding out.

The sheriff found he could not speak, could only shake his head, his mouth working like a banked fish. He waved a hand, palms up, at her and backed to his horse. His face felt hot and he guessed it was redder than beet juice. He was nearly out of the yard when he remembered to doff his hat at the ladies, and then he rode hell-for-leather on out of there.

As they watched his dust cloud swirl apart in his wake, Esperanza turned to Callie. "What are these 'womanly things' we are up to, Callie?" Espy did a poor job of hiding the humor she found in the situation.

"I have no idea," said Callie. "But we know that the sheriff has no idea either."

The women shared a laugh. Something that had not happened at the little house on the Dancing M in a long, long time.

Chapter 44

Later that day, Esperanza closed the door to the little bedroom off the kitchen and prodded the coals in the stove's firebox.

"Is Brandon better?"

"No, not better. Just sleeping."

"Esperanza . . . I—"

She faced him. "Call me Espy."

Brian Middleton stared at her a moment, then said, "Thank you, I will." He cleared his throat and sat up straighter with a wince. She hurried over and held in place the bunched blanket she'd put there to help keep him sitting upright. "You know Miss Grindle well, I assume?"

"Yes, her whole life. She has always been my good friend."

"She is exasperating." He looked up at the smiling face of his hostess as she carried an oil lamp over to the small bedside table and lit the wick.

Espy nodded. "If that really means that you are fond of her, then that is true."

His face flowered red, in strong contrast to his pale color. "Why, I . . . I'm not sure what you mean by that. . . ."

"She feels the same as you."

Brian Middleton frowned at the fireplace. "This is all quite vexing."

She wiped her hands on her apron and opened a deep drawer in the sideboard. She pulled out a bundle of letters, bound with coarse brown twine. "You think too much about things you should feel instead." She set the bundle of letters in his lap and nodded. "Take your mind off one kind of love and read about another."

"What are these?"

"After you went away to the East, and when I was still just Rory's cook and housekeeper, I also helped him to write letters to you. One letter each week. He never missed a week for years and years."

"But I never received a single letter from him."

"I know." She nodded at the bundle. "Those are the letters, returned to your father unopened. Rory understood. It was your mother's father. He hated Rory."

Brian said nothing, but stared down at the top letter, the handsome script flowing, straight, and well rendered, though faded on the brown-tinged envelope. He noted that the tops of the envelopes were ragged, opened. So these were the letters Brandon had told him of.

"He also sent gifts to you on your birthdays." She headed outside, but stopped in the doorway when Brian said, "At least he had Brandon."

She said nothing, then left the house.

Brian sat for a long time looking at the thick bundle, and thinking of the various birthday gifts he'd received over the years, wondering if any of them had been sent from this very house. Certainly none of them ever bore a label with his father's name.

Chapter 45

"Choctaw, that's what I said." Squirly Ross turned his back to the bar as if it offended him and rested his elbows there. Tom, the barkeep, raised his eyebrows and shook his head as he looked at the other drinker.

Mortimer Darturo sipped his beer, knowing he wouldn't keep his own mouth shut for more than a few seconds. He would worry this like a terrier on a rat. And it would be fun. "Choctaw, you say. . . ."

"Now, fella . . . ," said Tom the bartender, half smiling.

"No need to worry. I just want to get this straight." Darturo scrunched up his face, bunching his cheeks until his eyes disappeared in a knot of crevices. Though Mort was still on the green side of forty, time had not been his best friend. He looked older than his thirty-four years. But he had to admit he looked better than this pudgy little town drunk with his hairy belly poking through holes in his red long-handles, and on through the rents in his buckskins.

The hair on Squirly's head had long ago lost the battle with skin, but what little there was up there was gray-white and wispy, and it trailed down to a sparse fringe rimming his pink head, hairs squashed out like bug legs as if pressed by a hat.

"He is telling us that the reason he has been gone is that he's been off in the Choctaw Nation, pillaging and ransacking and plundering and generally having himself a grand old time. For two whole days. Do I have that right, Mr. Ross?"

Squirly stared ahead at the far wall. The dartboard hung there, its projectiles bunched in the center. He had wanted to instigate a conversation, somehow try to trap the stranger into admitting his guilt in the death of Mitchell Farthing, but for the life of him he didn't know how to go about it. Hell, if he was honest with himself, he wasn't even sure the fellow was guilty. Just because he had a gut feeling didn't mean the man was a killer. And yet something told him otherwise. Finally he turned his head and looked at the two men, then turned back to studying the dartboard.

"I'll take that as a yes. Wouldn't you, bartender?" said Darturo. "After all, it is your establishment and you should therefore be the arbiter of all civilized discourse. Wouldn't you agree, Mr. Squirly Ross?"

Squirly glanced sidelong at his bar companion. "Might be that's what I meant. As for your falootin' talk, I wouldn't know, bein' so long with the tribe and all." He shifted his chaw over to the right side of his mouth and continued working juice from it, like a cow with its cud.

The barkeep slipped a gray towel over his shoulder and said, "Squirly Ross, just because you ain't been in my bar for a few days don't mean you have to stand there and lie to us. Don't you forget that I've tossed you out of here for everything but relieving yourself on the floor, though I am sure that day's coming." He shook his head and shifted bottles on the counter behind him. "And don't think I ain't counted the drinks you've poured. Unless the Ojibwa or whatever you claim to have lived with paid you in cash for listening to your lies, your purse is most likely hanging a bit limp right now."

Squirly Ross turned with a smile and said, "I reckon you could use a swamper, Tom—"

The barkeep held up a meaty hand and said, "Nope, don't need one. Any spittoons need emptying, I can do it myself. Saves me from having to listen to more stories about your crippling rheumatism."

Squirly looked at the honey-color liquid in the nearly full bottle before him on the bar and licked his lips. He'd almost decided to raise his hands toward it, see what might happen, when the saloon door swung inward. Here was a fine distraction.

Squirly smiled wide. "Well, hello, young Mr. Grindle. Fancy meeting you here like this. Why, I was just about to tell the boys about that time I saved your father's filly from having to be put down. He ever tell you about that? Prize horseflesh, she was, as I recall him telling me. And him nearly in tears. Oh, not that he's a man given to womanly ways, not what I meant at all, Mr. Grindle. It's just that—"

"Tom," said Junior, weaving a bit. He licked his lips and leaned against the bar. "Why don't we set up Mr. Ross here in that table over there in the corner with that bottle and that glass? How would that suit you, Mr. Ross?"

Squirly straightened and licked his lips again. "Right down to the ground, Mr. Grindle. But I'm more than willing to stay right here and tell you all about my recent exploits with the Cherokee tribe."

Tom snorted and shook his head. Mort smiled into his nearly empty glass.

"Well, now, Mr. Ross, you may be willing, but I . . . well, I'm not willing to listen just now. It's not that I'm not uninterested, but I have a feeling that, just like the story of you saving my father's filly, I've heard it before. And what's more, I'm afraid I have to tell you that it's not true. Which I also think I told you before." Junior smiled and leaned on the bar top. "My father has had many prize fillies over the years. Won't handle one himself, though."

Chuckles circled through the three men and chased Squirly to his seat at the table in the corner.

"Why is that?"

Junior looked Mort up and down. "How's that?"

"I'm wondering why your father will not handle a filly. You just said—"

"Oh." Junior played with the shot of rye Tom had set before him.

Tom looked at Mort from under heavy brows, shook his head once. "Something to do with my mother, I reckon. Long time ago anyway." He knocked down the slug and poured another from the fresh bottle. Then nodded to Tom to set up the man next to him.

"I know you?"

The man shook his head. "I am new to your town. Perhaps you saw me a few nights ago. We did not converse much then—you were in your cups, as they say."

Junior looked at the character beside him. Most men around here were punchers in rough garb and sweat-stained hats. But not this gent. This one looked clean and smooth, somehow. Gambler, maybe. And that accent? Wasn't Mexican, that's for certain. Junior shook his head and sipped his whiskey.

"The Dancing M," said the man.

Junior looked at him, narrowed his eyes. "What about it?"

"I went out there just yesterday, looking for work. I assumed that since gathering time is coming . . ."

"Gathering is coming up quick." Junior looked at his glass.

"I am Mort, by the way. Mortimer Darturo." The men exchanged curt nods.

"To answer your unspoken question, Mr. Grindle,"

said Mort, "when I got to the ranch, his Mexican housemaid told me that the owner, Mr. MacMawe, had died.
And she said she did not need help." Darturo shrugged.
"She ran me off, eh?" He leaned toward Junior and
spoke in a lowered voice. "The interesting thing, though,
is that while I was talking to her, a young half-breed, by
the looks of him, came around the side of the house, his
head all bandaged up. He was tossing seed to the chickens." Mort tapped his temple with a slender finger. "But
he was not right, stumbling and falling over." He leaned
even closer. "From the look of him, he must have taken
a nasty knock on the head, eh?"

Junior straightened and set his glass on the bar. "You
mean Brandon?"

Darturo shrugged. "I never learned his name."

So, Junior thought, *Brandon is alive. Not good. Not
good at all.* What if he remembered seeing Junior from
that night? What if he had seen Junior's face? Could
that be possible? Junior felt a sudden, gut-tightening
urge to know. If Brandon was alive, well, that was one
thing. But there could be no way on God's green earth
that the big city fool could be alive. He was a dead man,
gut-shot as he'd been. Had to be dead. . . .

Junior regarded the silent stranger a moment, then
slid the bottle to the edge of the bar and lifted it by the
neck. "What say you grab your glass and we'll find us a
table to sit at? Could be we have some openings at the
Driving D for gathering time. No promises, but I'm what
you might call the foreman, so we'll see what we can do.
All right?"

He wove his way to a table a few yards off. Mort
leaned in toward the barkeep. "Before I dig in too much
deeper here, who is this royal pup anyway?"

Tom laughed. "That's a good name for him—he's Wilfred Grindle, Junior, son of Wilf Grindle. But folks call
him Junior." He paused, expecting the man would com-

prehend. Nothing doing. "Of the Driving D." He paused again. Still no response. "Biggest outfit around."

Mort winked, then smiled. "I know all about it. I just wanted to hear how important it is—from the lips of a local." He straightened and poked his brim back with a trigger finger as he watched Junior pour himself another drink. Under his breath he said, "It looks like I have found myself a new job."

Junior caught his eye. "You comin' over here or what, stranger?"

Mort smiled and crossed the room. He stood over the table and said, "Of course, now it all occurs to me, now I place you. You are Junior Grindle, son of Wilf Grindle, founder of the famous Driving D. I was headed out there in the morning to see if I could scare up some work."

"Well, I saved you the trouble, didn't I?" Junior nodded to the chair opposite him and splashed whiskey into Mort's glass. "So, Mr. Darturo. You say you've worked cattle. Funny, you don't look much like a cowhand."

Darturo stared awhile at Junior, then smiled. "It could be I did a poor job of explaining myself. It has been a couple of years since I've been following a herd. Time has a way of tricking a man. I took some time off the trail to try my luck at the tables." He gestured at the empty green-topped poker table to his left.

Junior nodded as if he'd been down the same path only yesterday.

"Let us cut to the chase, eh, Mr. Grindle?"

Junior looked up, watery eyed. "I ain't 'Mr. Grindle.' That's my father, damn it!" The young blond man slammed his shot glass on the tabletop. Drops of honey-colored whiskey flew upward. "I am Junior. Just plain ol' Junior and nothin' but. I'm beginning to wonder if I will ever have my own name."

Mort smiled, wet his lips with his own whiskey, and

leaned forward. "All right, then, Junior, I am betting you need more than another ranch hand." He watched the younger man, but Junior studied his glass as if it were a book. Mort continued. "I am betting you have a problem you need taken care of. Something you cannot possibly do on your own, it being of a sensitive nature." He leaned back. "Am I right?"

The saloon doors pushed open and three young men, spruced in clean shirts, kerchiefs, and fresh shaves, shoved into the saloon, laughing and each trying to get in front of the others to be first at the bar. One looked toward Junior and his smile gave way to a serious expression. He poked the other two, who also looked, nodding and becoming quiet as they stepped up to the bar.

"Think you know something, do you?" said Junior, not seeing the men.

"Come, now, Junior. You invited me over here, remember?"

The young man sighed. "Course I remember." He fiddled with his glass, turning it in circles between his fingertips. Then he leaned forward, hunching over the small round table. He waited for Mort to lean in too. "It's like this. Say there was a couple of fellas. Say they were half brothers who stood to inherit a certain ranch because their father just up and died."

Mort nodded once, no trace of his wry smile left on his face. His eyes pinned Junior's and held the boy still for a moment.

Junior licked his lips and looked back to his glass. "And there's this other fella ... oh ... about their age, who'd be the best one anywhere to own that ranch. This other fella's got money enough, but his father won't back his play. The old man wants it all done legallike. But that ain't likely, leastwise not with them two half brothers gumming up the works." Junior leaned back and poured another drink. "You savvy, Mort?"

Darturo nodded, eyes half-closed like a lizard's. He stared at the boy a moment, then leaned forward. "I understand perfectly. And what is more, Junior, I know who you're talking about. Like I said, I have been around." He leaned in and said in a low, hollow voice, "One thing that's unexplained. This young man, the son of the rich rancher, how can he be sure he will end up owning the dead man's ranch?"

Junior smiled and shook his head as if explaining something fundamental to a child. "Shoot, Mort, my father's got more money than God himself." Junior's smile dropped and the two men regarded each other for a moment. "Well, not that much, but—he wants something, he buys it. Problem is, he's on and on about making it all a legal affair." He leaned forward again, crowding the little table. The bottle slid a few inches, and Mort reached up and quietly moved it out of harm's way. Junior never noticed. His eyes narrowed and he warmed to his subject. "He's going to ruin everything. With thinking like that, we'll never get the Dancing M. He needs to let me do this my own way ..." A scowl hardened the young man's features. "Or he needs to get the hell out of my way ... for good! I'm through living under his thumb."

"Understood ... Mr. Grindle. For that is truly your name, is it not?" Mort stood, his chair squawking on the plank floor. He downed his shot and said, "You will be hearing from me."

Darturo crossed the room and as he passed the bar, one of the newly arrived cowhands, a tall fellow in a blue shirt, older by a couple of years than his companions, stared at him. Darturo stopped, his thumbs resting on his gun belt. They regarded each other for a moment; then Darturo ran his tongue over his teeth, his mouth fixed in a sneer. He smoothed his clipped mustache and walked out into the dark. The jangle of his spurs and the echo of his boots on the boardwalk could be heard for the half minute of silence that followed his departure, only broken by the sound of Junior's bottle neck clinking the rim of his glass as he poured himself another drink.

Tom slid beers to the three men and leaned in. "You boys got to see if you can yarn him out of here before he busts up the place again like the other night. I don't care if he does pay. It's nothing but a load of extra work for me."

One of the three, a large, round-faced fellow, nodded, said, "Okay, Tom," and turned to rest his elbows on the bar. He cleared his throat. "Mr., uh, I mean Junior. . . ."

The boy looked up, focused on the speaker, and said, "Chester, you ox, how're you tonight?"

"Fine, just fine." Chester walked closer, his hands on his hips. "Me and the boys, we're just about ready to head back to the Drivin' D. Wondered if you wanted to ride along."

Junior squinted and looked from the bartender to Chester, then the other two men. They all stood silent, watching him. "What is this?" He stood, flipping the table forward as he rose. The bottle, almost empty, rolled across the floor and the glasses both broke. "The bum's rush? No, no, no." He swung his head from side to side, the action dizzying him. "I have had it with people telling me what to do, when to do it. Had it up to here!" The thin wooden chair flew from his hand and clattered against the wall, knocking free the glass globe of a sconce. It shattered against the floor as Tom rounded the bar, headed for the door. "Keep him from breaking anything else. I'm getting the sheriff!"

All three Driving D men rushed the boy and pinned his arms down. Despite their size and strength and his drunken infirmity, Junior lashed out, striking at the faces and torsos of his suppressors with surprising vigor.

By the time Tom returned with Sheriff Tucker, the three men had shucked Junior's pistol and had him pinned to the floor. He'd gone limp and his head lolled, the booze now washing fully through his system.

"Okay, boys. If you don't mind, I'll ask you to transport him on over to the cells for the night. And tell Wilf he can come for him tomorrow. I'll not turn him loose before then. I, for one, have had enough of his foolishness. Wilf had better do something about him, and soon."

The men nodded and heaved the limp form of their boss's son up onto his feet, then eased the lolling drunk on out the door.

"Fight's gone out of him, I'd say." Squirly Ross wheezed out a ragged laugh as if he'd told a real ripper. "Boy ought to learn to pace himself if he ever hopes to make it to a ripe old age."

"And end up like you, I suppose, eh, Squirly?" The sheriff shook his head and turned back to the bartender. "Tom, when these boys are done at the jail, set 'em each up with a beer and a whiskey, on me. And tally up this mess. I'll be sure Wilf pays you tomorrow."

The bartender nodded and resumed sweeping up the shattered glass.

"Might be you want to ask about the stranger young Grindle's been jawin' with, Sheriff." Squirly sipped his glass and licked his lips.

Sheriff Tucker stopped in the doorway and looked down at the pudgy little wreck seated in the corner. "And I suppose he's the one you told me about, eh? The one who you claimed killed your old friend, what's-his-name the cowhand?"

Squirly fixed the sheriff with his bleary eyes. "That'd be the man, yes, indeed."

"When I want something from you, you'll be the first to know. But until then, Squirly Ross, keep your mouth shut. I'm the one wearin' the badge, in case you forgot."

The little drunk's eyes widened in mock surprise, and he raised his hands as if he were the victim of a holdup.

But he didn't say another word as he watched the sheriff leave.

Hours later, after the last Driving D hand had staggered out to his waiting horse, Squirly grunted to a standing position and weaved out the door himself, and into the dark of the alley.

Chapter 46

"So, you think the sheriff might be interested in talking with me, huh?"

The snagging purr of the voice, like rawhide dragged over rusted steel, crawled out of the dark of the alley, over Squirly's shoulder, and into his ear. He peed on his own foot and didn't realize it. "Who. . . .?" But he knew who it was. And for the first time in years, he wished he wasn't drunk.

"You . . . I thought you was gone." Squirly couldn't see more than a dark outline, but he knew it was Darturo. He had hoped that the man would just ignore him. That maybe word hadn't gotten around to him that he'd said all those things about him to the sheriff. Now he knew he was wrong. No matter who told, or if they told—this foreigner seemed to know a little bit of everybody's business. He wasn't sure how, but the man seemed to be everywhere.

"Yes, Mr. Ross. It's me." He advanced on the little man in buckskins. The only light in the alley came from the faint glow of an oil lamp across the street, beyond the mouth of the alley, and the glow of the quarter moon high above. Squirly remembered what he'd been up to and fidgeted to stuff his trousers back together. His heel clunked an empty bottle spinning back against a crate. Other than that noise, his own stuttering breaths, the town sounded utterly still to Squirly. The man backed him up to the far side wall of the saloon. He'd spent enough time back here, either as swamper for the Doubloon or urinating in the dust, that he knew he was still a dozen yards from the rear mouth of the alley. "What do you want of me?"

"Of you, Mr. Ross? Not much. Nothing of yours, in fact. Not yet anyway."

"Wh-what, then?" Squirly swallowed and wished he had a tall glass of cool water.

There was that loose chuckle again, like little coils of dry paper rattling together. "That friend of yours? You found him well, I presume?"

"I . . . I found him, if that's what you mean." A vision of Mitchell's picked-over corpse came to him, just enough of the face's flesh left to let Squirly know it was his old friend. A spark of anger flared in him. This was the man who had killed Mitchell, and they each knew that the other knew it. *And what's more, it was all my fault*, thought Squirly. *If I hadn't opened my mouth and let this killer pour booze into it, Mitchell would still be alive.* They'd be planning a way to buy the Dancing M with his poke, whooping it up in fine shape, talking about old times.

At the thought of all that money, of the future that might have been, Squirly grew even angrier at the damned killer. He pictured the thin foreigner standing there just in front of him in the dark of the alley, and something within him tensed. He guessed it was the spirit of Mitchell, fighting for revenge over the awful end he'd come to. Squirly crouched and lunged at Mortimer Darturo.

Though his heart was in the right place, his mind was nonetheless addled by drink and Darturo slammed the butt of his pistol hard against the back of the little man's head. The little drunk sprawled forward in the dirt, his face mashing hard against the hard-packed alley. "Where is the poke, as you call it? Where is your friend's great stash of money?"

Squirly's head was swimming, his ears buzzed, and a righteous hammering had begun at the base of his skull. He was used to it, hangovers being part of the job for him, but this was odd, as if the man had a knee to his neck. Squirly tried to rise, but couldn't. The man did indeed have him pinned. Then the man's questions seeped into his brain and he stopped squirming. Had he just asked Squirly where Mitchell's poke was? Did he really not have it? Had he not taken it when he killed Mitchell?

"What do you mean, you damn killer? You robbed Farthing when you killed him."

He heard a long sigh, as if the man had become too tired to discuss the matter.

"Alas, Mr. Ross, there was nothing more of value on the man when I last saw him than a half-empty sack of tobacco. Not even a good brand. Just something cowboys indulge in—cheap and of poor quality, like so much they spend their time and money on."

"What are you on about?" said Squirly, managing to get his face turned so that his cheek rested in the dirt. He still couldn't see the man, but he could hear him better. Sounded to him as if he were becoming increasingly disappointed in the way things were turning out.

"So that means if you don't have it, you must think I have it," said Squirly, raising his voice a notch or two in hopes someone might hear them.

"*Sh-sh-sh-shhhh* . . . Hush, now, little soak, or some-one will mistake you for a diseased alley cat and kill you."

Squirly stopped struggling and tasted grit as he licked his lips. "So," he said, in a lowered voice. "You think I have Mitchell's money?"

Another sigh, then, "That was my fondest desire. But I am beginning to think that we have both been had, eh? I think your friend, the old cowhand, Mitchell Farthing, was as destitute as you are. A fine pair of ranchers you would have made, without the means between you to buy even a single bull calf."

"I don't understand—he always had a wad of money saved. Always had a poke. . . ."

"Things change, my friend. I have no doubt that at one time, many years ago, your friend Mr. Farthing was a well-off man, at least by the low standards against which cowhands measure themselves. But look at you—I am equally as sure that at one time you had more to offer the world than a foul stench, a smile that shows no more promise than a mouth half-full of rotted teeth, and a lecherous desire for alcohol. But again, those days are long in the past. Then for a time, you and Mitchell had in common the fact that you were both useless."

"I . . . I ain't useless. I know where there's silver—that ledge of silver. I can take you there."

"*Shh-shhhh.*" Darturo pressed harder between the little man's shoulder blades. "I don't believe for a single minute that there ever was a ledge of silver, and cer-tainly that you could take me to one now."

"No?"

Darturo shook his head. "No, Mr. Ross. But you do have something else in common with your friend, Mitch-ell Farthing, and a good many other people in this crazy little town."

"What's that?"

"You all seem to want to get your hands on that dead man's ranch."

"Don't you?"

Darturo eased off his pressure on Squirly's back and shuffled backward a pace, but remained crouching beside the little man. "I thought that I did," said Darturo, seeming to consider the question for some time. "But now, now I am only regretting this detour. I think that tomorrow, I will finish what I promised to do, perhaps see if there is something else to be had, and then I will be on my way."

Squirly inched backward as Darturo spoke, hoping to keep the man chatting long enough to get up and run. He didn't know quite where he would go, but he figured that if he could slip by him, he might get out front to the main street and whoop it up enough that someone might take notice and save his hide from this killer.

"Where will you head?"

"So kind of you to ask, Mr. Ross. I believe I will head to Mexico. There, I will be able to relax for a time and live the life of a bandit king, eh?"

Squirly scooted his backside farther away from Darturo. "Sounds like a good plan. I wasn't so attached to Turnbull, I'd tag along."

Darturo chuckled. "While your company is . . . interesting to me, Mr. Ross, it is hardly such that I would wish to detain you from your previous engagements."

"I don't know what that means, really, since I ain't got no dance card filled up yet."

"No, but you have another thing in common with your good friend Mitchell Farthing."

"Oh?" Squirly eased himself up onto his knees, all the while keeping his eyes on the foreigner, who appeared to be lost in thought, still squatting beside where Squirly had lain moments before. "What might that be, then?" Squirly lunged to his feet and, abandoning his plan to skirt the foreigner and make for the front of the alley, bolted for the rear of the alley. He might race behind the buildings and rap on a few doors in the process, all the while shouting his head off.

He had barely gotten to his feet and staggered back a few lengths deeper into the alley when he realized he wasn't nearly as quick as he thought he might be. For the foreigner was there, looking down at him. He could see the man better now, dull moonlight reflecting off eyes that otherwise looked as black as the clothes he wore. The moonlight also glinted dully off the various silver conchos and other decorations adorning the man's black garb. The man crowded him, forced him backward amid a jumble of old crates and sparse, dry grasses.

"Yes, Mr. Ross, there is one other thing you have in common with your dear old friend Mitchell Farthing." Darturo's breath smelled to Squirly like food gone fly-blown and rank on a hot summer afternoon when nothing at all moves, when rocks sizzle if you look at them, when lizards are the only things enjoying the vicious heat. Squirly tried to respond, but the words "What's that?" came out as a soft whimper.

The man smiled down at him and said, "You are both dead men."

Sharp lancing pains radiated upward from somewhere down low in the drunkard's guts. He felt a seeping wetness, as if he'd peed himself worse than ever. Then he heard a wet slapping sound, and by the time Squirly Ross thought to scream, hot, thick liquid filled his gorge and all he could manage was a gurgling sound that soon strangled in his throat in a cough. The man before him stared down at him, still smiling, the last of the moon's glow reflected in those black eyes, slowly giving way to full dark of the shadowed alley.

Darturo wiped off the thin-bladed knife on the grimy buckskinned leg flopped at his feet. He pulled in a long, slow draft of night air. "Pity the saloon is closed," Darturo said in a quiet voice as he wandered out of the alley and into the silent, empty little main street of Turnbull. "A nice glass of milk with perhaps a splash of whiskey would be soothing right now. Ah well. Tomorrow is another day."

Chapter 47

"What's wrong, Chester?"

The broad-shouldered ranch hand, though he towered over his employer, curled the brim of his boss of the plains. "Oh well, sir . . . nothing's wrong with the ranch, Mr. Grindle." He hurried his words.

Wilf smiled and said, "Something's on your mind, Chester." It never failed to impress him, even after all these years, how men twice his size would squirm before him, and only because he owned land and they didn't. Odd, but he had to admit he still liked the feeling. A lot. He stepped to the side and waved an arm inside the house. "Just having breakfast. How 'bout a cup of coffee?"

Chester's eyebrows rose, and then he looked down again. "I better not, Mr. Grindle. You see, me and the boys, well, we drew straws and I . . ."

"Got the short one. Okay, out with it." Wilf, still smiling, eyed the man more closely now. "It's Junior, isn't it?"

"Yes, sir. He's . . . in jail."

Wilf stared for a moment, then took a deep breath and let it out slowly. "Drunk?"

Chester just nodded. "Me and a few of the boys went into town last night for a drink or two." The big man warmed to the telling and stopped fidgeting with his hat brim and looked at his boss. "But he'd been there awhile before us, it looked. So we said we'd call it an early night, tried to get him to come on back with us, but he wasn't having none of it. He commenced to bust up the place."

"Again?" Wilf felt his face redden. "Then what, Chester?"

Chester sighed and said, "Then the sheriff came in, looked fairly put out, if I read him right." Chester licked his lips. "Marched right over to Junior, give him a quick tongue-lashin', though I don't think Junior took in much of it. Anyhow, he had us muckle onto him, bring him to the jail." The cowhand reddened.

"So Junior spent the night there?"

Chester nodded. "Yes, sir, but we tried—"

Wilf clapped the man on the arm. "I know, Chester, and I appreciate it. But you shouldn't have had to." The old rancher crossed his arms and shook his head. "Might be a night in a cell will do the boy some good."

"Yes, sir, I'm sure it will." Chester looked up again, eyes wide. "What I mean is that Sheriff Tucker told us to tell you he'll hold Junior there until you pick him up this mornin'." Chester leaned in toward his employer and lowered his voice, as if they were in a crowd, "Said he wanted to talk with you."

Wilf sighed. "All right, Chester. Appreciate it."

The big man nodded once, plopped his big hat back on his head, but remained facing his boss.

"Something else you'd like to say, Chester?"

"Yes, sir. Well, no, sir, but . . . what I mean is there is something else."

"Out with it, then." Wilf almost smiled again.

"Well, me and the boys noticed this fella Junior, your son, was talking to at the Doubloon."

"No crime in a conversation, is there, Chester?"

"Well, no, sir. But this one, well, F.J., you know, the fella who hired on last month?"

Wilf nodded.

"Well, it come to him later on that he recognized this fella Junior was jawing with over at that table in the corner. Then the fella up and left and later F.J. told us he'd seen him before. Didn't say how he knew him, just that he'd crossed paths with him a few years back. Said he was a bad, bad seed. Felt sure the man was wanted somewhere for at least a couple of killings."

Wilf didn't say anything, just watched Chester's face. Finally, in a small voice, the cowhand said, "We thought you might want to know."

Wilf nodded. "Appreciate it."

Chester made it halfway down the path to the front gate before Wilf spoke again. "Chester."

The big man spun, eyes wide, and hands reaching for his hat.

"Tell the boys I said thanks. And ask 'em to keep it to themselves, not that it matters all that much."

"Yes, sir, count on it." Chester headed for the gate.

"Oh, and, Chester, one more thing. . . . I might as well kill two birds at once and take the long way into town through the east pastures, see how the boys are making out. See that the barouche is rigged and ready up here for me."

"Yes, sir. I will surely do that." Chester spun again and jogged his big bulky frame to the bunkhouse.

Wilf stood watching him go, but not seeing him. In his mind he was already deep into what he knew would be a one-sided conversation with a hungover son who was fast turning out to be the biggest disappointment of his life.

Chapter 48

"And just who are you to make such a request?" The young deputy slid his scuffed brown boots off the bare desk and rose to full height.

"Easy now, pup. Easy." Mort Darturo worked his slim hands in a patting motion. "There is no reason to get yourself worked up. My boss sent me to get Junior Grindle out of the jail. He is needed back at the ranch. I was told to tell the sheriff he appreciates what he did and that he would be in town later to talk with him."

"Who's your boss?"

"Who else? Wilf Grindle."

"You work for the Driving D?" The deputy looked the well-dressed man up and down. "You don't look much like a cowhand."

Darturo nodded. "I am new to his employ."

The deputy chewed the inside of his lip. Finally, he stood and said, "I reckon if it's good enough for Mr. Grindle, it's good for this chicken too." He smiled and slid the steel ring off a hook under the desk. The keys jangled as he worked the latches on the outer door and the cell in the back.

"Mr. Grindle, time to wake up. Your father's man is here for you."

The young man lay on his side, his back to the cell door. He didn't move. The deputy coughed once. Nothing. So Deputy Sweazy let out his held breath and clanged the door hard. He hated to do it, but something had to happen, even if it was Junior Grindle, no older than himself but a heap richer. He secretly wanted to dump a pail of cold water on the young spoiled drunk, but he knew that was no way to get ahead in law enforcement, even if it was only Turnbull that he was working in. He'd need connections to wealthy and powerful people if he was ever going to work the bigger towns like Dodge or Phoenix. Still, the reaction he'd get from the drunk would be worth it. Sweazy smiled.

The clashing ring of the steel cell door whipped the sleeping man upright. "What! What's wrong?"

Deputy Sweazy really wanted to laugh, but didn't dare. He cleared his throat. "Mr. Grindle, your father sent a man for you. Said they need you at the Driving D."

Junior held his surprised pose for a few moments more, then swung his legs over the side of the cot and sat there, his head resting in his hands. He said nothing for a full minute.

"Mr. Grindle . . ."

"Yeah, yeah, yeah. Enough already. I'm leaving."

Sweazy let the cell door open hard. It clanged and he smiled as he headed back toward the front of the jail.

"Hey," said Junior's voice from behind him, back in the cell.

The deputy stopped but didn't turn around.

"Who came for me? Was it Mica?"

"Who?"

"Big black man."

"No. He said he's one of your father's men. Probably waiting for you."

Grindle pushed to his feet and headed out of the cell. He glanced back, saw his hat, crown down, on the floor, went back, and snatched it up.

By the time he made it to the office, the deputy was pouring two gray tin cups of coffee. He handed one to Junior.

"Call me Junior," he said, rubbing his eyes. "My damned old man's 'Mr. Grindle.' Where's the Driving D man?"

"Dunno. I got back out here and he was gone."

Junior went over to the door, leaned out, and looked up and down the street, but saw no one.

"What'd he look like?"

"Thin, not overly tall. Dark hair, had an accent too, sort of Mexican, but not really, if you know what I mean. Had a low, black hat. Real neat clothes, now that I think on it. More like a dandy than a cowhand."

At the mention of the man's hat and clothes, Junior raised his eyebrows, looking over the cup's rim at the young deputy for the first time. "Black hat, you say? And nice clothes?"

Sweazy nodded, sipped his own coffee. "Yep."

Junior stood there a moment, staring at the plaster wall behind the sheriff's desk. "Darturo," he muttered. Then his eyes widened and he said, "Oh Lord. . . ."

"Here's your gun and belt, Mr. Grin—uh."

Junior grabbed them from him and strapped on the belt as he raced for the door.

Sweazy followed, shouting after him, "Sheriff said your horse is with Silver Haskell at the livery. . . ."

Chapter 49

Wilf heard the first shot after he felt it. His right arm jerked as blood sprayed outward. Unimagined pain raced through the dangling limb and burst into his chest. He gritted his teeth and fought the fogging, fuzzy feeling that threatened him, and watched red-black blood flower into his puckered blue shirt at the shoulder. He still gripped the reins hard with his good left hand and as he fought to stay conscious watched the single horse fidget in the traces. Wilf shook his head and blinked to try to keep his vision focused. Was it an accident, a stray shot? Had to be—who'd want to kill him? He knew he should climb down, hide behind the buggy and wait to see if the shooter intended to come closer. But he wasn't thinking right. The best he could muster was to jerk hard on the reins in his left hand and turn the barouche around, head back to the ranch.

In his raw pain and confusion, he was pleased to note that earlier he'd taken off his dress coat and folded it on the seat; otherwise it too would have been ruined. As the reality of the situation slapped him, he realized the folly of such thinking. *So much for seeing Miss Gleason today*, he thought. *And if the shooter intends to kill me, I'm to be shot in the back and it won't matter anyway. But who?* he wondered as he snapped the leather reins hard on the back of the confused horse.

Wilf crouched low and waited for another bullet to tear into the black canopy he'd had raised to ward off the sun as he drove to town. He slipped the looped reins over his good arm and worked one-handed at the knotted kerchief about his neck, then stuffed the wadded silk under his shirt, gritting his teeth at the hot, slicking pain. There was little more he could do, but he knew if he didn't make it back to the ranch soon he'd bleed out. Unless he was shot again. He leaned his head out the side of the rumbling carriage, but no one thundered close by on horseback. No one followed.

Who would do this? And why? It surely must have something to do with the Dancing M and the tangled mess it was becoming with that damnable Mexican woman. But to shoot him? He knew Esperanza was angry with him, as was Rory's boy, Brandon, and even his own daughter, Callie, but he expected no less. After all, she was a woman, weak with emotion when it came to her friends.

Who else, then? Mica? No, they might have exchanged harsh words, harsher than Wilf had ever intended them to be, but never in a hundred lifetimes would Mica shoot him; of that Wilf was certain. Who, then? One of the ranch hands taking potshots at coyotes or buzzards? His head ached with the effort of thinking.

But a new face flashed in his mind. Perhaps it was the boy, Brandon. Rory's bastard son. He'd never liked the youth, and since Rory's death the boy had taken a definite turn for the worse—drinking in public and at all hours, making a nuisance of himself in town. Junior had complained to him about the boy on more than one occasion, even though he had been playmates with the half-breed.

It could well be the boy, he thought, as pain bloomed anew through his arm and across his chest with each jarring slam over a rock or through a rut. Why was life dealing him and his family such dire blows lately? Hadn't they suffered enough over the years? His dear Carla, gone nearly twenty years now. Damn that filly that threw her. He'd had to bury his wife and shoot her prize horse. But he thanked God every day Carla had seen fit to leave him with two beautiful children, troublesome though the boy could be. . . .

And at that moment a sudden thought came to him—Junior. His own boy. The person he hoped to pass everything to. No, the thought that Junior would want to kill him was ridiculous. But then everything Callie had said about Junior, about how Wilf rode him too hard, it all made sudden sense. And the boy had been nearly unrecognizable to him these past few months, until now he seemed almost like a stranger to him, coming home less frequently, long enough these past few weeks only for clean clothes and food—and hardly at all these past two days. As one thought led to another, so Junior's last words to him echoed in his fevered head: *"I will kill you. . . ."*

A fresh rush of nausea rose from Wilf's boots, and his teeth chattered. He was close to passing out, he knew, but he had to get back to the ranch. With the last of his waning strength, he snapped the reins hard against the poor lathered horse's back and managed to shout, "Heeyaa!" once. Then he pitched off the seat and to his knees on the floor of the barouche, the reins slipping from his hand. His breakfast of ham and eggs and bread and coffee rose in his gorge, then left him, spattering the side of the black carriage. His last thought before losing consciousness was of his boy, Junior, and of how it very well could have been his own son who had shot him. But why?

Wilf never felt the second shot.

Chapter 50

Junior reined up at the fork in the road from town, looked to his right, to the west branch that led to the Dancing M, and for a moment he held the stamping horse, his thoughts on the people he'd wronged there. But he shook his head and knew that right now it was his father who needed his help. He touched heels to the horse's flanks and shouted, "Haaa!"

He rode hard the last few miles, his horse lathered and breathing like a demon as they barreled into the dooryard outside the bunkhouse. Chester, Chaz, Dilly, and a few other men filed out.

"Junior," said the big man, eyeing the overworked horse as he grabbed the reins. "Your father left here early to fetch you back from jail."

"I know, Chester, but which way did he go?" Junior slipped down off the horse, shucked his hat, and scanned the rolling terrain to the east.

"Well, he said he was going to take the east road.... Didn't you see him?"

"East road? No, no, he wasn't in town when I left. And he wasn't on the road back home. Must still be on the east road."

"Why wasn't he in town, Junior?"

Junior continued to scan the horizon, but said nothing.

Chester eyed the boy hard. "As I say, he went out the east way to check on the boys while he was headed to town. To get you out of jail."

Junior returned the look and said, "Look, Chester. I don't give a hang about your problems with me right now. There's something more important than all that. I have to find my father. I think he might be in danger. Because of something I did. I think."

"Boy, you're not making sense, but if I find that something's happened to your father because you did something stupid, you can rest assured there will be hell to pay."

"Yeah," said Chaz. "We've all had it up to here with your crazy ways."

Junior nodded as if he were agreeing with a child. "I understand all that. But right now I need to find my father." Even as he said it he snatched the reins from Chester and mounted up.

"Hey, Junior! No more worries on that score. Here comes your father's buggy now." They all looked to where Dilly, the cook, pointed, and there was the barouche, but it was led by a man a-horseback, not wasting any time.

"What's this?" Chester strode forward to intercept them, waving his big arms.

Junior climbed down from his horse and stiffened. Wilf was nowhere in sight. He ran ahead, past Chester, and jumped up on the side of the dusty black barouche.

There lay his father, slumped on his side on the red leather seat. Junior jumped over the low door and lifted his father to him, touching the gray face with the flat of his hand, patting. "Papa, Papa, come on, it's me, Junior. Papa?"

He turned to the handful of cowboys gathered and watching. "You fools! Don't stand there. Someone get the doctor! Where's Mica? He should be here. Mica!" He shouted the man's name, but his shouts were ridden down by those of Picket Jim, the man who'd brought the buggy in.

"Too late for that, boy. He's dead." The tall, mustachioed cowboy had been with the Driving D for most of Junior's youth, knew Wilf well, and by the grim set of his mouth, the resigned droop of his eyes, all the other hands knew that it must be true. Their boss man, Wilf, was dead.

"Shot?" said Chester in a low voice.

Picket Jim nodded. "Twice, from the looks. Don't know by who."

"No!" They all watched the boy, angry with him but not sure why. Then Junior vaulted out of the buggy and gripped the near wheel, looking back at all of them, a wild, hard look in his eyes. He grabbed at Chester's shirtfront. "Where's Mica? Where's Callie? Don't any of you know where they are?"

"Take it easy, Junior," said Chester, gripping the boy's wrists. "They both went off to the Dancing M. Mica left early. Callie went over just a short time ago."

"The brothers are in trouble, don't you see?" said Junior, wrenching himself free of the big man's grip. "It's them he's after now. And now Callie and Mica are there. Oh God . . . I have to go. . . ." Junior bolted for his horse, the men after him.

"Leave him be," shouted Chester. "We'll get Mr. Grindle in the house, then get to the Dancing M. Chaz, get on that little bay, the spirited one, and ride for the sheriff. Tell him what's happened, tell him Junior knows something about who did it, but that he's gone to the Dancing M. Tell the sheriff we'll meet him there."

The little man nodded, taking it all in.

"Now go!" shouted Chester, pushing him toward the stable.

Chaz had made it but a few miles from the Driving D when he saw a cloud of dust up ahead, from the direction of town, boiling closer to him, the midday sun causing him to squint, his horse to shudder and blow. Still, he could tell she didn't want to stop. As Chester said, this was a spirited little filly.

The dust cloud drew closer and Chaz knew it was a rider. He slowed the horse to a lope, hesitant to meet the rider, half wondering if it might be the man who shot Mr. Grindle. From what he could gather, it hadn't been the boy who shot his own father, but maybe that man from the bar last night.

Relief like a cool drink on a hot day washed over Chaz as he recognized the two riders as Sheriff Tucker and his deputy, Sweazy. He reined up and flagged the men to a standstill, but the lawmen didn't look pleased with the interruption.

"Sheriff, I was sent for you—"

"Have you seen Junior Grindle? And Wilf? I aim to give them a piece of my mind. Had enough of people thinking that money gives them the right to skirt the law. Not in my—"

"Sheriff, listen to me! Mr. Grindle is dead, shot. And Junior took off to the Dancing M. I was coming to get you."

The sheriff's face slackened. "Wilf ... dead? Shot? Not by Junior ..."

"We don't think so, but Junior said something about that stranger from the bar last night. You know the one, Sheriff. . . ."

The lawman nodded. "That foreign one," he snapped, his distaste evident in the sneer on his face. "So that's what Squirly was on about. And Junior too. Deputy Sweazy here tried to tell me."

"Junior also said something about how . . . the brothers are in trouble? And now Callie and Mica. . . ."

The sheriff's gaze sharpened. "What? Where are they at? Where's Callie?"

"At the Dancing M. Chester and the boys are headed there now."

Sheriff Tucker nudged his horse into a gallop and shouted, "Good! We'll meet up with them, form a posse. I don't understand what's going on, but I don't like it one bit. I am not riding into trouble without better odds. Let's go, Sweazy!"

The deputy nodded and sank spur, riding just behind the sheriff. Chaz fell in line behind the deputy. A short time later, they met up with five Driving D ranch hands down the lane toward the Dancing M.

As they rode, Sheriff Tucker had a good bit of time to mull over just what it was he might be facing. First off, there was that young Grindle whelp. He gritted his teeth at the thought of that boy, whom he'd known his entire life, drinking up the town and expecting no consequences of his actions. Then there was that big dude from the East, MacMawe's oldest boy. The man, Middleton he called himself now, was Rory's son, no doubt about that—one glance proved it. He looked like a younger version of Rory, had the same hair, same big build, same way of walking. And yet he was as city as any you'd find in Frisco or Chicago.

And then there was that Italian rascal, Darturo. He'd found out the man's name after too much pestering and snooping. Didn't like to do that normally, but the man wasn't forthcoming with information and it was his job, after all, to make sure anybody who came to his town was not an unsavory. This one was too much of a bad thing. Something about him that the sheriff didn't trust in the least. And try as he might, send as many telegrams as he liked, he couldn't turn up paper on him. He could have sworn there was a notice on him in the stack, but he'd be jiggered if he could find it.

Even Sweazy, his deputy, who had a nose for such things and a solid memory too, swore he'd seen him in the stack, but when it came time, nothing.

The most galling knowledge of all to Sheriff Tucker was the fact that Esperanza and Callie and Mica had kept a shooting from him. Did they honestly think that someone would get shot in these parts and he'd not find out about it? He'd ridden out there to the Dancing M the morning after the Driving D boys told him about the shooting. They'd heard it from Wilf, they said. But when he rode out there, Esperanza hadn't let him in. He'd asked to see Brandon, but she said he was gone, didn't know when he'd be back.

Callie stood right there lying to him too. Little girl he'd known all her life, same as Junior. Friends with her daddy and all. Got that stubborn streak from Wilf, he'd guess. And then he was winded by the sudden thought of his old rich, cranky friend—and friendly rival for Miss Gleason's affections—gone, shot by someone.

As they thundered down the road, gaining ground on the Dancing M ranch house, Tucker cursed himself for not investigating that shooting more seriously. He'd come to the conclusion that something had happened between Brandon and Middleton. But it wasn't like him to just take someone's word for it. But that's exactly what he'd done—take Callie and Esperanza's word for it that Brandon and that Middleton fellow were both alive, if not unhurt. He figured that as long as they knew that he was aware of the incident, that would be enough, and that they could solve their own problems. But now that Wilf had been shot, he knew he'd been a fool to be so lax about following up.

And as much as he hated to admit it, he'd been a double-damned fool for not paying attention to Squirly Ross, who'd warned him just the night before about that rogue, Darturo. Tucker heeled his horse harder as the little ranch house came into sight, and vowed never to take anything his old gut told him, or even what a little drunk like Squirly Ross told him, for granted ever again. If it proved the little drunk was right, he'd owe him a big apology. And a drink . . . or three.

Chapter 51

"I honestly don't understand this savage behavior. It's as if everyone out here is afflicted with a sort of . . . madness, an anger. . . ."

An hour before Junior took off for the Dancing M, Callie had ridden there herself. And now as she rode, Brian's words echoed in Callie's thoughts. She and the horse were both well rested for the first time since the attack days before. As the words echoed in her head, she recalled staring at the face of Brian J. Middleton, the man who'd said them, and for an instant anger much as he described flared up in her. But it was an anger with herself for allowing feelings for this citified oaf to veil her judgment. And then that anger passed and she saw him for what he was—a stranger here in more ways than mere presence. He might have been born here, but that was a long time ago. He was raised in a different place, a different world as removed from this one as if she were called to visit a city back East.

She worried this thought over and over, like a frayed end of rope, as Butter carried her, at a steady lope, toward the Dancing M.

The last half mile before she thundered into the dooryard of the Dancing M had been the hardest to bear these past few days. She didn't know what she would find, but she knew what propelled her forward, faster with each day. Not just her feelings for Esperanza and Brandon, people who were like family to her, but concern for Brian too.

Mixed with this was her worry that it could have been her own brother who had attacked the brothers. But as eager as she knew Junior was to please their father, would that really be enough to drive him to kill?

As she thundered into the dooryard of the Dancing M, Callie saw that strange horse tied out front. It was a fine-looking animal, a buckskin, and wore a gleaming black leather rig, adorned with modest but expensive decoration and accoutrements. Something unknown niggled at her, but she ignored it. It was not uncommon for even the remote ranches to have visitors on occasion. But then again, what if it were an unwanted person? Someone the sheriff sent, perhaps? He had been steamed and not a little embarrassed when they sent him packing the day before. She didn't think it would take him long to figure out a way to get into the house and find out just who had been shot and why. Neither of the boys would be in much of a situation to help Espy should she need it.

Callie cursed herself for being so caught up in her own thoughts that she didn't see potential danger until she was in it. *Always the way with me,* she thought. *Can't see the forest for the trees, Mica would say*. Instead of reining up to the house as she usually did, she rode straight for the barn, through one of the big, open double doors. She swung down and looped the reins through a ring mounted on the wall.

That sound—it was Espy's chickens, but these were not the long, drawn-out clucks of a hen on the nest, but the short, clipped sounds of agitated hens unaccustomed to missing their morning feed of cracked corn. Espy never neglected her brood—something must be wrong. Other than the chickens, there were no sounds, no songs in Spanish floating on the scents of fresh tortillas from the kitchen, no odd mumbling from Brandon as he walked about the place, scuffing from one task to another, not finishing much of anything.

She looked again at the other stalls. They were empty save for one. There was Mica's horse, the big gray he called "Horse." She half smiled. That was a good sign. Mica surely would see to it that no harm came to Espy or the wounded brothers. She cursed herself again. It was later in the day than she meant to get there. She had overslept, and woke with Mica's old saw ringing in her ears, "You wouldn't have slept if you didn't need to."

"Sleep or no," she whispered, "I'm here now." And reached for her rifle on Butter's saddle. But the boot was empty. She had forgotten it back at the Driving D stable. "You fool!" she cursed herself in a harsh whisper.

"Come on, little girl! We are having a grand old time in here. I insist you join us."

The man's voice, shouted from the house, froze her. Who was that? Callie swallowed hard, her throat dry and her mind a blank. What should she do? None of this made sense. But something was definitely wrong.

Callie stepped through the big barn door and walked with care toward the little quiet house. Smoke crawled slowly up and out the chimney. A gallinipper buzzed and rattled in a thicket of mesquite a few yards away, the buff-and-white hens scratched closer to their night pen, eyeing her, still complaining loud enough for Callie to look toward them. As she did she heard Mica's familiar voice. "Get out of here, Callie! Go for help! Go—"

His pleas were cut off by a loud thudding sound and a drawn-out groan.

"Mica!" she yelled, and ran toward the house, hearing but not heeding his warning. She took the two steps into the kitchen as one quick stride and just inside the open door stopped short. Sprawled on the floor at her feet lay Mica, an upturned chair kicked to one side, dark blood pooling under his head.

Espy snatched towels and half-dried shirts from behind the stove, anything to stanch the flow of Mica's blood. He moaned softly as she tended him. Espy made no sound, but Callie saw sparks of hate dancing in the little woman's eyes at the smirking man standing just behind them, half in the shadow of the rear of the room.

"Who are you? What have you done?" Callie spat the words, no fear showing on her stern, tight face. She dropped to her knees beside the groaning man and stole a quick glance toward the trundle bed where Brian lay, white-faced and unconscious . . . or worse.

The sound of the hammer clicking back into the deadliest position of all seemed to echo outward from the shadows. Callie and Espy looked up at the man, who was shaking his head and clucking his tongue as if he were disappointed with what he saw. "You should back away from him, little miss. He already has one wet nurse."

Callie and Espy exchanged glances. The older woman nodded once in assurance, and went back to tending Mica. Callie stood, her jaw thrust outward, raw hate narrowing her eyes.

"As for who I am, why, I suppose there is no harm now in telling you. I am Mortimer Darturo, at your service, little miss." The man offered a quick bow, then said, "But not really at your service. That is merely something one says in such social situations."

"What do you want here? You don't belong here." Callie stood firm, tried to control her breathing. Her hands formed hard fists at her sides.

"Now, is someone going to tell me who this gut-shot fellow is?" Darturo nodded once at Brian Middleton's still form.

Callie held her breath until she saw Brian's chest rise and fall beneath the thin quilt covering him.

"He is nearly done in, eh? In fact, I would say he is knocking hard on death's front door. I would guess they'll let him in soon enough. No need to waste lead on a foregone conclusion."

Callie's gut tightened. Minutes ago she was sure everything in their lives would somehow turn around, that it was going to work out for the best. But now a stranger she'd never seen or heard of held them all at gunpoint and Mica's face was distorted with lumps and one eye had puffed shut. What was going on here?

A scuffing noise outside drew their gaze to the doorway. Brandon weaved into view and peered into the dark of the cabin, the bandage on his head smudged and unraveling. Several feet of it dragged behind him, though he seemed not to notice.

"I had forgotten about the boy—he looks 'tetched in the bean,' as an old miner I once knew would put it. There is no denial from any of you, so I guess he must be crazy, eh?" Darturo stared at the oblivious boy, smiling and on the verge of a laugh. "I will deal with him in a moment.

"Now, as touching as this family scene is, it is not feeding the baby, is it? Eh?" Darturo looked around the room at the faces staring back at him. "All of you make my plans more complicated than I expected to find here." He paced back and forth behind them, wagging his gleaming pistol in emphasis. "But, then again, when we are faced with the unexpected, well, that is often where the sweetness of life comes from, eh?" He looked at each of them in turn. No one said anything.

"You people." He smiled. "You need to relax. Understand that very little in life works out as we hope it might. I came to your dusty little turnip of a town in the hope of finding an angle for myself, some way to take something for Darturo, eh?

"But the drunken rich boy I think will not be worth much when he is held upside down and shaken out. That is too bad, as I have had much luck in the past with putting people in painful situations and forcing them to buy their way out of them. It's not a bad thing, you see? They end up happy and so do I. And I can always return to them later, as if they were a bank, should I need more money down the road. It makes good sense."

He leaned down and peered at Espy. "Are you listening to me, you mother hen?" He brushed a loose length of hair from her forehead with the barrel of his pistol. She jerked away from him, sneering but saying nothing. "Your look, it is angry, eh? How much angrier could you be with me if I were to put a bullet in your man's brain, eh?" He poked the snout of the barrel into the wound on Mica's head. The man's groans hitched in his throat.

Callie bent to help Mica. "Stop it! What do you want? You want money? Is that what this show of yours is about?"

Without warning, Darturo pounced like a barn cat on a mouse and grabbed Callie's wrist, slamming her backward into a chair. "You will sit there, little miss, until we are ready to leave." The entire time a sort of smile stayed on his face, his lips pulled tight against his teeth.

"Why are you doing this?" croaked a voice from the other end of the room.

Mort turned to him. "Oh, so you are still among us, eh? Allow me to explain, as being an Easterner, you would not understand the ways of the West. . . .

"When I left Denver, it became all about the land, the land, the land, the land. It was all I could think about. I heard of an opportunity there that I thought might make me a wealthy man, an important man. I thought to obtain a ranch where I could live out my days in peace, get fat, settle down with some women, that sort of thing. But this is not turning out to be the case. For that, I blame that fat, bigmouthed lawyer in Denver. He talked this place up, but this is not very pretty land, is it? It is hot and dry here. I see few trees that can proudly wear the name." He thrust his bottom lip outward and shook his head as if he were lamenting the passing of a friend.

"But this is the way of things. I am no richer than when I arrived in Turnbull, and then again, I am no poorer." He shrugged. "I took the chance on seeing it through, and now it is time to cut my losses and get the hell out of here, eh? But I'm just going to have to slow you all down so you are not tempted to follow after me. Now, who is the first loss to be cut?"

Then, as quickly as it began, his laughing ceased and he looked at them all in a sweep of the room. "The only way to fix a problem is to get rid of the things that cause it. At least that's the only way I know of. In this case it was the rich old man and the two half brothers. That's what we talked about in the bar the other night."

"Who's this 'we'?" said Mica, who had pushed himself up so that he leaned against Esperanza. "You got a mouse in your pocket?"

Darturo's eyebrows rose. "I do not know what that means, but it was a business arrangement between myself and . . . Aha! No, not a mouse." He wagged a finger at Mica, and one side of his mouth rose in a smile. "But a young man. Someone I think you all know very well. . . ." He watched their faces and nodded as the recognition hit them. "Yes, yes, you see, you see. . . . Now I wait here so we can talk about what I get out of all this. For I am owed something."

Another noise from outdoors drew Darturo's attention. Brandon tottered into view and pointed at Darturo. "Out of my mother's house now, or I will come in after you." It seemed as if just saying the words drained him of strength.

Darturo sighed. "You again, you addled whelp." He sighed. "Pardon me, good people. I will stop the madman from interrupting our proceedings and then we can get back to the matters at hand." He hoisted his pistol and walked to the door, eyeing the four figures in the room as he walked, the gun outstretched before him. He raised it as Brandon, wobbling in the yard, assumed the stance of a drunken pugilist, both fists raised in the air before his chalky, wobbling face.

"No, you don't!" Callie crouched low and whipped her chair at him, catching the small Italian in the thigh. The man trained the pistol on her, his eternal smile replaced with the sneer of a cornered wolverine.

"Callie! Get down!"

The startled girl turned and dropped to the floor just in time as the boom of a shotgun filled the small room. Everyone winced and Darturo slammed against a shattered wall of shelves, half of the contents now ruptured, debris filling the air. The stricken man groaned and staggered to the doorway. Impossibly, he remained upright, leaning against the doorframe. Smoke and the stink of burned powder filled the room. He thrust upward once more with his pistol and squeezed off a shot out the door.

"No, not my brother!" Mere seconds after the first shotgun blast, another followed it. Darturo's body whipped out the door as if yanked, pitching headfirst down the steps. He rolled onto his back in the packed dirt of the yard, his horse stamping and thrashing, but held fast to the hitching rail. Brandon too was flopped on his back beside the dead Darturo, the youth's soiled white shirt flowering with blood. They all stumbled outside. Brian dropped the shotgun and held his gut with one hand as he staggered down the steps. He dropped to his knees beside Esperanza in the dirt at Brandon's side.

Brandon's lids fluttered open and he swallowed, looking with new clarity up into the face of Brian. "Oh, so you are my brother." He smiled, one hand held tight between Brian's massive white hands, the other squeezed tight in Esperanza's hands. And then Brandon's last breath left him.

Esperanza pushed away the last of his ragged cap of

bandage, smoothed the boy's coarse red hair. "So like his father. So very like his father." A single tear slid down her nose. "A hard life . . . but he is now at peace."

The chickens slowly approached, their wary clucks rising into the stagnant midday heat.

Callie and Esperanza carried Brandon inside and laid him on his father's bed by the fireplace. Esperanza silently arranged his hands on his chest, pulled a blanket up to his chin as if he had taken ill and needed warmth.

Brian stood at the table, leaning hard against a chair back. Callie checked his wound, her hands trembling from the madness that seemed to have dropped on them all.

"Where did you get the shotgun, Brian?" she said in a whisper, as much to fill the awful silence as any need to know about the gun.

He managed a weak smile and looked over at his nurse. "Esperanza suspected trouble was coming for days now. I don't know how, but she knew. She taught me how to use it, though we never shot with it—I think she was afraid it would open up her fine stitching."

"Pardon me," said a weak, deep voice, little more than a whisper. It was Mica, propped up on sodden blankets in front of the cook stove. "But I think you'll find those whipstitches are mine—pure cowboy sewing job there." He grunted and leaned back again, gray-faced.

"Please . . . stop talking." Esperanza focused on her young son's face.

No one said anything else for several minutes. Soon the familiar sound of rapid hoofbeats drew closer. Callie ran to the door. "Junior!"

Junior Grindle dismounted, drew his Remington, and stared down at the body of Darturo. Callie had to tug on his arm to get him to speak. Finally he looked up as if seeing her for the first time. "Who shot him? I came here to kill him, but someone beat me to it. He's a bad man, the worst kind." He turned to face the people on the step. "I didn't know. Callie, you have to believe me. I didn't know. I do now, but then, I was drunk, a fool! You have to believe that, Callie."

She hugged him tight. "Junior, whatever it is, it's okay now. You're among friends."

Junior shook his head. "No, no, it isn't, sis."

She pulled away and looked at him. "What's wrong?"

"Wrong? Wrong, Callie?" He doubled over as if gut-punched, as if he'd just heard the funniest thing he'd heard in years. "I guess to hell it's funny."

"What do you mean, boy?" Mica squinted at the young man.

"I did this." He waved his arms wide. "I think I hired him. But I don't know."

"What do you mean, 'you don't know'?"

"I was drunk, damn fallin'-down drunk. I don't remember."

Callie held his arm, and led him inside. "But why?"

"For the ranch, the Dancing M."

"But it is not yours. It never could be." Esperanza's voice was edged with a growl none of them had ever heard.

"I know that now, Esperanza. . . . But now it's too late, too late for us all. . . ." He stood just inside the door and looked up for the first time, and saw Brandon. "How is Brandon?"

"He is dead." Esperanza's words quieted the room.

"No, not Brandon!" He staggered across the room and collapsed at the boy's side, grabbing at the blanket covering him.

As they dragged him away from Brandon, Junior looked back outside, stared at Darturo dead in the dust, then looked up at the faces staring at him. These were people who had known him his entire life. Then his eyes settled on Brian as if seeing him for the first time.

"It wasn't Brandon who did this to Middleton. It was me. Me!" He gripped his head with his hands, knocking his hat to the floor and pulling at clumps of his sun-colored hair as if to pluck his head clean in his white-knuckle rage.

Callie tried to put an arm around his shoulders, but he pushed her away. "I was drunk." He slumped, shaking his head as if he was denying everything he'd ever done wrong in his life. "I don't know why. I suppose I was trying to make the old man realize I wasn't a kid anymore." He looked up, an innocent half smile on his mouth. "I thought that if I could just get the Dancing M for him, free and clear, wouldn't he be so proud of me?"

He smiled, his tearing eyes looking up at the ceiling, his head slowly shaking side to side as if in slow disagreement with his words. He looked at the gaping faces, at the hurt on his sister's face, at Mica's disappointment, at the anger burning hard in Espy's face, at Middleton's disgust and confusion.

"If I could change this, make things different ... but it's too late, too late for Papa, too late for us all."

"What do you mean it's too late for Papa? Junior, you're worrying me. Has something happened to Papa?" Callie grabbed his shoulders and shook him. "Junior?"

The boy's sudden racking sobs filled the room, his fist bunched around the grip of his pistol. "I killed him, sis. Killed him, sure as I pulled the trigger myself!"

Horses thundered in close out front. Junior jumped to his feet and fingered back a curtain on the little window over the table.

"It's the sheriff," he said, as if to himself. "And the boys from the D."

The lawman's voice boomed from without: "Junior, it's Sheriff Tucker. We know you're in there; we see your horse here." He paused, waited for an answer, then said, "Did you shoot this man, Junior? Can you hear me, boy? Come out and we'll figure out this mess together."

Inside, Junior's face relaxed for the first time since he had arrived. He smiled as he shucked the bullets from

his revolver's cylinder. They dropped, one by one, plink-
ing to the floor. In a small voice, he said, "If I could only
make it right. Even just a little bit . . ." And he walked to
the door.

Before anybody could stop him, he raised his .36 Remington and aimed it as if he were about to fire at the gathered posse members. There were shouts as the men
dropped to the dirt and fired in self-defense. Junior's body
spasmed on the top step. The bullets that didn't drive into
him flew past, twanging inside and splintering the wood
of the opened door, pocking the rough log-and-stone
adobe structure, inside and out.

As the shooting ceased, Junior half turned toward the
roomful of stunned friends as if he were about to take a
bow. He smiled at them, a look of sad apology in his
eyes; then he tumbled backward down the steps and into
the dirt to lie beside Mortimer Darturo, the dead outlaw.

The echo-filled air of the little farmyard cracked with
Sheriff Tucker's voice as he staggered, unharmed, into
view and looked between the dead boy and the kitchen.
"Oh God, Junior, this is not what I wanted. Not at all,
not at all."

The sheriff turned to face the silent men behind him,
thin wisps of smoke still curling from their pistol barrels.
"Squirly was right all along," he said, shaking his head.
"And I ignored him. So help me, I should have listened
to Squirly Ross."

Chapter 52

Two weeks later

"It was good of you to sign over the Dancing M to Esperanza."

"I have no real claim to it. Besides, it's rightfully hers." Brian stared at the wide blue river before him.

Callie nodded. "And there's no one alive who knows more about ranching than Mica Bain."

Brian's brow creased for a moment. Then a half smile formed on his face. "Are you saying . . . Esperanza and Mica are a couple?"

Callie looked up at him as if he had just asked her if water was wet. "Of course. Mica will ask her to marry him any day now. I think he would have already if all this hadn't happened. . . ."

The big man nodded. They stood silent for a few minutes. Then he said, "So, do you think Sheriff Tucker will go back to his job?"

"I hope so. He's a good man. I know he blames himself for all the killings. He was close friends with my father, and misses him." She pressed a hand to her mouth. "Then finding Squirly Ross murdered in the alley. I think that was what drove him to quit."

"I remember Mr. Ross. He helped me with my baggage the day I arrived." Brian looked at her, a wry smile on his face. "I'm afraid I wasn't overly friendly to him."

"What an absolute shock, Mr. Middleton. Surely you don't mean you are a prickly pear?" Callie feigned surprise, a hand to her chest.

Brian smiled and shook his head. They stood quietly together a few moments more, watching the river, the far-off hills, and then he said, "You know, Callie, when I first met Junior, he told me that land is everything out here. And while I understand that sentiment, I have to disagree."

Callie tensed, turned a sharp glare on him. "My brother's dead now. Can't you just let it rest? He's not here to argue with you anymore."

"Please hear me out," said Brian. "Yes, land seems to be the reason behind so much that is good and bad here—everywhere, for that matter—but there is so much more to the notion. It is the urge to possess this land that is at the root of all this evil." He faced her, stared into her light blue eyes. "But it's the people, the *people*, Callie, who are the most important part—it's the people who are everything out here. I see that now. See it as clearly as I saw nothing of the sort before."

Callie turned back toward the river. They stood side by side, but separated by the weighty silence of their thoughts.

Finally, Callie shivered. "I can't stand wearing these mourning clothes." She stood beside him a moment longer, hugging herself as if in a chill wind. She looked out beyond the river. "You'll be leaving on Tuesday's train, then."

Brian stared at her long enough that she finally looked at him.

"I have thought about it," he said. "Lots. And the best reason I can come up with for staying is if you'll marry me, Callista Grindle." He watched her face closely, but saw barely a flinch. Those blue eyes seemed to him to burn brighter, though.

She didn't unfold her arms. "I will not marry Brian T. Middleton."

He felt as if he were struck hard across the face with a quirt. The only question applicable formed on his lips. He almost spoke. . . .

"But I would consider marrying Brian MacMawe."

Again, he felt as if he were smacked hard across the mouth. "Lucky for you, then, for according to that telegram from my grandfather, should I choose to remain in the West, Brian T. Middleton ceases to exist."

She stared up into his eyes. Was it hopefulness he saw there?

"I own very little now, Callie. An old family Bible, this suit of clothes . . . but no land."

"That's all right," she said. "I do. Plenty of it. Besides, the Driving D is just too big for one person." Before he could speak, she stepped in close to him and plucked off his battered derby. "But I would not consider marrying even Brian MacMawe if he wore such an atrocity on his head." And rabbit-quick, she threw the misshapen thing hard with a snap of her wrist.

"Hey! My hat!"

The much-dented mouse-colored topper curved south and landed smack in the middle of the rolling Maligno Creek, where it bobbed for a moment, flipped over, and sank from sight.

She looked up at him and said, "I'll help you choose a proper rancher's hat when we go to Gleason's tomorrow. And while we're in town, you can return that cantankerous little mare to Silver Haskell."

He smiled as if he knew a secret, then shook his head. "No," he said, staring at Callie, then pulling her in close. "I think I'll keep her."

Brian bent down and kissed her. Callie tried to say something, but he kissed her harder. And they stayed that way for a long, long while, beside the slow-moving river on their own hard-earned land.

Don't miss another exciting Western adventure
in the *USA Today* bestselling series!

ONE MAN'S FIRE

A Ralph Compton Novel by Marcus Galloway

Coming from Signet in May 2012.

Wyoming Territory
1883

The wagon was supposedly secured against any attempt to rob it. At least, that's what was said by all the men hired to protect it before it had left Omaha. Enough iron plates were fixed to the sides to make it necessary to add an additional pair of horses to the team pulling the monster on wheels. Slits had been crudely cut into the plates so any of the three men riding inside could fire at anyone foolish enough to approach the wagon without permission. The man who might grant such a boon rode up top in a seat partly surrounded by a thick wooden shell that wrapped around the driver's back and sides. Another man sat beside the driver, carrying a shotgun that had been stored among several other weapons in the box at the driver's feet. Strictly speaking, the wagon should have been close to impenetrable. To the young man gazing down at it from atop a ridge south of the trail, it was a big fat egg dying to be cracked apart.

"What do you think, Eli?" another man asked from behind the younger one. He had a thickly muscled torso wrapped in a duster that had been with him through more hard days than most men saw in a lifetime. Dark brown eyes gazed out from behind narrowed lids set within a heavily scarred face that looked like something a goat had chewed up and spat out. It was difficult to discern which dark streaks on his chin and cheeks were dirt and which were wiry stubble.

The younger man kept a pair of field glasses close to eyes that were the color of a sky smeared with mist from an approaching storm. His voice had a faraway quality when he replied, "I think I can take her."

A second pair of anxious men crouched behind the first two and hearing that didn't do anything to alleviate their situation. The bigger fellow with the dirty face waved back at them as if he were shooing away a pair of annoying hound dogs. "Either one of you messes this up," he snarled, "and I'll use yer carcasses to trip up the team pulling that wagon."

Both of the other men settled down quick enough.

"You sure we can take that thing?" the scarred man asked. "Looks like a rolling fortress."

Eli lowered his field glasses to get a look at the wagon with his own eyes. Smiling at what he saw, he said, "You brought me along this far, Jake. You about to stop trusting me now?"

"Ain't about trust. It's about a job that we can or can't do. I won't charge into a slaughter just so you can scratch that itch you always got for stealing."

"That itch has served this gang pretty well so far."

"Sure has," one of the men farther down the rise said. He was definitely older than Eli, but carried himself like the youngest of the bunch. A wide, round head made his eyes look more like holes knocked into a pumpkin with a roofing nail. White knuckles were wrapped around a

Spencer rifle, and every muscle in that arm trembled at the prospect of putting the weapon to use.

"Shut up, Cody," Jake snapped. "When I want your opinion, you'll know about it." Once Cody was sufficiently cowed, the scarred man hunkered down and gazed down at the trail where the wagon was still rolling. "How many men you think are on that thing?"

"There's two up front," Eli said. "Couldn't tell you for certain how many are inside."

"Hank?"

The fourth man in the group was the most raggedy of them all. He resembled a scarecrow thanks to his wiry build as well as the tattered clothes he wore. Even his long hair was stringy enough to look more like strands of wet straw plastered onto his scalp. Three guns were strapped under his arms and at his hip. For all Eli knew, Hank could have had three more besides the .44, .45, and derringer. Ever since he'd lost his left eye, he seemed one twitch away from gunning down anyone in his sight. That twitchiness made it awfully hard for anyone to sneak up on him and he prided himself on being able to get to anyone before he could be hurt again. Those things made him a perfect spy. "There's five in all," he said with absolute certainty. "If you see two up front, that leaves three in the wagon."

"You'd stake our lives on it?" Jake asked. "Because that's what we'd be doing."

"I watched them load up myself."

Jake showed Eli an ugly grin and slapped the younger man on the shoulder. "All right, then. I suppose we should get moving before all the money in that wagon gets away."

Eli looked down at the trundling wagon as if it were a fat, limping goose on Christmas Eve. "No danger of that. We'd be able to hear it from a mile away even if we did let it get out of our sight."

"How much money are we talking about again?" Cody asked.

Jake was looking down at the wagon hungrily as he told him, "At least twenty thousand. You hear any different, Hank?"

The scarecrow man shrugged. "They loaded up a few strongboxes. If I could get into them things, we wouldn't need the young'un."

Patting the youngest member of the gang once more on the shoulders, Jake said, "That's right. Eli here can crack open the devil's own coin purse. Ain't that so?"

"Yeah," Eli said. "It is."

Neither Jake nor any of the other men in the gang knew for certain whose money was down there. They'd heard rumors of a bank shipping funds to cover a payroll or provide a loan to a large customer with deep pockets, but none of them had cared enough to ferret out the truth. There were even rumors that some businessman was shipping a bribe to a politician, but when there was a large batch of cash involved, speculations were bound to arise. Those fires were stoked even higher when that money was ferried about in a rolling spectacle like a crudely armored wagon. More than likely, the money was just a payroll being shipped by a company that had been robbed one too many times already. All most of the gang cared about was that the money was inside the wagon and there was lots of it.

But there was a different kind of glint in Eli's eyes when he stared down at that trail. It was a dull, yet intense thing that hinted at a hotter fire deep beneath his surface. "Yeah," he said. "Let's get moving."

The gang mustered like a disciplined army regiment. They kept low so as not to skyline themselves before enough of the ridge was between them and the men riding on the wagon below. When it was safe to move faster, they broke into a run toward the horses that were tethered to trees nearby. Having already scouted out the area while waiting for the wagon to roll by, all of the men knew their way down the narrow path around the ridge, through a stand of trees, and across a short stretch of bushes that had been turned into scorched brambles by an unforgiving sun.

It was no surprise for Jake to fire the first shot and when Hank joined in, Eli's world became a mush of cacophonous sound. Despite the horse's jostling movement, he kept his eyes locked upon the wagon. Even as the animal wove between pits left by deep puddles or jumped over a fallen tree, Eli kept his eyes glued to the wagon. As soon as the ground in front of him leveled out, he snapped his reins and rode ahead of his outlaw pack.

"You two move around to the other side of that contraption!" Jake shouted. "I'll see to it the kid don't get himself killed!"

Cody and Hank peeled away to circle around the back of the wagon. Compared to the horses that had swarmed around it, the iron-encrusted vehicle might as well have been standing still. It was far from defenseless, however, as rifle barrels poked out from the slits in its side to spout smoke and lead at the gang. Bullets hissed through the air past Eli's head, causing him to duck down as if that would be enough to keep him safe for the remainder of the journey. Before the rifle rounds could get any closer, they were diverted toward a greater threat.

Howling like a mad dog, Jake gripped his reins in one hand and a .44 Smith & Wesson in the other. Rather than fire wildly at the wagon, he gazed along the top of his barrel as if he had all the time in the world to take his shot. When he squeezed his trigger, sparks flew from the edge of one of the slits in the wagon's armor and angry curses echoed within. More shots cracked through the air on the other side of the wagon as the second half of the gang was greeted by another batch of riflemen. Eli tapped his heels against his horse's sides and surged forward as the spark in his eyes grew to a roaring flame.

"Bring this thing to a halt!" Jake bellowed.

The driver responded with a barking command directed at his team. The horses pounded their hooves against the rocky ground even harder as leather straps slapped against their backs. The shotgunner emerged from behind the wooden barricade atop the wagon like a target in a shooting gallery to unleash a smoky payload from one barrel and then the other. Jake had already veered away from the wagon by the time hot lead ripped through the air and fired at the shotgunner, clipping his shoulder and spinning him around to collide with the driver. Both men wobbled atop the wagon before becoming entangled in the reins. Once that happened, the team was pulled to the right, causing the entire wagon to lurch.

Eli was close enough to see in through one of the rifle slits by now. When the man behind the weapon poking out through the opening looked his way, Eli had plenty of time to grab hold of the rifle and yank it from him. He could have taken it away completely if the slit had been just a bit wider. As it was, the rifle clanged against iron while the man inside struggled to regain control of it. The driver's predicament caused the rattling iron monstrosity to swing away from Eli, taking the rifle barrel from his grasp and causing something of a panic for Hank and Cody on the other side.

Jake fired two more shots before snarling, "Bring this thing to a stop or I will!" Although the driver had gotten his team pointed in the right direction again, the wagon had slowed to something slightly better than a crawl. This allowed Jake to grab on to a post at the front corner of the wagon as if he meant to hop from his saddle and onto the driver's lap.

With the blood pounding through his veins amid the hammering rhythm of his heart, Eli felt as if he were charging down the trail at a breakneck speed instead of keeping pace with a wagon that was barely moving at all. Now that Jake had gotten under the driver's skin, the wagon slowed even more. The riflemen inside were still ready for a fight, but were preoccupied by Cody and Hank. That meant Eli was able to get back to the slit on his side a second after the rifle barrel poked through it again. Still rattled from his last confrontation as well as the unpredictable movements of the wagon itself, the rifleman on Eli's side pulled his trigger before he even had a target.

No bullet chewed through Eli's skull, but a mighty loud screech pealed through his ears. Apart from his hammering pulse and the dull thump of his own horse's hooves against the ground, he couldn't hear a thing. And yet, not so much as a hint of panic showed on his face as he pointed one of his .38s at the rifle slit and shouted at the man on the other side. Eli only had a vague idea of what he said, but it was enough to get the man to relinquish his grip on the weapon.

The wagon came to a halt and the gang surrounded it like a pack of dogs vying for the biggest chunk of a discarded hunk of meat. Eli was still mostly deaf as he came up alongside the wagon and stared in through the slit. His eyes were searching for one thing, but found another as all three men within the armored box turned to face him. The pair that had been dealing with Cody and Hank still held their rifles and the man on Eli's side had gotten to the pistol holstered at his hip. They all looked through the slit back at Eli and struggled to get their weapons pointed in his direction. From the corner of one eye, Eli could see the shotgunner on top of the wagon swing his weapon around to aim at him.

For that brief instant, Eli felt as if he'd drifted outside his own skin to watch everything from afar. Even if his ears hadn't been ravaged by the close-range gunshot, he doubted he would have been able to hear much of anything. He recalled folks talking about something like that when they'd been about to die. Their bodies drifted up and everything got real quiet. It was said to have been peaceful. As far as Eli could tell, he was about to find out firsthand.

Just as well, he figured.

Once more, the gang acted like a well-oiled machine. Jake brought the shotgunner down with one shot while Hank stuck the barrel of a .44 in through a slit on the other side of the wagon and pulled his trigger. The gunshot sounded like a muffled thump to Eli's tortured ears, and the bullet rattled around inside the wagon like a pebble being shaken in a tin can. All three riflemen flopped onto their sides or bellies in their haste to clear a path for the bullet or any more that might be following on its heels. Even Eli could make out the dull murmur of those men's excited voices, but he couldn't see any blood. When he felt the rough hand slap down on his shoulder, Eli twisted around while bringing his pistol up to bear.

Jake took his hand away and stepped back. His other hand kept his .44 pointed up at the driver while Cody made his way to the top of the wagon. Although Eli couldn't make out the words coming from Jake's mouth, there was no mistaking the victory etched into the gang leader's smile.

"A writer in the tradition of Louis L'Amour and
Zane Grey!" —*Huntsville Times*

National Bestselling Author

RALPH COMPTON

**Available wherever books are sold or at
penguin.com**

Charles G. West

Outlaw Pass

When impetuous Jake Blaine doesn't return home
from a prospecting trip in the gold-rich gulches of
Montana, his staid older brother Adam sets out to
find him. But his investigation draws unwanted
attention from some very dangerous men who are
more than happy to bury Adam to keep their secrets.

Also Available
Left Hand of the Law
Thunder Over Lolo Pass
Ride the High Range
War Cry
Storm in Paradise Valley
Shoot-out at Broken Bow
The Blackfoot Trail
Lawless Prairie
Death Is the Hunter

GRITTY WESTERN ACTION FROM

USA TODAY BESTSELLING AUTHOR

RALPH COTTON

NIGHTFALL AT LITTLE ACES
AMBUSH AT SHADOW VALLEY
RIDE TO HELL'S GATE
GUNMEN OF THE DESERT SANDS
SHOWDOWN AT HOLE-IN-THE-WALL
RIDERS FROM LONG PINES
CROSSING FIRE RIVER
ESCAPE FROM FIRE RIVER
GUN COUNTRY
FIGHTING MEN
HANGING IN WILD WIND
BLACK VALLEY RIDERS
JUSTICE
CITY OF BAD MEN
GUN LAW
SUMMERS' HORSES
JACKPOT RIDGE
LAWMAN FROM NOGALES
SABRE'S EDGE
INCIDENT AT GUNN POINT

S909

No other series packs this much heat!

THE TRAILSMAN

Follow the trail of Penguin's Action Westerns at
penguin.com/actionwesterns